FATAL ILLUSION

THE FATAL FAE SERIES: BOOK ONE

TEACUP
DRAGON
PUBLISHING

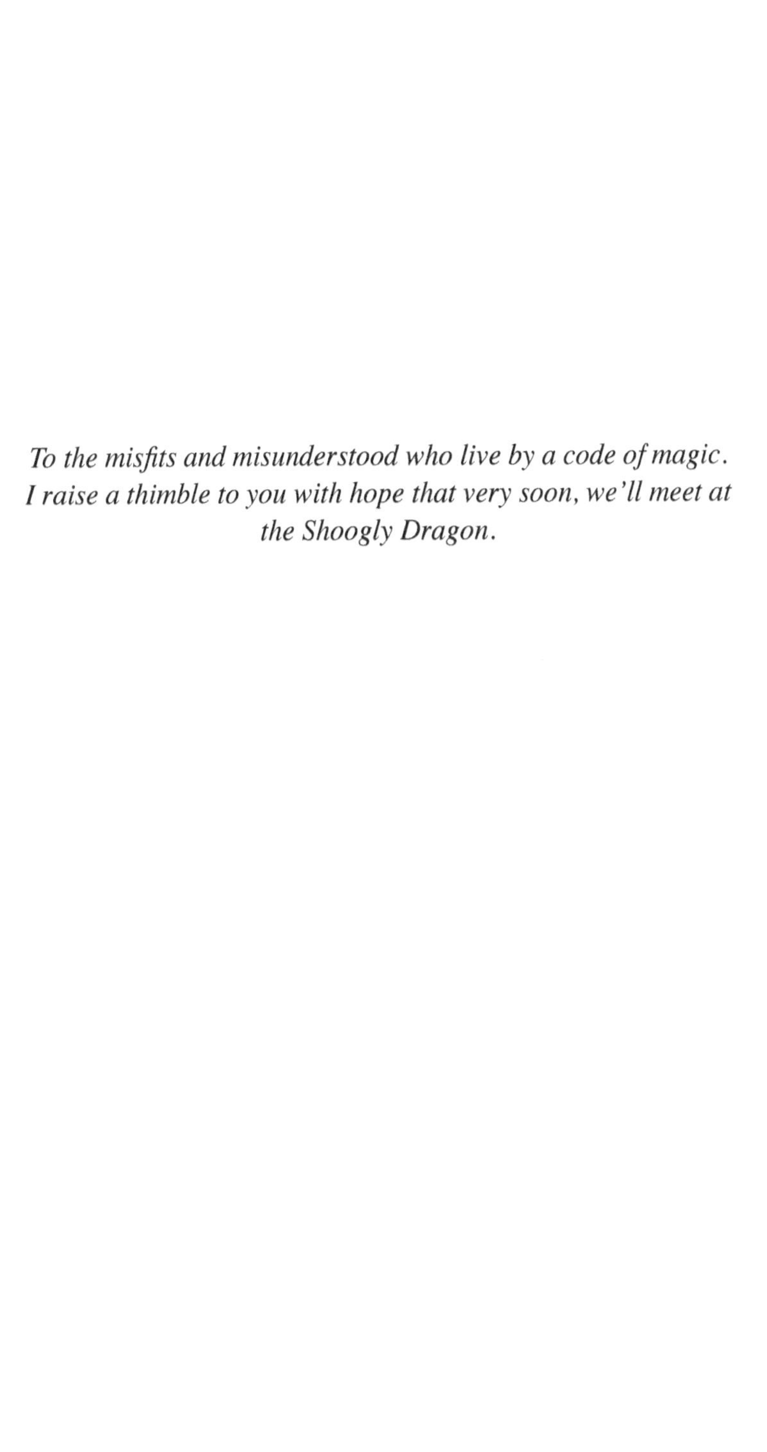

*To the misfits and misunderstood who live by a code of magic.
I raise a thimble to you with hope that very soon, we'll meet at
the Shoogly Dragon.*

BOOKS BY TAMERI ETHERTON

*Song of the Swords**

The Prince of Dragons

The Stones of Resurrection

The Temple of Sacrifice

The Ruins of Betrayal

The Veils of Deception

*The Fatal Fae**

Fatal Illusion

Fatal Assassin

Fatal Legacy

*Court of Stars**

Sunset in Shadow

*Chronicles of Eidyn**

Child of Fire

Dragon Mage

Short Stories

UnBroken

*Books that are part of the Aetherverse: The fantastical realms of Tameri Etherton. Characters and storylines intersect within the books with magical consequences.

FATAL ILLUSION

THE FATAL FAE SERIES: BOOK ONE

USA TODAY BESTSELLING AUTHOR

TAMERI ETHERTON

Death crept through the forest.

From branch to branch, through dirt and root, an ominous pall clung. Rori lay on the ground, her back stiff against the gritty earth. She stared above her, where trees heavy with blooming foliage spread from one side of her vision to the other, choking the light and leaving her in dappled darkness. Whether it was night or day, she couldn't tell. She inhaled deeply, expecting to smell familiar scents of loam and lichen, but beyond a hint of perspiration, she was left wanting.

This was no forest she knew. And Rori MacNair knew every forest in Faerie. Every forest except one.

She strained to listen, but heard nothing. No twittering of birds, no crunching of leaves, no breaking of twigs, nor howling of wolves. All around her was a still hush. Despite being surrounded by thick timbers and sprawling vegetation, the desire to cover herself, to hide from an unseen enemy, scratched at her senses. Sweat dotted her skin, but her throat was too dry to swallow. Anxiety pooled in her gut, distorting her focus. She couldn't shake the sense that she was on display, with all her weaknesses exposed.

Caged, yet under a microscope.

She curled into herself, as if to hide all those bits she dreaded being discovered.

"Get up, Aurora. Never show fear. Never give your enemies a weakness. If you don't win, you're dead. Get up!" Her father's voice echoed in her mind. Demanding as always, yet she knew he wasn't with her. Not this time.

Then why was she hearing him now, after a decade and half of silence? The use of her formal name did nothing to alleviate her confusion. What had she done wrong? The stern warnings— those were familiar. She'd heard them repeated every day of her childhood until they became etched against her skull. A mantra of sorts meant to comfort, but more often than not, only emphasized her failures. So, she shut them out. At least, she thought she had. But now she heard her father as if he stood beside her, commanding her to get up, to fight.

Beaten or bruised or broken, she always got up.

If only she knew what had knocked her down. Her head pounded as if she'd drunk an ogre's bath worth of mead.

She rolled to her side and the woods shifted in terrifying dizziness. The churning of her stomach matched the swirl of muddled thoughts that bounced through her mind. Goat's balls, what was wrong with her?

Gingerly, she rested her head in the crook of her arm. From that angle, trunks and ferns filled her sight. Just beyond, a gravel path led between two massive trees. Warmth emanated from the sandy soil, and she sniffed the ground. Dust, rock, dirt. Something was missing. She dug her fingers into the earth and flinched at the strangeness of its texture. She inhaled and closed her eyes. An acridness lay just beneath the surface. Her nostrils burned with the scent. Nothing about this place was right. Beyond the plants, there was no life.

Except her. Unless, of course, she was dead.

A forest of death. But, no decay.

If she was dead, then why did her body hurt so damn much? Even if she were dreaming, the same rules applied. Or did they? She couldn't remember a dream where every muscle and sinew ached, from the tips of her toes to the roots of every single strand of hair on her head.

Maybe she wasn't in Faerie. Her head rested on her leather jacket, comfortable against the worn folds. Her human clothes weren't any help. She'd long ago stopped changing into Faerie garb after returning from a mission. Queen Eirlys didn't approve, but then, the queen—and Rori's mother—would've been quite content to have her dress in the flowing, gauzy, half see-through gowns popular at court. No thanks. Dresses were dreadful to fight in, and she'd never been one to flirt and giggle like a simpering idiot. Better to dress for the job, and that meant jeans, boots, and dark colors that didn't draw attention.

The forest might be in the human realm, or anywhere, actually. She shook her head against the thought, regretting the movement immediately. It felt as if trolls banged their wicked spiked clubs against her skull. *Think, Rori. Focus.* She took a deep breath to clear her mind. The raging headache stubbornly remained, but she was able to ease the circling panic that settled at the base of her neck.

Even though magic was nearly exhausted in the human realm, she'd never come across a forest as devoid of living organisms as this one. Besides, she'd returned from the human realm that morning, hadn't she? Jumbled timelines danced through her head. She'd finished the mission in the human realm and definitely returned to Faerie. Yes? No. No, definitely yes. Yes.

The mission had nothing to do with a forest, of that she was certain. Gods, but it hurt to think. The memories she'd kept buried pushed against her brain, insisting she revisit them more. Try as she might to ignore the pressure, her mind circled back to her father. To that day. The day that changed everything.

Faerie's greatest spy, Hagan MacNair was a legend. Of course, she'd heard of his exploits, and a part of her was impressed beyond measure, but all she ever wanted was a dad who came home every night. Each time he left, she saw the anguish in her mother's eyes and felt the same fear that this might be their final goodbye.

Stars, but she missed him. Despite everything, he was her dad, and she loved him. Even when it was dangerous to do so. Like now, when she wasn't even sure where she was and she was imagining him being there, urging her on as if it were just another day of training.

An ache cramped against her heart, and she squeezed her eyes shut against the tears that wet her lashes. The last time she truly saw her father and heard his voice, she was eight. He'd kissed her forehead and admonished her to be a good girl for her mother while he was gone. Then he'd taken her brother Cian out on a secret father-son adventure. She'd been jealous of their time together, yet also grateful that Cian got some much-cherished time alone with their father.

"Stop," she whispered to the memory. But it continued, tearing at her heart with the same vigor now as it had then. She didn't want to relive that day. For fifteen years, she'd fought to suppress the events that had scarred her more than she'd ever admit. "No more." But her mind ignored her.

While her father and Cian were away, she'd worked hard to perfect a tricky spell her father had taught her. She'd hoped to be able to show him what a good daughter she was, how well she listened, and that she was ready. Instead of succeeding, she'd failed. Not just failed, but she lost control. Her magic spiraled out, tendrils grasping at something she couldn't see. The only explanation she came up with was that her magic had turned wild.

She'd heard tales of what happened to those with wild magic. Although no one had been prosecuted for over one thousand years, the punishment was brutal and swift. Those who survived were little more than flesh-covered rag dolls. The loss of control had only lasted a few moments, but long enough to instill fear into her that, even now, made her hesitant to use her magic.

When Cian returned later that day and said their father had died, she knew. In the marrow of her soul, she knew she was responsible. Her dad died because of her and her fucking weakness.

A MacNair does not lose control. Of magic, of emotions, of anything.

She pressed the pads of her palms against her closed eyes and fought against the memories that flooded her mind. It had been years since she'd allowed herself to think of that night and how she'd watched the light ebb from her mother's eyes. Labhruinn MacNair was a warrior, one of Faerie's finest, and Queen Eirlys's captain of the guard, but that night, she was a woman whose heart was broken. As Rori attempted to comfort her mother, their tears combining as they pressed their faces together in their grief, she closed off her heart to the kind of love that brought such heartache. Fates be damned, she swore she'd never love another the way her mum loved her dad.

Fresh tears tracked over her cheeks as she stared into her past. She might be a lethal weapon now, but the sharpened edges of her pain from that day never left her.

She swiped at her cheeks and glared at the forest as if it were the enemy. Perhaps it was. She gazed at the trees anew. If this was the forsaken Unseelie forest, then she had to be extra cautious with her thoughts. It wouldn't do to have her inner-most shame revealed.

No one knew—about her loss of control, or the guilt she bore—and she'd rather die than reveal her secret. Since that day, she'd lived with the fear and anxiety that she'd be discovered. All through her time at the Academy, she'd trained harder and longer than the other students, honing her skills in areas that guaranteed she'd never be called upon to use her magic. All to hide the fact that her magic had once turned wild.

How could her mother or Cian ever trust her again if they knew?

Cian. Gods, what would he think of her now? Disappointment soured her tongue, but not from what her brother might say—from her own stupidity. How the hell had she ended up in a deserted forest? And where in the ever-loving snickertits was she?

"Keep it together, MacNair. Remember your training," she told herself. Remember not just what the Academy taught her, but the years of discipline her dad had instilled. "Remember who you are."

She was Rori Fucking MacNair. She did not cower because of a little discomfort. With a grunt and a fresh wave of nausea, she scrambled to all fours and panted through the wave of pain that thrashed against her. She cocked her head and concentrated on what she couldn't see, relying on her inherent skills to give clues to her whereabouts. Even if she wasn't wary about using magic, to do so in an unknown situation would be idiotic. Instead, she closed her eyes and focused on listening. Blood rushed through her veins, her heart beat too fast, and her breathing came in labored drags. Beyond those sounds, there was nothing. The forest kept its secrets with quiet insistence.

"Hello?" she called out. The word floated on stale air. She flicked a lock of cobalt hair from her face and stood, hating the effort it took for such a simple task. Aside from a few scratches, she found no obvious injuries. Her fingers brushed past the dagger secured to her left thigh and relief swept over her. A second dagger hugged her right hip. Tucked into the inner pocket of her jacket were her phone, some human cash, and two fake IDs. All necessary for the human realm, but useless in Faerie.

If robbery wasn't the motive, then what? Question upon question zipped through her thoughts. She tugged the phone from her pocket and held it close. *Battery low, signal nonexistent.* If she were in the human realm, it was somewhere far from a cell tower. Tech wasn't allowed in Faerie, at least tech the queens didn't approve of, which was most everything found in the human realm. She always turned her phone off after returning home. Maybe she'd forgotten this time? Would her phone still work in Faerie?

She shrugged against her leather jacket, jostling it to a more comfortable fit. Pain ricocheted from forehead to ankle with the effort. She swayed where she stood, swallowing the sickness that crept up her throat. Several swearwords, the ones Cian didn't approve of, hissed from between clenched teeth.

There was a lot Rori did that Cian didn't approve of—like rhyming his name with "pee-in," for starters. Or elongating it into a whiney Keeeee-innnn. Gods, but she was an annoying little sister. How many times had he asked her not to be such a pest? About as many times as he'd begged her not to follow his path at the Academy.

Maybe that's what big brothers did. Still, it wasn't fair that at only sixteen, he'd had to take on the role of big brother slash father figure when their father died. The poor sod. She'd turned her pain of losing their father into anger and rebelliousness—with Cian bearing the brunt of her internalized despair. Through it all, he'd been patient and loving. She both idolized and loathed him because of it.

She bent at the waist and placed her palms against her knees to steady herself. When she got out of this hell, she owed her brother a huge apology for how she'd treated him. She was twenty-three, for goddess' sake. She wasn't a child anymore. It was time to stop teasing him and treat him with the respect he deserved.

"Fuck Cian," she said aloud, with a defiant lift of her chin. The tiniest fraction of guilt cut through her impertinence. It wasn't her brother she was angry with. That honor went to herself and no one else. Somehow, she'd gotten herself lost. *Somewhere.* A fresh ripple of anxiety swept across her chest to settle just behind her belly button.

It would take months before anyone thought to look for her. Since she first began working missions, it was well-known that Rori MacNair worked alone, always. She preferred it that way and didn't need anyone getting in her way. Self-preservation, she called it, but that was a lie. If she let people get close, if she cared for someone, how could she trust they wouldn't leave like her father had? Everyone—the queens, her brother, her mum, they all thought her father was dead, and perhaps he was. Publicly, she went along with what they believed, but deep inside, she refused to accept he was dead with the same vigor she refused to accept love in any form. Being a loner served her well—it protected her in a macabre sort of way.

Except now, she could perish here and no one would ever know. They'd think she simply disappeared just like her father had. It came with the job, sure, but the thought of dying alone filled her not with regret, but resignation. This was the reality she'd created. She'd closed herself off from love, keeping everyone at arms' length out of fear they might get too close and discover the wild magic locked deep inside her. It was best this way. She deserved to die alone.

Rori squeezed her temples between her fists and groaned against the force that compelled her to think the morose thoughts. She was a loner, yes, but no one *deserved* to die alone.

"Get out of my head." She grunted the words to whoever or whatever was messing with her. Because if she knew anything for certain, this little trip down memory lane hadn't been of her own volition. She'd worked too damn hard to lock the past in the deepest, darkest cell of her mind. This enchantment, or whatever it was, had somehow found a key.

Was she finally going mad? Or was someone else orchestrating the manipulation? That was the question. And if it wasn't her own insanity, then who? And why?

Therron rubbed the spot above his heart and scowled at the mysterious pinching. Intermittently over the past few days, he'd be struck with a sharp pain, with no discernable reason why it happened. He was too young for heart trouble, having just celebrated his twenty-eighth year. Besides, elves weren't known for having illnesses that affected their internal organs. He pressed against his chest and whispered an elven spell to ward off evil. The pain dulled to a soft throb, enough to be a nuisance, but not enough to kill him. He hoped.

His gaze went to the inn across the street. If the enchantress knew he tracked her, she might be retaliating. But, at the same time, if she were aware of his presence, why hadn't she confronted him before now?

He pulled his hood lower and took a sip of mead, wincing at the sourness. Times like this made him miss his soft bed and the decadent food in Elvenwood. He bit into a hunk of day-old bread and chewed as if his life depended on it. Whatever had possessed him to accept the job from the Unseelie queen?

That's right. War. Or rather, stopping one.

Queen Midna must've been desperate to hire an elf. The fae ruler knew the history of their races and yet, she'd entrusted him with the secret mission. Quite possibly, it was exactly because he was an elf that she sent him. If he died, so be it. Even if she knew his real identity, no one else at the palace did. None of them would miss a lowly thief. Although, he did wonder how she would explain his death to his father. If she deigned to tell him at all.

From what he learned about her during his short stay at the Unseelie Court, she had an exceptional skill at avoiding scandal. Most likely, she would deny any and all knowledge of Therron. Even if there were a portrait of them both, Midna would find a way to explain it away. She was slippery, that Unseelie queen, but then, that's what the fae court of the dark was known for, wasn't it? Scandal, salaciousness, seduction. And at the heart of it all was the gorgeous faerie queen.

Sending him away gave Midna a convenient excuse to end his spying on her. At least neither of them had pretended he was at her court for any other reason.

Truth be told, he was happy to leave behind the queen and her lonely, hungry gaze. She knew far too much about him, and he'd uncovered far too little about her. That she wanted to bed him was obvious. It had taken a strong resolve to deny her the dozens of times she'd asked—sometimes commanded—that he join her in her private quarters.

But she wasn't his queen; therefore, he wasn't beholden to her demands. Out of respect, he refused her suggestive offers, but respect for whom? The queen? Or himself?

He rubbed his chest again and let out a long breath. The pain subsided, but his unease did not. No stranger to the affections of women, though hardly a womanizer, Therron had never allowed himself the luxury of loving his bedmates, and he suspected Midna wanted not just a playmate, but a soulmate. That, he could never offer.

He'd taken the job from her not only as a means to escape her court, but also for the chance to see more of Faerie. Midna had given him precious little instruction, only that he was to find an enchantress called Acelyne. According to the Unseelie queen, she was a danger to both kingdoms of Faerie, as well as Elvenwood.

When Therron had questioned the queen further, she grudgingly admitted that Acelyne had stolen something from her. He was to retrieve the missing item, even though he had no idea what it was. Midna swore the enchantress would tell him. Fool that he was, and desperate to flee Midna and her increasingly vulgar demands, he'd taken the job on the scant information he had. At the moment, bedding Midna seemed like the easier choice.

A door to the inn opened, and he looked up to see a pair of trolls lumber through the opening and shuffle to a table in the corner. Therron took the opportunity to study them, as he'd not seen their kind this close before. They weren't as tall or as bulky as giants, but these trolls were still two heads above the height of an adult elf and a goodly two men wide.

The pair wore loose-fitting tunics and breeches over their furry bodies. Their thick fingers gripped tankards made specially for their size. Unlike Elvenwood, Faerie was accepting of other species and races found across their world. Except elves. Midna might have tolerated him in her court, because he was a novelty—someone to be studied for usefulness or possible stud for breeding, but outside the palace, he'd had to keep his ears covered, his identity concealed.

He watched the pair laugh at something he didn't hear, and sighed. If only the elven king could see there was value in the other races. King Thane only saw the worth of elves, and unfortunately, a large section of the population agreed with him. Elves kept to themselves within their closed borders, rarely allowing outsiders to trespass their lands. Not only did that make the other kingdoms mistrust elves, but that narrow-minded thinking would be the king's undoing.

Therron allowed himself the traitorous thought, knowing it would stay unspoken lest the king find even more reason to be vexed with him. The elven king's meddling was what prompted Therron to flee the mountain palace and seek a life in Faerie as a thief. It was better this way. Perhaps he'd taken Midna's job to escape her meddling, as well. Kings and queens…why did they always think they should dictate the fortunes of their subjects? Why not leave well enough alone? If he was going to make a fool of himself, so be it. He didn't need an egotistical know-it-all wearing a crown to tell him they knew what was best for him. Bah!

Therron's gaze flicked out the window to the inn. What the blood and ashes was Acelyne doing? He'd been following her for the better part of a month. She traveled throughout Faerie, stopping at small villages as well as large towns without any plan or obvious direction. At each stop, she'd go to a seemingly random pub, sleep at an inn, and then leave. If she was up to mischief, he didn't see it, yet his gut told him something was going on—something he could feel, but not see. This was powerful magic, if what she was doing made it appear as if nothing happened.

Perhaps Midna was paranoid? Or jealous? Acelyne was certainly beautiful, although only half as stunning as the Unseelie queen. Whereas Midna's skin tone and hair color changed from mood to mood, as did her magnificent wings, Acelyne's sun-hued hair and olive skin never wavered. Nor did she ever show her wings. Therron rubbed his chin, trying to recall if he'd ever seen another fae expose their wings. He hadn't. Only the Unseelie queen. Something in the back of his mind thumped with a reason, but that damn pinching in his heart started again.

He rose from his seat and adjusted his sword so the belt

hung low on his hips. As inconspicuous as possible, he left a coin on the table for the serving girl. She hustled over before he could escape and stood close enough he could smell garlic on her hands. Probably from preparing the midday meal. He'd spied her in the kitchen on several occasions, usually hunched over a large chopping block with a knife in her hands. As a general rule, he tried to avoid anyone with a deadly blade in their grip.

"Where are you off to this early?" She tossed a glance at the kitchen and returned to him with a grin. "I've got some time before the mistress comes down. We could take a tumble in your room if you'd like."

It was the same offer she'd made a dozen times since he'd arrived.

"Thank you, but I must decline."

"Got a girl back home, do you?"

"Something like that."

"Well, she's a lucky lass. I hope she knows that."

He pulled his hood lower and stepped around the woman. There was no lass in his life, lucky or otherwise, nor would there be one in his future. Fate had sealed his future when he was born. He rubbed above his heart and grimaced at the jab of pain. Once this job was complete, he'd return to Elvenwood and seek out a healer. This was getting ridiculous.

Dappled spring sunshine met him as he stepped out from the cool dimness of the inn. He positioned himself behind a pillar, half-hidden by a covered walkway. From this angle, he could see Acelyne's inn, but she wouldn't see him. If she left her room today. He settled in for a long wait, one leg bent to lean against the wall in a casual stance as to not garner attention. His gaze roamed over the quiet street. Acelyne had chosen an inn off the main road, not unusual for her, but it marked this town as different, somehow. But why?

As far as he could tell, Cere was much like any other town

of Faerie, with a central market square, airy spires, and marble-arched colonnades. Pedestrian bridges spanned the streets with what looked like lacy, delicate buildings crowding overhead. Ivy and blossoms in a riot of color covered the stone walls, sometimes hiding a doorway or entry to a close, the narrow alleys every town in Faerie had in abundance. It was these that Therron hated most about the godforsaken places. They were like labyrinths, leading sometimes to a large avenue, and other —most—times to nowhere. For a man like Therron, they were veritable traps, best to be avoided.

Grudgingly, he admitted the fae were accomplished architects. Not as skilled as his kin, but the lightness they captured using stone was lovely.

Cere was a large town with several inns, and enough coach houses to suggest it was popular with travelers. Contrary to Acelyne's previous stops, she'd been in this town for four days. After the first night when she went to a pub, she'd stayed holed up in the same inn. As far as he knew, she hadn't spoken to anyone, nor had she sent any messages. That meant nothing. A message could be hidden in a pint of ale, a threat delivered through the snap of a fan. Whatever the reason for her extended stay, Therron was determined to find out what she was up to.

A skinny figure lurched from the inn and scrambled across the street, narrowly missing a cart being pulled by two goats. The merchant driving the cart yelled at the boy, but he ignored the man and kept on until he saw Therron. Immediately, his posture changed and the chaotic movements of his limbs slowed. He slunk against the wooden slats of the building as if that would keep him from being seen. Therron kept from rolling his eyes, but only just. The lad had delusions of being a great spy.

"Sir, I have news." The boy stage-whispered without looking in Therron's direction, and indicated he follow him.

"You can tell me here. You're safe."

"Nay, sir. She's in the breakfast room. It's the first window on the left. She's been there all morning, sipping tea as you like, and peering out the window. I can feel her gaze on me now, sir." He rolled along the building to the corner, where he disappeared. A slim hand stuck out and waved Therron on.

He suppressed a chuckle at the lad's dramatics and eased from his position. His gaze scoured the street, not seeing anything to give him alarm, and then moved up to the window of the inn. His breathing deepened, but the table where Acelyne had sat was empty. Disappointment lodged in his gut. He might be a thief, but he didn't lie and wouldn't tolerate those who did.

"Well?" Therron crossed his arms as he approached the lad. "What news?"

"Payment first." He held out a freshly scrubbed hand.

"That's not our arrangement."

Reluctantly, the boy lowered his arm and wiped his hand on his shorts. "The lady met with someone during the night. I didn't get a name, but me mam says it was a weaselly looking fella who's up to no good. She didn't like him at all. The gist of the meeting had something to do with the market. The lady wasn't happy with the man, or the news. That's all I can tell you. Oh, and the lady likes her eggs soft and tea scalding." His hand thrust out again.

Therron counted out the agreed-upon amount, adding another silver to the pile. "Thank you, friend, for your assistance. And for your mam's help. You make sure she sees some of this, you hear?"

The boy nodded, with a huge grin transforming his face from solemn to full of glee. "I will, sir. Do you want me to go through her belongings while she's out?"

Therron appreciated the lad's enthusiasm, but he couldn't endanger him any more than he already had. "That won't be necessary. You've been a great help. Keep out of her way today, understand? Make sure she doesn't have reason to suspect you of helping me."

The boy looked as though he might say something else, but Therron turned abruptly and strode toward the town square where he assumed the market would take place. Just as he neared the main street, he caught a glimpse of golden hair and a crimson dress. His belly twisted at the sight of Acelyne strolling down the street as if she hadn't a care in the world. She stopped momentarily to speak with the man who'd nearly run over the boy.

Therron moved into the shadows and strained to hear their conversation. Elven hearing was much better than the fae's, but the town was awakening and the sound of people going about their lives drowned out much of what Acelyne said. He managed to make out that she needed a ride to the market immediately and the man was to wait for her at the rear entrance to the inn.

The driver snapped the reins, and his goats hurtled toward the street that would lead him to the back alley as Acelyne had instructed. The enchantress returned to the front entrance and disappeared into the well-appointed building. Ivy grew up the white walls and curled up the dark timber frames. If needed, Therron could climb the ivy, but not in broad daylight.

A shout came from inside the inn, followed by a wail that sent birds screeching from the trees. Deadly silence followed. Therron hesitated a moment, not wanting to jeopardize his position. Fresh screams sounded from deep inside the inn, and Therron launched from his hiding place. Each step twisted his belly; his thoughts swirled with dark visions he hoped weren't real.

Acelyne was nowhere to be seen when he entered the inn's foyer. Hysterical sobbing came from his left, and he pivoted toward the sound. The kitchen was a hive of chaos when he entered. A streak of gold flashed outside the open door as the little cart disappeared down the street.

Two women clung to each other, their faces ashen, cheeks wet with tears. Both muttered incoherently as they stared in horror at the floor.

Therron's gaze slowly tracked down to where two bodies lay huddled. A woman half-lay over a smaller figure, and the churning of his belly tightened, the sour mead he'd drunk curdling. From where he stood, he could clearly see that their ears had been sliced off, their mouths slashed to gaping maws. The young lad, with so much future ahead of him, held in his lifeless hand the silver coins Therron had given him, now stained with blood.

$\approx$ 3 $\approx$

Rori pressed a hand to her heart and winced against a jab of pain. Great, now she was having a heart attack. Just what her brilliant morning needed. Although, it might explain why she wasn't herself today. Weeping more than she had in her whole life, reliving her worst memories, doubting herself to the point of loathing: this wasn't like her, and she didn't like it one bit. She breathed in through her nose and out through her mouth, attempting to calm the anxiety dancing along her every nerve. Her breathing evened, the pain in her chest eased, and her thinking cleared, somewhat.

She would not die here.

Whatever madness stalked her, she'd not succumb.

Gods, but the last time she felt this awful, she'd spent a miserable few nights in Paris. Magic was dying in the human realm, a fact that vexed both queens of Faerie. Even still, threats of a time long past were present. It was due to those threats, and her familiarity with the city, that Rori had been sent to Paris to investigate a spate of sightings involving creatures that shouldn't exist at all, and definitely didn't belong in the human realm. Lycans were a myth to the fae, something mothers frightened their children with in an effort to get them to behave.

In Paris, she'd found not one, but two lycans, which had surprised the crap out of her. Brothers, if she recalled correctly. She strained to focus on the details more to center herself in her mind than anything else. Cling to something known. Regain equilibrium. Focus. She'd been on an intel mission—observe only, do not engage. Honestly, the worst kind of mission. It was akin to babysitting, in her opinion. What she had discovered in the cold and desolate backstreets of Paris was far more than mythical beings roaming free in the center of Paris.

After two days of trailing the pair, she got bored of their aimless wanderings and decided confronting them would be more expedient. She could've sexed the info out of them—gods knew it had been ages since she'd had sex and considering lycans were part wolf, part man, it might've been interesting as hell—but she chose combat. Which was much more effective, anyway. For the price of one broken rib and several bruises, the lycans had given her loads of intel. Apparently, the best way to get a lycan to spill his secrets was to kick his ass.

Between punches, they taunted her for being fae, threatening that the humans would come for her next if she wasn't careful. A few well-placed jabs to their handsome faces revealed that humans were killing their kind for freaky pseudo-magic spells. That alone was a huge problem. Humans weren't supposed to know about lycans or faeries. Queen Eirlys had been rather keen to know why, but the lycans didn't know. Or, they wouldn't say. Rori had left them licking their wounds in a dark alley somewhere near Notre Dame.

That was two years ago, but her body seemed to remember every bruised muscle and broken bone as if it had been this morning. Rori cricked her neck from side to side. What exactly had she done last night? She straightened and surveyed her surroundings. No beasts, lycans or otherwise, here as far as she could tell. Just more saplings, more of the silty gravel, more ferns, more silence. In the distance, she saw taller shrubs, but here, in this little patch of dust, was only her.

Wherever she was, she needed to escape. An instinctive buzz in her gut told her this wasn't her time. She'd been in far stickier situations and wouldn't perish here. The key was to keep steady. Not freak out or lose it completely. Think through the problem. Solve one thing, then another, and then another. Rori reined in her impulsiveness and remembered her Academy training. She hadn't survived the trials by panicking. She hadn't graduated top of her class because of her name. She'd earned the honor by working hard, training harder, and not letting her emotions run riot.

If you don't win, you're dead.

She took a tentative step and another, moving with care and caution. The hard soles of her boots crunched against gravel with each foot she set upon the ground. Even breathing hurt in this wretched place. The only way out was to keep moving forward. With each step she took, Rori retraced the previous evening for clues to how she'd ended up here. The last she could recall, she'd been at the Shoogly Dragon, so, definitely in Faerie. Tug was there, as were his merry men, and Sal, too. She'd played darts with some trolls—who soundly walloped her even though she was considered the best dart player in the area. Who knew trolls had that kind of control and dexterity? Not her, that's for damn sure.

Had she drunk at the pub? Yes, she'd had a pint or two, but nothing to cause this much damage. And certainly not enough to pass out in a foreign forest nowhere near the Shoogly Dragon.

A soft breeze lifted the hair at her neck, bringing a chill to her sensitive skin. Even the air was off, as if tainted by this place. Stale, cloying. Yet a breeze meant wind and that meant an opening to the thick foliage. If she could follow the source of air, she could find a way out—then she could get back home. She paused and lifted her face, but with her halt, the air settled. When she took a step, a breeze followed. Her excitement died as quickly as it had come.

Frustration coiled around her sore muscles, ready to spring at the slightest provocation. She turned in a circle, noting three separate paths she could take. No single one looked more inviting than the others. Each path was a crapshoot. Each would either bring her closer to freedom, or closer to death. Without giving herself time to doubt, she headed for the path in front of her.

Step after step, her strength returned, but the throbbing in her head continued. If someone had left her here, why? To kill her? Or trap her? Was this some bizarre ritual where she'd become the prey for someone to hunt? Was this someone's idea of a sick game? She shook her head and regretted the movement immediately. It would serve no purpose to let her imagination run amok.

Focus. Why was she here? She licked the underside of her wrist and sniffed. No lingering odor indicated poison. A bit of bad breath, maybe, but at least no one had tried to kill her. At least, if they'd tried, they failed.

Who would want her dead? Names and faces floated in her mind. Plenty of people had a grudge against her—it came with the job. Upon reflection, she'd probably made more than one enemy in her four years working for the Seelie queen.

So, not poison. Then what? How long had she been in the forest? It could've been hours or even days. If she was drugged, then how? And by whom?

Why? Why? Why? beat through her mind to the tempo of her heart.

The who part of this mystery concerned Rori the most. What if she hadn't been drugged, but spelled to sleep? There were many people in Faerie, and even Elvenwood, powerful enough to knock out a full-grown fae, but who would do that? And to what end? Everyone had magic. She couldn't remember a time in her history, or the distant past, when magic was used against one of their own. Magic had rules. The two Faerie queens saw to it that people—no matter their race or species—respected the rules. And the elven king did the same in his kingdom. Magic might be commonplace, but it was precious and not to be squandered or used to harm another.

So, which was it? Poisoned, drugged, or spelled?

"Futnuckers." Rori stood at a Y in the path, unsure which way to turn. She glanced behind her, but could only see a few yards before foliage blocked her view. For all she knew, she could be walking in a giant circle. With a quick flick, she snapped the dagger from her thigh and held it at eye level, blade facing her. She took a calming breath and closed her eyes. Her arm pulled back, and then she thrust the dagger forward.

Ever since she could remember, she'd had a gift with weapons, especially blades. The steel obeyed her unspoken commands, which gave her an advantage when fighting.

This time, she let the dagger choose her path.

A dull thud came from the tree to her right. She opened her eyes and retrieved her dagger. To keep from getting lost, she carved a tiny X into the bark, just large enough to see without harming the tree more than necessary.

She'd been trained to survive the elements, whether it be snow-covered mountains or humid jungles. She knew how best to make shelter with what was on hand, but without food and a water source, she wouldn't last more than a few days. At the thought of food, her belly grumbled loudly, the sound echoing on the silence of the forest. She placed a hand protectively over her tummy and cocked her head to listen for sounds of a river or even a tiny stream. Nothing. Her glance went to the ground, but the leaves held no dew, and the grasses, although green, were as dry as her cracked lips.

Rori's sense of dread grew from a nagging thought to a fully formed panic hovering just to the edge of her consciousness. Time stretched and snapped in this place. Had it been hours or minutes? Or was it just exhaustion and hunger playing tricks on her mind? Thoughts of despair—of giving up and curling into a ball to sleep—bombarded her senses.

At least she wasn't dwelling on the past anymore. Small mercies, indeed. This was even more insidious. With each step, she fought against the pull to quit. With each tree marking, she struggled to keep her focus. When her stomach tightened and loudly protested its empty state, she stopped walking to search for something edible. Even this was fraught with subtle messages—she didn't need food. She needed sleep—the more she thought of food, the more powerful the desire to rest became.

Food. She shoved the word in front of everything else drifting through her mind. Not sleep. *Food.* The pull lessened, but there was definite pushback happening with her psyche. The mental gymnastics she had to endure intrigued her to the point she almost crouched to sit—not to rest, just to sort through what was happening in her muddled brain.

She leaned against a tree, resting her head on the back of her hand. It could be that whatever drug she'd been given was still in her system, lulling her back into unconsciousness. Or it could be something even more sinister. Her magic sparked in her veins, but she pushed aside the desire to let it free. What if that was a trap? Whoever had kidnapped her was just waiting for her to use magic—possibly even get her to unleash her wild magic.

Kidnapped. Snickertits.

But no, she wasn't bound. What lunatic kidnaps a faerie and leaves them free to roam a forest? Someone unhinged enough to use magic to trick their victims into succumbing to the long, dreamless sleep, but only after making them relive their most painful memories. That's not just unhinged, that's malevolent.

"I am Rori MacNair," she said aloud. "I am descended from mages, daughter to one of the greatest spies, and to the fiercest warrior ever to protect the Seelie throne. I am not afraid of you, nor will you defeat me. I will not die here." She shouted the words to the treetops, her body shaking with righteous indignation.

From far away, the sound of laughter rang out, but there was no joy or mirth, only mocking.

$\mathscr{H}$ 4 $\mathscr{H}$

The enchantress lifted her face to the sky and cackled as if mad. Her golden hair spun wildly behind her as the cart careened around a corner. More wild laughter followed in her wake. Therron pushed himself harder, running as fast as he could on the uneven cobblestone streets. What could be so funny to make her laugh loud enough to wake a mountain dwarf?

Her laughter faded, and he spat a curse to the sky. The enchantress had disappeared from his sight. Again.

It was useless. Acelyne had led him on a merry chase through the backstreets and outskirts of the town for the better part of the morning, and now she was mocking him with her cackling. Well, no more. He skidded to a stop and bent at the waist, his breath coming in labored drags. The sun shone bright overhead and sweat streaked his forehead. The leather cassock he wore didn't help.

For the hundredth time, he asked himself, Why had he taken this job? It wasn't for the coin, that was for damn sure. Queen Midna had made it clear he only got paid if he killed the enchantress, even though he'd not agreed to that condition. A thief he might be, but a murderer of women? Not yet.

Although, if the enchantress continued to toy with him, Midna would get what she wanted. Especially after what she did to that lad and his mam. He scanned the buildings and shook his head. Why murder that innocent child so brutally? If she was sending a message to him, he received it, but not in the way she might've imagined.

All the murders did was spur his anger. He'd been content to follow Acelyne this past month, but now he wanted her captured to stand trial for her crimes. This was the first time the enchantress had done something publicly and it once again made him question, Why this town? Why now? She'd been careful in her previous stops. Did his presence unsettle her? He rubbed above his heart and grimaced. She'd be coming for him soon enough. Might as well save his energy and be ready when she did.

Ashes, why had he thought it would be a good idea to run away from home and become a thief? He had a good life in Elvenwood. With that good life came a dragon's treasure of expectations, too. Better to leave them to his brothers. Although, Therron doubted that Thaddeus could stop womanizing long enough to become respectable. And Theo? His baby brother always had his face stuck in a book—he doubted Theo even knew he was gone.

The scar on his left cheek thrummed with its own kind of heat, and he brushed a thumb over the oddly curved marking. He'd have to return someday, just not yet.

Therron slunk into the shadows and took a moment to get his bearings. A sinking tugged at his belly. Acelyne had led him about as far from the market as she could get without actually leaving town. She was much quicker in the little cart, and Therron suspected she used her magic to give the goats endurance to keep racing through the streets. Perhaps he had it wrong and Acelyne wouldn't seek him out. The entire chase had been to lure him away from the market.

He shrugged off his ire and started off toward the center of town. Acelyne could've lost him at any point during the chase, but she'd kept her speed just fast enough to give an advantage. She enjoyed the game too much to lose him. And he'd played right into her deception perfectly. Like a damn cat chasing a mouse, except he was fairly certain Acelyne thought herself the cat. The cackling laugh, though…it didn't feel directed at him, but who else would she be taunting?

The sprawling town made him nervous. Elvenwood, the city proper and the palace, were built into mountainsides, using the cliffs and rocky surfaces as natural barriers. Faerie was too spread out, too open, and too exposed for his liking. Even with the covered walkways and tightly packed houses, he preferred the cool interiors of Elvenwood, with its granite walls and ancient trees.

He walked with purpose, rubbing the spot above his heart more out of habit than from any pain. His fingers lowered and traced the silver embroidered elvenwood tree on the front of his cassock. Elves would recognize the tree, and its importance, instantly, but the silver threads were woven with elven magic so that anyone else would only see a blurry depiction of something resembling a tree.

The elders said the elvenwood was the source of the elves' magic, a gift from the First Goddess. An actual tree that grew within the mountain palace at Elvenwood, through the floors right up to the top of the highest turret. Whether a gift from the gods or not, it was a sight to behold. If he lingered his thoughts much longer on the palace, he would become homesick.

Thinking of Elvenwood brought back memories of glorious summers chasing sparkbugs in the gardens, and laughing with his brothers. It had been a more innocent time then. Before Therron knew of the curse placed upon his family. The curse that would one day kill him unless he found his fated mate and she returned his love.

Before the king began looking for a reason to bring war to Faerie. Their kingdoms had experienced peace for millennia, but now King Thane was determined to destroy all fae and anyone who supported them. Therron rubbed the scar out of habit. It made no sense. The fae princess Ishnara had cursed his family ten thousand years earlier, and aside from a male child being born every hundred years to the curse, most elves had forgotten about the fae princess and the origins of the curse. So, why now? Nothing had changed in the kingdoms that Therron could see, but the king didn't confide in him, so he could only hypothesize.

His footsteps crunched on the gravel road as he walked, scanning the streets for a glimpse of Acelyne, alert to danger.

The more Therron saw of Faerie, and the more fae he met, the more he found similarities rather than differences between their races. There was no doubt elves were more serious and sterner than their mischievous counterparts, but both races were highly attuned to nature. In fact, their magics complemented one another. Of the fae healers he'd witnessed, they were skilled, but not nearly as gifted as the elves. Where faeries excelled was at elemental magic. The two courts of the Faerie queens used their powers effectively to keep the lands fertile, the weather temperate, and the races peaceful.

They needed each other—the fae and the elves. If only King Thane could see that, too. War would only serve to weaken the world as a whole, and divide the races, perhaps permanently. That benefitted no one. Especially not the elves. He had to find a way to convince the king war wasn't the answer.

The hairs on Therron's neck rose, and his blood quickened with apprehension. Acelyne was near. He continued walking, his gaze whipping from one side of the street to the other. The only sounds he heard were of townsfolk going about their day. On his right, he passed a stall with root vegetables and fruits stacked in neat baskets.

He tossed the merchant a coin and pocketed two apples in his coat. A smallish face peeked from behind a bushel of thrashes, and he waved. The little urchin ducked behind the basket, where he hoped they would stay until he was far away and the threat of Acelyne gone.

She'd already killed two people this morning; he couldn't risk her harming anyone else. Guilt sliced across his heart, and he grimaced at the truth of the matter. She'd killed the boy and his mam because they gave him information. Their deaths were his burden to avenge, and he would.

A dark flash lit from behind a pillar, and Therron rolled out of the way, narrowly missing being struck. He leapt up, his magic whirling around him like a protective shield. Ashes, he was hoping to avoid a fight, but he couldn't leave the towns-folk exposed to her malicious schemes. Acelyne peeked from behind the pillar and jerked her head back, but not quick enough.

Therron pounded across the street, a snarl on his lips, a growl bursting from his sternum. Acelyne stepped out into the daylight, her glorious hair glowing bright. A wave of magic punched him hard, forcing his feet to slide backward. He'd always heard faerie magic was softer, gentler than that of the elves, but this was ferocious. Someone with lesser power than he would've been knocked unconscious or killed immediately.

A small crowd gathered a short distance from where he stood facing the enchantress. Therron motioned for them to back away, careful not to make eye contact with any one of them for fear Acelyne would assume there was a connection. Despite his warning, the townsfolk inched closer. He'd do what he could to keep them safe, and with Acelyne's focus on him, he hoped she would leave them out of the fray.

Another thrust hit him with deadly efficiency, leaving him breathless for a moment. He swept the crowd, but none of them seemed to be hit with Acelyne's magic. Just him. If only her magic was as admirable as her accuracy. He sensed rather than felt what lay behind Acelyne's power, and dread clouded his thoughts.

All elves were taught from an early age to respect their gifts. Magic was never to be used to harm another, nor was it to be wasted. Between their lessons of warping and weaving, or spell making and healing, they were taught the dangers of dark magic—and how to recognize the telltale signs that someone meant harm. Beneath the guise of ordinary magic, there was always a stain, sensed more than felt, but there, like a claw ready to tear the world to shreds if given a chance.

Against his elven magic, Acelyne's dark magic battered with impotent fury. This must be why Midna was desperate to have the enchantress killed.

Forbidden in all the kingdoms, dark magic corrupted the user until they had no goodness left in them. Kindness and compassion were replaced with cruelty, a viciousness that became insatiable.

"Well, well, well, this must be my lucky day. Although, I can't quite fathom what you're doing in Cere. Aren't your kind too superior to sully themselves with us lowly creatures? I have to ask myself, why are you following me, elf scum?"

Therron winced at the slur. Not because of the insult, but from what the onlookers might do next. He'd kept his race hidden thus far, but if these citizens believed the rumors that elves were baby killers, or whatever worse lies were spread about them, then he was in for a difficult time.

"I'm merely taking a walk. I don't want any trouble." Therron kept his hands loose and circled the enchantress.

The crowd edged backward a good distance from where he and Acelyne faced off in the middle of the street. She strutted across the gravel as if she walked the finest halls of the Unseelie palace. This woman was accustomed to getting her way. Not only that, but she had the arrogance to believe she was superior in her powers. Saying elves were snobbish wasn't a lie, but coming from her, with her haughty attitude, was hypocritical to say the least.

Therron didn't want a public fight, nor did he enjoy the constant thrum of Acelyne's magic against his own magical barrier. He needed to capture her and to do that, he needed to outsmart the enchantress.

In a blink, she was at his side, a small dagger stained red gripped in her fist. Small cracks formed on the outer edges of her otherwise unblemished skin. Unlike natural magic, the dark arts exacted a price, and it appeared Acelyne's was vanity.

She thrust the dagger forward, but was blocked by Therron's magical barrier. Her eyes narrowed and nostrils flared. With a grunt, she thrust again, but was once more thwarted. Again and again, she shoved the dagger forward, but it never reached more than a hands' width from Therron's midsection.

Her lips curled in a venomous snarl, and she glared at him as if he'd betrayed her somehow. "Who are you?" Her eyes searched his, but he kept his mind locked to her intrusive prodding. The cracks deepened, and she snarled like a cornered wolf.

"Do you always underestimate your opponent?"

"Is that what you think this is? I'm merely searching for a weakness." She sneered, her lip curling almost to her nostril.

"And have you found one?" He redoubled the lock on his thoughts and made her his sole focus.

"I have. Kindness." She lifted her hand, and a silver coin winked in the sunlight. "He was giving it to his mam, just as you directed."

Therron's blood spiked as though with fever, and

murderous rage rushed through him, barely controlled. "You didn't have to kill them."

"Oh, I know I didn't. But it was fun."

Her cackling nearly broke his resolve, but he sensed that's what she wanted—for him to unleash his magic in anger. Dark magic thrived on fury.

He reached for her, but she spun aside. He threw a rope of magic after her, snagging her wrist before she disappeared into the crowd. A cry rose up, and then the group parted to reveal Acelyne struggling against his hold.

That wasn't all. She held a young woman by the neck with her bound hand, and pressed the dagger to the woman's neck with her free hand.

"Let her go, Acelyne. You've already killed two people today, reason enough for the Seelie queen to sentence you to death. Let's not give her more cause to have you executed." No sense letting her know he was working for Midna. Besides, it was true. Murder was punishable in any kingdom.

He stepped slowly forward, keeping a tight grip on his magical rope and barrier. If he pulled on the rope, it could cause Acelyne to slit the woman's throat. The woman's face turned ashen, and he suspected the enchantress was stealing her magic. Another punishable offense. She really didn't care for the rule of law.

The woman whimpered and struggled against Acelyne's hold, but she was far too weak against the enchantress.

"I won't ask again." Therron stared down the enchantress, hating the choice he knew he'd have to make.

The cracks in Acelyne's face had all but disappeared, and she cricked her neck from side to side. She released the woman and, too quick for him to stop her, clutched a young boy to her bosom. He yipped and kicked, but her blade at his throat stopped the thrashing.

"I'll kill them all before I let you take me. Release your

hold over me, and I'll let them live. All of them." Her gaze went to the stricken woman. "Well, except for her."

Somewhere behind him, he heard sobbing and knew he couldn't let Acelyne kill anyone else. "Release him first, and I'll remove my bonds."

"How do I know I can trust you?"

"I give you my word as a thief you may have safe passage as long as you swear not to kill anyone else today."

She pouted and stamped her foot. "Oh, pooh. You're no fun." She tapped a finger to her lips and smiled. "Deal."

She knew he would let her go to save one life. She'd used that fact against him brilliantly, but Therron had no regrets. He hated letting her get away, but would set a trap for her at the market and capture her there—without any more deaths to burden his troubled heart.

＊   5   ＊

I f Rori didn't eat something soon, she needn't worry about who was behind the magical force that continued its incessant compulsion to rest. Something, or someone, didn't like her moving or having her own free will.

She set her shoulders and held her chin aloft while she scanned the area for food. Whatever sought to influence her mind, she'd need strength to fight and that meant nourishment.

Red berries dangled from a tree, tempting in their plumpness. She tentatively sampled one, shaking her head at the chalky bitterness that stung her tongue. This was no berry she recognized.

Immune to one hundred thirty-seven poisons, not much could kill her. Still, she didn't fancy testing the odds of finding number one hundred thirty-eight. Hunger or no, she hesitated to subject her body to possible ills from this wicked place. She swept past the berries to a patch of clover growing near a rock. At least clover wouldn't harm her. She pinched several stalks to munch now and filled both pockets for later. There was no telling when she'd find more.

She stood on wobbly legs and listed sideways, bracing

herself on a tree. This wasn't hunger—this was muscle fatigue. But she hadn't been fighting or running, and walking wouldn't produce full-body exhaustion—as if she'd been sick for a week.

With more effort than it should've taken, she pushed away from the trunk and stumbled down the path. A few feet on, she stepped around a circle of tall mushrooms, being careful not to disturb the faerie sleeping within.

Wait, a faerie? Here?

It was tiny, no bigger than her thumb. Even pixies weren't that small. She squinted at the wee thing, noting the veins on its wings, the curl of her teeny toes. This was a fae, she was certain of it. All the faeries she knew were the size of a human —some taller, some shorter, some average like her—but she'd never met another faerie so small. There were rumors of fae long ago who could alter their sizes, but Rori had yet to meet one in the flesh.

She gazed up at the trees, as if they could give her answers. This might be a trap. Everything in this forest was some bizarre version of reality. The wee fae might be an enchantment, one meant to lure her into compassion, to lower her defenses only to destroy her. Well, it wouldn't work. Compassion served no purpose and was best locked up tight where it couldn't impede her mission.

The smart thing to do was leave the fae sleeping in the mushroom circle. Keep walking and forget she ever saw the stupid thing. Even the mushrooms looked shady.

This forest wanted her dead, and apparently would use any trick it could to achieve its purpose. She glared into the distance. Adrenaline-fueled rage lifted her lagging spirits. Whatever this hell was, she would prevail. She took ten steps down the path before she let out a loud groan and turned back to the sleeping faerie. On the off chance it wasn't a trap, she couldn't leave the wee thing in this wretched place. It wasn't compassion, she told herself, but a sense of duty—hadn't she sworn an oath to Queen Eirlys to protect all fae when she became her spy?

Rori held a dagger in her right hand, ready for a surprise attack. She bent low and examined the tiny thing. From the clothing, she guessed the fae to be female. It didn't move when gently nudged. Skin the color of pale chestnut, life still flowed through the fae's veins, yet she stayed curled in a tight ball. Gossamer wings covered her like a protective embrace. All faeries had wings, including Rori, but they'd long since kept them tucked safely beneath their skin. Wings were awkward and uncomfortable to maneuver. At least, she assumed they would be. She'd never unfurled her wings, and didn't plan to, because for a faerie to reveal her wings meant this one was either royalty, or close to death and had lost control of her magic.

This forest, wherever or whatever it was, would not claim the sleeping faerie. She only hoped it wasn't too late.

Rori gently scooped the wee one onto her palm. The poor thing didn't even flinch at the movement. Never had she known a faerie to sleep this deep.

But then, until a few hours ago, she'd been slumbering just as deeply. Her thumb traced the fae's wing and a memory of long ago, before her father's disappearance, fluttered to the front of her mind. She must've been three or four at the time, still young and so very innocent. She'd found an injured sparrow in the woods with a thorn lodged between its feathers, preventing him from taking flight. As gently as her little hands had allowed, she'd removed the thorn, but the sparrow's wing was hopelessly damaged.

Tears stung the backs of Rori's eyes as she recalled how she'd stroked the soft feathers, begging the fragile wings to mend. She didn't know the words a healer might use, but she'd wished with all her heart for the bird to recover. The joy she'd felt when its little beak squawked and its wings flapped was unparalleled. It was also short-lived.

She'd run to her father and excitedly declared she'd healed a bird and wished to become a healer. Instead of applauding her efforts, her father had calmly taken the sparrow into his big hands and very efficiently broken the bird's neck.

Her tears dripped from Rori's cheeks as she remembered seeing the cool indifference in her father's eyes.

"We are assassins, Rori. We kill. We do not heal." He'd bent low, seriousness etched into his features. "Promise me you won't be foolish again? Yes? That's my girl. This will be our little secret." He'd stroked her hair and pinched her chin. "You wouldn't want to upset your mother, would you?"

Until that moment, she'd forgotten the elation she'd felt from healing the sparrow. Even now, recalling details hurt her brain. Tiny spikes pricked against her skull. She wiped her eyes and pushed the memory far from her thoughts. No use mourning the past, especially when her present was fraught with much bigger problems than an injured wing.

Still, the desire to heal—to help—was undeniable. It went against everything her father had taught her, but he wasn't there to criticize or condemn. Her legs wobbled at her tiny rebellion as she snuggled the fae into an inner breast pocket of her jacket with hope that the sound of her heartbeat would give the lass some comfort. Perhaps even wake her.

The sleeping fae was the first living thing she'd found... were there more? Or had this fae been kidnapped the same time as she? Had there been faeries at the pub? She scrubbed a hand over her face, trying to recall. Yes, two. Or three—she couldn't be certain—and full grown. Pixies weren't allowed in the Shoogly Dragon on account of their penchant for mischief, and inability to hold their liquor.

So, yes, there was at least one faerie at the pub. She strained to recall more details from the previous night. She'd met Tug, had dinner and a few pints, played darts. A groan rose from deep in her sternum as she remembered singing a rousing rendition of "Give Yer Goats to Mam for Milking"—always a crowd-pleaser—with Tug and his merry gang. She might've even danced. And who wouldn't with Tug around? He might be a giant, and twice the width of a full-grown man, but he was light on his feet and an absolute delight. Dear, sweet Tug…was he worried about her?

No, she wouldn't get mushy. She had to focus. What happened next? She struggled to focus, but after the singing and dancing, everything became fuzzy.

Her stomach gave a vicious pinch, reminding her she was still hungry. The mushrooms wobbled when she prodded them with her boot. They looked edible, but skepticism won out and she left the fungi alone. If she became desperate, she'd make her way back to the spot, but secretly hoped she'd be out of the forest before that happened. Even when non-poisonous and cooked properly, she hated the taste. Gods, but she wished Cian were there to advise her. Not that she'd ever admit it.

Where the hell was Cian, anyway? Rori continued through the forest, chewing one clover leaf at a time and marking every third tree she passed. The last she'd heard, Cian had been sent to the Unseelie Court. Not an outrageous assignment. Eirlys was trying to maintain peace with Queen Midna, after all. But why Cian? Surely Eirlys wasn't thinking of murdering the Unseelie queen? Nah, that would be too outrageous, even for Eirlys. Not to mention, it would destroy any peace the two courts shared.

If ever there was a man who could take out a public figure like Midna, it was Cian. Dashedly good-looking, charming, but never let his feelings distract from the mission, her brother was as lethal as they come.

Rori stopped so suddenly, her boots skidded on the dirt. What if Cian actually was involved in a plot to kill Midna, and she'd gotten caught up in it somehow? It would be just like him to drag her into his messy business.

She scanned the trees with renewed interest. This definitely could be the forsaken forest in the Unseelie kingdom. Filled with dark creatures and witches who practiced ancient, some would even say forbidden, magic. Rori had heard tales of ogres that ate their victims raw. And of tree-dwelling creatures who only traveled by the light of the moon. An involuntary shudder tightened her shoulders. Ogres and goblins and horrible beasties could stay far away from her. Although, at the moment, she wouldn't mind seeing one living forest creature who wasn't in a coma. She patted the pocket where the fae slept. Just something to let her know this wasn't an eternally damned place.

If this *was* a forbidden forest and she were captured, Queen Midna might hold her for ransom—which wouldn't be paid because she wasn't of noble blood and Queen Eirlys would deny any knowledge of Rori—or she might be forced into service for the Unseelie queen. A strange jag, not of pain, but something not entirely terrible, ran the length of her. A long dormant thrill warmed her in places she'd almost forgotten existed. Curiosity and excitement tightened her belly.

Forced into service to the Unseelie queen didn't mean digging in the diamond mines. That, Rori wouldn't mind. According to her sources, Midna exacted other forms of payment from her prisoners. Payment in the form of sexual pleasure. Whether that meant for the prisoner, or the queen, Rori wasn't sure. And she sure as hell didn't want to find out.

Liar.

6

That stupid pinching in her heart started again, and Rori glared at the trees. She had to find a way out of the forest before she relived every single failure she'd ever endured. This slow dive into madness would surely kill her as painfully as scaphism.

Especially in conjunction with thoughts about Queen Midna and her palace of seduction.

It wasn't just prisoners who entertained the queen sexually. The Academy might've given Rori her erudite education, but Midna's Unseelie Court was the reputed unofficial institute for higher learning where select spies from the Academy went to broaden their skills. What they taught at the Unseelie palace—so the rumors went—had nothing to do with textbooks and everything to do with intelligence gathering of a more intimate kind. The students who entered Midna's program were referred to as her álainn obedience. Beautiful obedients who swore to obey the queen's every command. While in her service, the álainn obedience gave up freedom and free will.

Rori kicked at the dirt and suppressed a shiver. How could

anyone voluntarily give someone else that kind of power? And for what? Sex? No thanks.

Queen Eirlys ruled her subjects with a stern resolve, but also with compassion and empathy. As long as those in her kingdom followed the law of the land, they were allowed to live their lives as they pleased. No one was forced into submission or kept a sexual prisoner in the palace. And to think, those who went to the Unseelie Court did so of their own volition.

It wasn't just students from the Academy who sought Midna's teachings. Subjects from all over Faerie, no matter rank or position, even elves from Elvenwood were said to seek out the Unseelie queen. Cian undoubtedly studied there.

"Eww, gross. Don't even go there, MacNair." She gagged a little at the mere thought. Or what about her father? He might've been one of the obedients, too. "Even grosser. Sweet biscuits, now it's in my brain. I can't ever unthink that."

What if they had? Sure, she'd heard tales of the debauched acts Midna made her álainn obedience perform on one another. All-night orgies played out for all the court to watch. Couplings of every sort of combination, no matter the gender or race. In Midna's court, anything was allowed. And all the while, the álainn obedience had to fulfill the court's every desire. What if her brother and father had gone there, or even her mother, and what if they'd enjoyed it? Not everyone was as timid sexually as her. She wasn't a prude, just…sexually awkward. Sex meant letting someone close, even if only for a shag. Closeness meant vulnerability. Another jag, this one tinged with nervous desire, surprised Rori.

If captured, would she be thrown in a dungeon, or offered a chance to become one of Midna's álainn obedience? If so, wha —she stopped the thought before it bloomed into full-fledged treason. She was a true subject of the Seelie Court. She was Rori MacNair, assassin and spy to Queen Eirlys. Her loyalty was now and forevermore pledged to protecting the Light. Her father had served the Seelie queen, and his father before him. Her mother was Eirlys's most trusted captain of the guard until she retired a few years ago. Rori's family connection to the Light went back ages.

The past rulers of Faerie had been as loyal to the MacNairs as they were to the Seelie throne. Eirlys believed in Rori, and she wouldn't do anything to abuse that trust. Rulers always had an agenda, one which Rori wasn't privy to, but she trusted that Eirlys had her best interest at heart.

The Dark court, with its promiscuous queen, was better left to men like Cian, who viewed their family's history to the crown far differently than Rori. But then, he could get away with breaking the rules. It was part of his charm. And he had far more experience than her. With women, with court politics, with life in general. As much as she loved her brother and was quite possibly a little jealous of his achievements, she didn't envy him an assignment at the Unseelie Court.

He had no problem sleeping with the enemy for information. She snorted and lifted her chin in defiance. Obviously, Cian had received different training from their father. She often wondered whether their father was as demanding with Cian, but she'd never had the nerve to ask. Everything came so easy to her brother, maybe their father didn't have to push so hard to get results. Maybe if he hadn't disappeared, once Rori reached puberty, she would've been sent to the Unseelie Court for specialized training. She'd never know. But it was clear Cian excelled at his job—in all aspects. Best not to dwell too deeply on any single area.

The ground rocked, and Rori braced herself on a nearby tree. Even though she felt the movement, the leaves didn't flutter, nor did the gravel move. A touch of vertigo, perhaps? Delirium from lack of water or food?

Every nerve went on high alert. Not using magic hadn't helped thus far. She was running out of options and had to do the thing she really didn't want to do. Just in case she was being watched, and not wanting to call attention to herself, Rori opened her magic a fraction, being extra careful to keep control. If she were attacked, she wanted to be prepared, but she also knew showing too much magic was like setting a beacon above the treetops, especially if her long dormant wild magic decided to make a sudden appearance.

Magic encircled her like a lover's embrace, sloughing off her lagging energy and renewing her spirit. Though her body still felt as if she'd been trampled by a pack of mountain trolls, that tiny spark of power gave her an adrenaline jolt she desperately needed. Way better than an espresso, which she desperately craved, with maybe a pain au chocolate on the side. *Focus, MacNair.* She tilted her head back and stared up at the leaves. What if she did send a beacon to the sky? Who would see it? Even if the Unseelie queen captured her, and forced her to become an álainn obedience, surely that was better than being trapped in these endless damned woods.

"Stop it, Aurora. You're talking nonsense." Rori spoke in her best Cian voice—using her full name, which he knew would annoy her—and tried to sound as authoritative as her big brother.

"You're right, as usual." Under her breath, she added, "Bastard," then laughed at the ridiculousness of having a conversation with herself as her brother. "I'm losing it." She peeked inside her pocket at the sleeping fae. "I'll get us out of here before I go completely mad."

The faerie didn't move, but Rori could've sworn she saw the slightest flutter of a wing.

Yes, she'd get them out of there before they both perished. The tiny thread of her magic swirled around her like a planet to its moon, keeping her upright, on course. Purpose renewed, she strode along the trail, marking trees as she went, and making mental notes of the minuscule changes in the forest. Here, some trees were thick-trunked and covered in ivy; over there, some had ferns growing from the valleys between branches; farther along, tall, slender trunks in muted greys stretched above the leafy canopy. This was absolutely no forest Rori knew. And she began to suspect it wasn't in the Unseelie kingdom, either.

What if, somehow, she'd stumbled into an enchanted forest in the elven kingdom?

Her heart thumped against her ribs and throat tightened, choking off vital air. If this was in King Thane's kingdom, then she was dead. The elves kept to themselves, not interfering in fae business and vice versa. The elven king didn't tolerate fae being in his lands. His punishments were harsher than Queen Eirlys's, and Rori didn't think Thane had a dungeon. She imagined he would tie a trespasser to a tree and leave them to slowly fade. Left to the elements, birds would peck out their eyes and rodents would eat their flesh. Probably starting with the softest tasty bits that would hurt the most. Blech.

"No more of that, please." Her imagination didn't need further prodding, at least not in the varied ways she might be tortured to death. She cupped her hand over the place where the fae slept. "I've never understood the rift between the kingdoms, have you?" Only silence came from her pocket.

Fae-elven distrust went back centuries, with no one recalling now what started it or why it continued. Elves were allowed to cross into Faerie, but she rarely saw them in the two kingdoms, and when she did, she kept a wary distance. Whatever caused the quarrel between Faerie and Elvenwood might've been forgotten, but the animosity between the kingdoms grew over time. Rori knew both queens kept elves at their palaces as spies, but where were their loyalties? How could the queens trust their intel? She'd always wondered about double and triple agents. Who did they really serve?

Rori served Queen Eirlys. She had no reason to mistrust

elves, but she saw no reason to court danger by befriending one, either.

If this forest was within King Thane's borders, she might have to do more than make nice with the sworn enemy of her queen. The last thing she wanted was to give Thane reason to start a war with Faerie. Capturing a faerie spy on his lands would be an excellent reason, indeed.

7

Thoughts of war never ended well, so Rori banned the subject from her mind. At least, she tried to. But the more she tried to not think of war, the more she envisioned her beloved homeland in flames, her friends suffering. Their screams tortured her ears; their burnt bodies lay at her feet. Even though she knew it wasn't real, she felt responsible all the same.

"It's an illusion, MacNair. There is no war. Your friends are fine." Rori said the words over and over like a mantra, but the more she spoke, the deeper her fear.

Panic joined her burgeoning dread and she fought them both with each step forward. The more her anxiety rose, the harder breathing became. The air thickened with her increased pulls of oxygen. She paused and forced herself to think of happier times. A vision of when she was young and Cian would chase her around their garden, pretending to be an ogre, popped into her mind. Then a memory of when she first entered the Academy and the pride she saw on her mum's face.

Her breathing slowed and the air thinned.

Curious.

Rori continued on, being mindful of her breathing. When her thoughts careened toward despair, the air became thick and she'd repeat the process, thinking happy thoughts until she calmed. This deep into the woods, she couldn't afford to waste energy or oxygen. Pacing herself, she came to yet another fork in the road and took the right. Trees clumped closer the farther along the path she traveled, until her shoulders brushed the trunks on either side. A slim line of gravel led through the moss growing at the tree bases. She trudged on, sometimes sidling between two ungainly trunks until absolute darkness made continuing difficult. Even with her enhanced fae sight, she couldn't make out what was beyond her outstretched hand.

Snickertits. Rori pressed both palms to her forehead and stomped a circle twice before she bent over, hands on her thighs, and considered her choices: go back the way she came and take the left path, or carry on into the darkness and hope for the best. The obvious move would be to retrace her steps, but Rori wasn't known for making the obvious choice. Which was why Queen Eirlys chose her to become a spy. Her targets never saw her coming, and if they did, they wouldn't know what to expect from her. Chaotic savant, the queen had called her. Now, she hoped it served her well.

She stood to her full height and set her shoulders. The forest would not win this day. She took out her phone and prayed there was enough battery life to get her through this patch. The light illuminating from the flashlight app wasn't much, but at least it cast a small circle through the inky blackness. Mobile in one hand, dagger in the other, she lunged forward with the determination of a general marching to war. If she'd had enough battery, she would've put on a badass playlist to boost her confidence.

Her boots crunched against gravel with each determined stomp. She might've swung her hips a bit, too, just for the swagger. A dozen steps in, the light flickered on her mobile, then went black. She took a tentative step forward, but there was no sound. Even the soft hush of her breathing vanished, and she was left in a noiseless vacuum.

Indecision racked her thoughts, and her pulse fluttered. Waves of nausea rode over her, with not-so-subtle messages to turn back. She struggled to step forward, but was buffeted by an unseen force. This was beyond a compulsion to turn around. This was powerful magic. Someone or something didn't want her to travel any farther. Bile inched up her throat, and she swallowed hard. If this path was forbidden, she'd be damned if she turned back now.

She wasn't a quitter. When she'd faced magical trials at the Academy, she'd persevered even though she'd nearly shit herself with how scared she'd been that her wild magic would be discovered. When the lycan brothers were hell-bent on killing her, she'd dug deep and bested them without using magic. When her father died, she'd continued training, pushing herself so that if, impossible as it may seem, when he returned he'd think her worthy.

If she didn't win this test, none of that would matter.

Rori tucked the useless mobile into a pocket and held the dagger aloft. Her faerie magic swirled around the blade, giving it a comforting glow. For one mad moment, she debated searching for her wild magic, thinking it might be what she'd need to help her escape. That was foolhardy reasoning. She didn't need forbidden magic, nor could she trust it. It might destroy her and quite possibly all of Faerie. Or, it might be exactly what the forest wanted from her. It had dragged every last bit of shame and remorse from her; maybe her wild magic was the final ingredient needed to fully break her emotionally and mentally.

Whatever the forest's intentions, she wouldn't give in—her

fae magic would protect her. She allowed only enough to see one pace in front of her, no more.

Struggling through the unseen force, she took one, then two, then three steps, all the while listening. A death-like eeriness hung on every branch, cloaked every leaf. Her breaths came in short pulls without disturbing the air. Another step. Rori slammed into something hard, her dagger making an odd clinking sound.

She reached her free hand out and felt along a smooth surface. As high and wide as she could touch was an invisible wall.

What the ever-loving bloody freaking hell? Rori took a step back and surveyed what she couldn't see. Beyond the barrier, lights flickered. The ground shifted, and she steadied herself against the sudden movement. It could've been an earthquake, but of the few she'd actually experienced, this felt different. Her stomach buzzed with nerves, like a hive of bees hopped up on meth. This wasn't good, whatever was happening.

The trees were too closely spaced to give her any idea of what the sky looked like. No rain fell, nor did any wind blow, but the ground was rocking just the same. Violently. She returned to the wall and pressed both hands against it, but it wouldn't budge. The hilt of her dagger cut into her palm with the effort.

A flash of light, then another, and the rocking stopped. The world spun with terrifying speed and the buzz in her gut turned sinister.

She rested her head against the barrier, welcoming the coolness against her forehead. The smooth wall reminded her of glass.

Her heart raced with possibilities. A glass wall? In a forest? Ridiculous, yes, but then nothing here made sense. She hoped, however, if it were glass, it could break. And

sucked forward, through the barrier. The sound of shattering glass stole her hearing. Bright lights blinded her. Pain, acute and all-consuming, tore through her limbs. Something hard slammed into her, or she into it, and the air rushed from her lungs with one great whoosh.

Futnuckers and cocklesocks. That didn't go as she'd hoped.

🦋 8 🦋

The crowded market made it difficult for Therron to keep a guarded distance between himself and Acelyne. As soon as she'd released the boy, he let his magic drop. Before his next breath, she'd fled the street, and he heard the clop of goat hooves several blocks over. At least she'd kept her word. After making sure the boy was unharmed, and confirming the woman she'd stolen magic from was alive, Therron had left the townsfolk to heal their kin. It didn't sit right with him to leave without healing those who needed it, but he had to find Acelyne before she was in the wind.

He just hoped the young lad's information about meeting at the market was good. It would only add to Therron's guilt if it wasn't and his death was in vain. Acelyne's mocking sneer cut through his memory, and he winced at the delight she'd shown at having killed the boy. She was getting reckless and far too bold for his comfort. Now he understood Midna's need to eliminate the enchantress, but he still didn't know what she had stolen from the Unseelie queen.

As he'd entered the market from the north, he caught a

flash of red and gold as Acelyne wove in and out of sight. She carried a large floral carpet bag that he'd not seen before. In all the weeks following her, he couldn't remember her ever carrying anything more than a cloak for when it turned cold. Perhaps finally, he'd get answers, if only she'd stop darting to and fro, frustrating him to the brink of madness. He hadn't yet worked out how best to capture her, but for certain, the very busy, very public venue wasn't his first choice.

At an intersection of stalls, Therron paused. To his right hung the featherless bodies of ducks, geese, and chickens. On his left stretched a long line of brightly colored goods. More foodstuffs were laid in front of him. Why the market? Why today? If he was a betting man, which he very much was not, he'd put money on whatever was in the bag.

He dodged a large family laden with heavy trunks and tucked into an alcove to gather his wits. His senses were on high alert from the morning's events, and he couldn't risk missing whatever was to transpire next. There was something about Cere that had kept the enchantress here for several days. Aside from the wild chase this morning, and now the market, she'd not gone anywhere else in the city besides the pub a few nights past. The one with the ridiculous name, *Shoogly Dragon*.

A smile tilted his lips despite himself. The pub where he'd seen the beautiful lass with outlandish blue hair. He'd tried not to watch her, as he was supposed to be keeping an eye on Acelyne. Tried and failed.

The lass intrigued him, it was true. Her strange clothing consisted of tight black trousers and heavy black boots, and a leather jacket cut as he'd never seen before. Short, hitting around the waist, she wore a black shirt beneath with cutouts that would be scandalous in the elven court. Tiny glimpses of her belly showed through, enough to tantalize and tease. The fantasies he'd had that night of what lay beneath her clothing had stayed with him. Even now, at the memory of her, his blood warmed.

Best to nudge thoughts of the girl aside and concentrate on the job at hand. With a mournful sigh, Therron eased into a small crowd. A flash of red caught his attention, and he kept his focus above the heads of those surrounding him.

"If you wish to live, you won't move," a squealish voice hissed in Therron's ear.

"And if you wish to live, you'll remove your blade." Blood and ashes, he'd been so intent on his memories of the pretty lass, he'd not paid attention to his surroundings. He turned slowly to see who his would-be murderer was.

"Don't look at me. Stay where you are." Cool steel pushed against his midsection.

"Easy now. Let's not do anything rash. If it's robbery you've got in mind, I'm afraid you'll be disappointed."

"Why are you following me?"

This took Therron aback. The voice was certainly male, and by the smell of him, not someone acquainted with bathing regularly. An acrid wave of perspiration assaulted his nostrils. He breathed as shallow as possible to avoid the stench.

"I am not following you, friend."

"I saw you the other night. And again on the road. Now you're here. Did she send you? Is she unhappy with my work? I did as told—why does she want me dead, too?"

She who? The enchantress? Therron twisted his head enough to see the top of a greasy brown head. He'd said he was at the pub, yet Therron couldn't place him. "I don't know who you refer to, nor am I following you. As I've said."

"Don't turn around." The blade's sharp point cut against his ribs.

Therron slid his own knife from his sleeve into his palm. His hood slipped with the movement. "I don't like being threatened, nor do I like being told what to do."

A gasp came from the man. "You're an elf. What's she want with the elves? I thought it was only fae—" The man cut off his words and clamped his mouth shut.

"Who is this mysterious 'she' you keep referring to?" Therron eased his blade up to the man's soft belly. The last thing he needed was a fight in a busy marketplace.

"No one you need concern yourself with." At the pressure from Therron's blade, the man sucked in a breath. "Oy, what do you think you're doing?"

"I told you. I'm not following you, nor do I know who you're talking about. Either you remove your dagger, or I'll gut you right here."

The blade left Therron's ribs, and he turned to confront the stranger. He recognized the wide face and overly thick lips. The man had been at the pub with the girl—the attractive lass with wild laughter and daggers at her thighs. Details from that night blinked through his mind like picture cards being placed upon a table. Skilled at darts, not so much at singing. Her eyes, as deep and mysterious as the ocean, shone with merriment, and her creamy cheeks pinked each time she smiled, which she did often. Her odd clothing set her apart from the rest of the crowd and that only made her more intriguing.

But it was her confidence and easy grace that drew him to her like a dragon to its hoard. He'd wanted to simultaneously protect her, and follow her wherever adventure might lead. He'd yearned to speak with her, but didn't wish to jeopardize his surveillance. Before he could talk himself into it, she'd disappeared.

"Where's the enchantress?" Therron growled low, his irritation mounting.

The man blanched, and he shook his head. "Acelyne? Ain't gotta tell ya." Confusion danced in his eyes, followed by understanding. "You're following her, ain't ya? Why're you following the witch?"

"She has something of mine, and I'd like it back."

The man's laugh was maniacal and guttural. "If she's taken it, then it's gone. Gone, gone, gone. You should forget what she has and return to your kingdom." He repeated, "Gone, gone, gone," several more times, as if he were singing a nursery rhyme.

"What do you mean?"

The stranger shook his head violently, as if having a spasm. "No, she swore me to silence. I dinna want to help, but she made me. Made me hurt her. I dinna want to. No." The last word strung out into one long "ooooooooooo" and his whole body trembled.

His jerking caused Therron's blade to cut through the soft flesh of his torso. Blood oozed onto his tunic, making a small red stain. Therron cursed under his breath. There was nothing for it now. He'd have to get away from him as quickly as possible to avoid suspicion. He wiped the knife on the man's clothing and slid it up his sleeve. This made three deaths in as many hours that he was connected to. He doubted the constables would consider it coincidence.

With a quick glance around to make sure he'd not drawn unwanted attention, he clapped the man on his shoulder. "Well, friend, I bid you well in your endeavors. If you won't tell me where to find the witch, I'll just have to make do on my own."

As much as he wished to know, there wasn't time to ask what the strange ramblings meant, and Therron doubted he'd get straight answers from the cretin. It was best to leave him there, in the center of the crowded market.

The man grabbed Therron's jacket. "Tell her I'm sorry. She can trust Sal. I dinna want to." Tears streaked down his cheeks. His face twisted in torment. "She hurt me." He tapped his head. "In here. I can feel her."

Therron paused, his voice lowering with concern. "Who did you hurt, Sal?"

"I'm sorry. Tell her. Promise me you will. Tell her Sal dinna mean to hurt her." His eyes glazed and an ashen pall crept into his cheeks. Dark half-moons edged his eyes.

"I'll tell her. You should go have a lie down. You don't look well. Go home, get some rest. You'll feel better by tomorrow."

By tomorrow he'd be long dead. Therron's daggers were coated in a hard-to-find poison that acted quickly or slowly, depending upon how calm a person remained. He hadn't meant to cut Sal, but with his thrashing, he'd probably not last more than five minutes. It was best he wasn't seen with Sal when he collapsed.

Try as he might, he really did want to leave a good impression on the subjects of Faerie that elves could be trusted, but with the enchantress on a killing spree, and now Sal caught up in the mess, he feared he wasn't doing a good job of it. His father would be so proud.

Therron whispered an elven blessing before he turned and left the man where he stood. He pulled his hood low over his face and scanned the area for the enchantress. She was still here—he could feel it. At the end of a long row of stalls, he spotted her crimson gown and headed in that direction, keeping himself as hidden as possible.

A quick glance over his shoulder showed Sal standing upright, his knife hanging from his fingertips. Life had all but left his eyes. Therron was relieved to see he hadn't yet crumpled in the middle of the street. He needed to distance himself from the crime and quickened his pace until he'd put two more rows of stalls between him and the maniac. A sharp cry rose above the din of merchants and townsfolk. Someone shouted that they had discovered the wounded man named Sal. Therron ducked behind another stall, his focus on Acelyne, but keeping an ear toward the ruckus with Sal. If they came looking for Therron, that might be a complication he didn't need.

By the sounds of it, the search was heading in the opposite direction. He strained to listen, delighting a little too much at the mention of, "the little bugger deserved no less." The man might've shown remorse for his actions, but it appeared to be too little, too late.

That damn thumping began in Therron's heart, pinching with sharp jabs of pain. Maybe it had to do with Sal. After all, the mysterious pain started that night at the pub. At first, he attributed it to the stale beer, but three days on, he had to admit it was something else. Therron paused to rub his rib cage and muttered a curse. Whatever these strange pangs were, he wished they would stop.

He spotted the enchantress hunched over a table, midway down the row where he stood. He slowed his steps and made his way to the back of a booth selling pots and housewares. Acelyne bent to retrieve her bag and began placing caskets, small wooden boxes with highly stylized decorative scrollwork covering the tops and sides, on the table. She took each box carefully out of the fabric bag and set them down as if they were prized crystal.

A month of travel throughout Faerie without a whiff of fanfare, and now she's setting up shop in Cere's market. He glanced up and down the row. Was this what kept her in the city? And if so, what was she selling?

Intrigued, Therron slipped behind another stall, one festooned with scarves decorated in bright colors. A small breeze furled the wispy fabric to and fro, blocking his sight and increasing his irritation. He hurried to another booth, this one selling jewelry and trinkets. From this vantage point, he could see Acelyne clearly—see the minute details of the wooden caskets she arranged on the table.

Another sharp jab in his chest stole his breath. What in the name of dragon's breath was wrong with him? He could remember only a handful of days he'd been sick in his life, but nothing like the tightness he felt around his heart. That's it—after today, he'd head back to Elvenwood and have a healer fix whatever was wrong with him.

The enchantress opened one of the caskets to reveal glass vials enclosed in swirling metalwork. The trinkets he stood beside looked like child's play compared to the beauty of the amulets carefully resting on velvet. He did a quick count and came up with six amulets per box, twelve boxes.

Whatever Acelyne was up to, he was keen to discover what the glass pendants had to do with it. He cast his mind back to the night at the pub—he didn't remember Acelyne carrying a bag, nor did he recall her having any caskets. In fact, he'd been most perplexed why she'd chosen that particular pub. It wasn't her typical haunt of dark corners and murky conversation. The Shoogly Dragon was lively and filled with laughter. Most of that came from the blue-haired beauty he'd tried not to watch all evening.

The pub had a decent number of customers that night, a mix of fae, giants, trolls, a pair of brownies who kept to themselves, and an ogre tucked into a back corner. He noted the lack of pixies, but spied at least one goblin seated at the bar. An ogress serving maid kept the guests' tankards full while a muscular faerie with keen eyes and an impressive black beard worked behind the bar. Therron doubted he allowed any mischief to occur on the premises.

Each time Therron found himself drawn to the pretty woman with the odd clothing and sapphire locks, he'd jerked his attention back to Acelyne. Yet again and again, his gaze drifted to the lass. Her laughter was like a summer melody played at a festival. Brash and fast, and meant to be enjoyed by all those who were lucky enough to hear. It wasn't like him to be distracted, especially when on a job. But how could he avoid her? She drank and danced and played darts as well as any elf he'd known.

She and her friends made a merry group. They adored her, but she didn't seem to notice. Yet each one, especially the giant she affectionately hovered over much of the night, treated her with reverence, as if she were the fae queen herself.

Even though the trolls soundly walloped her at darts, she'd jested with them good-naturedly and offered to buy them another round. The trolls had chortled and mussed her hair with jolly familiarity. Only once had there been tension between the lass and pub goers when a satyr knocked over her drink with his tail. But even then, she'd clapped him on the ass and waved it off as an accident.

He was the first satyr Therron saw in Faerie, nay, the only one he'd seen in all his days there and he'd spent a great amount of time wondering what the lad was doing so far from home. Satyrs didn't often leave their lands in the south, but he'd overheard Midna telling an álainn obedience that she wished they would venture north more often.

Therron's veins chilled as if the Snow Queen herself had touched his soul. After the satyr incident, Sal had brought the beauty a drink. It wasn't long after that she excused herself to use the toilet. *Then...* Therron replayed every detail of that night.

He'd been watching Acelyne, with an eye to the lively girl, it was true. When she left the common room, the enchantress had followed. This was easy to recall, but Sal's role in the evening—other than bringing her a drink—that was clouded in his memory. It was as if a solid wall prevented him from remembering what happened after the girl left the common room.

The enchantress. He glared at her hard, his jaw clenched tight enough he might crack a tooth. Of course she would've tampered with his mind. After all, he was a witness to her quarrel with the beauty. Yes, he fumbled through the images scattered in his brain—the enchantress and the dagger-wielding lady had faced off in the courtyard. Angry words were spoken. What were they? Therron shook his head, trying to loosen the fog clouding his memories.

Blood and ashes, that girl could fight, that much he knew. She'd landed several punches, followed by hard kicks to Acelyne's midsection, some of which Therron was certain would've felled a giant. Yet the enchantress had barely reacted. Only when the girl connected her fist to Acelyne's face did she snarl and retaliate.

Therron's thoughts became muddied. The harder he tried to remember what happened next, the sooner his mind snapped to afterward, when he sat alone at the table, drinking his beer and wondering why he'd gone to the Shoogly Dragon.

Acelyne paced nervously in front of the table, her dark eyes scanning the rows as if waiting for someone. A woman approached, but the enchantress shooed her away. She was waiting for a buyer, by the looks of it, and a specific one at that. It was curious to see her anxious whereas before she always appeared confident, even aloof. She dug her nails into her palm and flicked dust off her gown as she walked a tiny circle.

As Therron studied this new development in Acelyne's behavior, he fought to remember every detail of what had happened at the pub. Fragments came, enough to piece together the puzzle if given enough time. One memory blazed clear in his mind—the enchantress had grasped a handful of that lovely blue hair and dragged the unconscious lass behind her, issuing commands like the queen's general.

It was a terrible thing to see the girl's body go limp, the fight gone from her. The strange pangs quickened, and Therron rubbed his temples. What did the fight between Acelyne and the lass have to do with anything? He stared at the wee amulets on their velvet beds and dragged a hand through his hair while blowing out a breath. What happened next? His mind pushed against the haze of his memories. More came, but they didn't bring relief.

Therron had chased after Acelyne and the girl, only to find they'd disappeared. Not as in they turned a corner and were gone, but vanished. He'd searched the area before returning to the pub in the hope they'd gone back inside. That's when he heard Sal telling the giant the girl had fallen sick and probably went home.

Sal had said he was sorry, that he hadn't meant to hurt her. Did he mean the girl? Therron glanced over his shoulder in the direction he'd left Sal to die. Had the beauty hurt him? Or did Sal mean Acelyne? The questions spun like a tempest through his mind.

A commotion at the enchantress's table drew his full attention. He moved to the edge of the jeweler's stall, half-hidden by the flowing scarves to his right. The giant from the pub strolled into view, oblivious of the enchantress or what lay on her table. He paused at a stall selling housewares and bent over to inspect an item. Therron debated approaching him to ask after the girl. His desperation to know whether she was safe was overriding his good sense to stay hidden.

A flash lit the area, accompanied by a mini boom that rattled nearby booths. A whooshing followed, as if he were in a cave and all the air was sucked out of it. If he'd blinked, he would've missed seeing the girl tumble from the table to the ground. Blue hair fanned around her crumpled body. He knew that hair, had dreamt of running his fingers through it more than once since that night in the pub.

His heart beat quicker, the pangs coming fast and sharp.

If this was death, he'd not have it. Not now.

The giant turned, his eyes huge in his broad face. "Rori? What are ye doin' here?"

Rori? Therron's mind spun, playing the deck of cards through his thoughts like a dealer at one of the pleasure houses. Aurora MacNair. Daughter to Labhruinn and Hagan, sister to Cian. Preferred to be called Rori. Employed by Queen Eirlys as a spy and assassin.

He knew this girl—as much as anyone could know someone from records and secondhand accounts. Yet there was more. The scar on his cheek burned, and he shook his head to deny the reality of what was happening. Not now. Not her. If the goddess had any compassion, then please not the pretty woman from the pub.

Once, long ago, a child had come to him in a vision and told him his destiny was tied to Faerie in the form of a woman who would alter the course of the worlds. He'd never known the woman's name, or what she looked like, but now, as he stared at the strangely dressed lass who was helped to stand by the giant, he knew her in his heart. His scar, the mark that he'd had since birth, the physical embodiment of the curse that spelled his doom, burned so deeply he felt it in his bones.

Therron Mistwalker, First Son to King Thane of the Elves, heir to the Forest Throne, thief, murderer, and sometime employee to Queen Midna of the Unseelie Court, felt, for what might've been the first time in his life, absolute, all-consuming, dread.

irt mixed with blood in Rori's mouth, making a silty metallic paste that choked what little breath she had left. Her nails scraped against the ground as she dragged her body up to rest on bloodied palms and knees. The last of her energy stores depleted, she crumpled in an awkward heap, making sure she didn't scrunch the fae in her pocket. It was then, when she was facedown in the dirt, that she heard Tug's deep baritone.

"Rori? What are ye doin' here?"

His strong hand gripped her arm, and she was pulled upward. Fresh pins of pain tormented her, and she whimpered.

A hand on each of her shoulders gave her support. She blinked at Tug in confusion. Her sight and hearing were stunted, and his words sounded like gnats buzzing. She glanced at the stalls and shoppers, all normal size. She looked from Tug to herself and could've cried that he was the same giant friend she'd always known. Except now, his sweet eyes, as soft and brown as a newborn fawn, were filled with worry and his kind smile, the one that he shared with strangers and friends alike, was drawn into a frown. A mop of black hair covered his head, with tufts sticking up here and there. Splotches of his breakfast stained the simple beige tunic he wore. At least that hadn't changed. Her sweet Tug.

She turned to take in the market and something delicate crunched beneath her boot. Splinters of glass glittered in the morning sun. Fragments of green leaves and shrubs were strewn a foot in diameter. To her right, she spied a velvet-lined casket with several pendants tucked into place. No bigger than her thumb, some looked like vials she would use for potions. A slim twig with tiny petals tucked into crevices snaked around the glass. Looping and scrolling metalwork held everything in place. Lovely beaded chains attached to the tops.

Amulets.

She peered closer at the decorated glass. Inside each was a miniature forest.

In another casket were crystals, also secured with beautiful twisted and twirling wires. Deep in the heart of each crystal, a soft glow emanated. The churning of her belly matched the tightening of her heart. She checked her pocket for the sleeping fae, breathing a sigh of relief when she saw a pale shimmering against the dark fabric. At least this faerie was safe. She scanned the pretty pendants, looking for signs of life beyond their faint glow. Signs she knew wouldn't be seen.

Rori pinched the skin on her wrist, wincing at the sharp pain. This was no dream. No illusion. How had she broken out when the other fae couldn't? They must all be drugged the same as she'd been, yet unable to fight their way out. She gazed up at Tug, at his size, and wondered again whether the sleeping fae in her pocket was truly that small, and if not, why didn't she return to her true height when Rori broke the amulet?

Her gaze swept the caskets. If they broke open the glass prisons, would they kill the fae inside? If they survived, would they stay miniature versions of themselves? She couldn't risk their lives. Until she knew how to break the enchantments they were under, they'd have to stay in the amulets.

A slender woman with hair as bright as the noonday sun stared at her, mouth agape, a stunned look on her face. As if jolted awake with a hot poker, she jerked to attention and darted to the back of the stall.

Rori sprang after her, regretting the movement instantly, and ignoring the torrent of pain.

"Where ye goin'?" Tug called, but Rori sped on.

She'd explain everything later. Right now she needed answers.

The woman darted between bright swathes of fabric, her scarlet gown whipping this way and that, making Rori dizzy with its speed. Her legs cramped and begged her to stop, but she continued, down one alley, through another. The longer she followed the woman, the clearer her sight and hearing became. At the crossing between New Town and the market square, the woman vanished. Not disappeared into a crowd, but just… vanished. One second, she was there—the next, she was gone. Empty air. No dress, no sunlit hair, nothing.

Rori raised her face and bellowed at the sky. A stream of curses left her lips as she kicked the dirt. If only it were the stupid woman's face beneath her boot. She jogged back to the stall where the woman had run off.

"What's gotten into ye?" Tug stood in front of the amulets, arms crossed.

Bless his heart, he'd waited for her.

"First, ye abandon us at the pub, then ye turn up bloodied and whatnot in the market three days later. Ye've done some crazy things afore, but nothing like this."

"Three days? I was gone three days?" Rori bent over and placed her hands on her knees. Breathing in deep drags, she waited for the roaring in her ears to die down before attempting to stand.

"Here, lemme help ye." Tug took her arm and wrapped it around his thick waist.

She leaned into him, appreciative for his support.

"Ye said ye had to use the ladies, that yur tummy was feelin' kinda funny. When ye didn't come back, well, we all thought maybe ye went home to sleep it off. Then I checked on ye the next day, and ye weren't at the cottage. Looked all over for ye, I did. Didn't find ye until just now."

Warmth spread from her chest across her body. Good old Tug. He wasn't the brightest spark in the sky, but he had a good soul. No matter how hard she tried to push him away, he never let it bother him, and somehow found a way to burrow even further into her heart. She couldn't imagine her life without seeing his joyful smile or hearing the deep baritone of his voice. Truly, she was grateful he hadn't let her force him from her life.

"Thanks be for that, my friend. I'm not really sure where I was, but I have a feeling these little trinkets hold a clue." She indicated the velvet-lined boxes. "Do you have a bag? I want to take all of these back to my cottage."

"Isn't that stealing? Ye chased the woman off who was selling 'em."

Stealing? After what she'd been through, he was worried about her stealing? She almost laughed but for the tears that stung her eyes. How could she explain to him where she'd been when she wasn't even sure herself?

"Please, Tug. I'll explain everything when we get to my place."

They put the caskets into Tug's bag, making sure not to break any of the pendants. The soft shimmering emanating from the center of the crystals nearly broke her heart. If they contained what Rori thought they did, she couldn't risk endangering the contents. That someone would trap fae in the crystals—to what end? Simmering rage kept her pulse heightened.

As they made their way down the high street, Rori stayed alert to danger. She held the bag in a protective grip that even Tug couldn't pry apart. The woman in the scarlet dress could be anywhere, and she'd be damned if she let herself be captured again. The fact that the woman got the jump on her once already stung, but now Rori had others to protect—Tug as well as those in the pendants she carried.

The wide cobblestoned streets, the buildings that her ancestors had built—hell, even the sky—looked the same as before. It was as if no one even noticed that she was gone. But then, why would they? Rori often came and went with zero fanfare. She'd spend months at a time in the human realm. Most of the folks she saw on the way to her cottage had never even traveled beyond the town's wall. They liked the sameness of their lives, believed in the safety of the sturdy bricks that enclosed the town.

Rori had once believed in those ancient stones, too. But now? Now everything had changed. The questions she'd feared asking loomed over her thoughts. Who was capable of drugging her, in a public place no less? And how had Rori let herself be captured? Some spy she was. Cian would be mortified to know she'd failed him this spectacularly.

He'd always believed in her. Believed in her abilities not just as a spy, but he'd always wanted so much more for her. Perhaps he knew, somehow, that she wasn't cut out for espionage. But that's all that Rori knew. Cian hadn't approved of their father training her at such a young age, but was powerless to stop it—as was their mother. And after their father's death, well, Rori refused to stop training and eventually Cian gave up trying to dissuade her.

It wasn't just Cian she was worried about disappointing. It was her queen. Eirlys had put her trust in Rori and now, someone had not only drugged her, but was able to trap her inside a tiny glass amulet. What kind of trust would the queen give her now? She'd be lucky if she were stripped of her position and put on desk duty. Or worse, forced to wear a gown and socialize with the courtiers as a palace mole. She'd rather die than succumb to that torture.

Whether sanctioned by her queen or not, Rori saw this as a mission she needed to complete. Who was the witch powerful enough to imprison not just Rori, but the others? Her palm covered her heart as if to protect the sleeping faerie. She had to solve the riddle for the good of the kingdom, but also to prove to herself that she wasn't an abject failure. She couldn't lose. If she did, it would be more than disappointing her queen. If she didn't win this game, it would cost the lives of innocent faeries, and that wasn't something she could live with.

Getting the pendants to Eirlys was her highest priority. The Seelie queen could protect the imprisoned fae against the witch's forbidden magic far better than Rori could. Eirlys would determine the next steps, but Rori was determined to find who was responsible, no matter the cost.

A sharp pang cut at her heart, and she grunted against it. Tug glanced at her with concern, but she shook her head to ward off any comforting he might give. Her nerves prickled, and she unsheathed the dagger at her hip. They were being followed.

10

Rori checked her hold of the bag and considered using a tiny amount of magic as a protective barrier. She couldn't risk it. Now that she knew a witch had kidnapped her, she wouldn't risk opening her magic to being stolen or abused. This was no ordinary kitchen witch. She was an enchantress or sorceress, neither of which Rori was prepared to encounter in her weakened condition.

Witches, wizards, enchantress, sorceress…what did the name matter if it all amounted to the same thing—they used spells to enhance their natural magic. It was all in the way they manipulated those tools, she supposed. But then, like everything else, there were good and bad witches. Evil and benevolent wizards. Yet Rori had never heard of an enchantress being anything but deceitful.

"Ye look like a mama carlix protectin' her kit. What's goin' on, Aurora?" Tug cut through her musings, and she forced a smile.

Only Tug was brave enough to use her formal name and compare her to a winged cat all in the same breath. "I don't know, but I plan to find out."

Her grip slipped on the bag, exhaustion winning out over her need to protect the caskets.

"I kin help ye." He took the bag from her and snugged it against his hip with a nod. "Ye might need someone t'look after ye, seeing as yer not quite yerself today."

Rori glanced up at his innocent face. "This could be dangerous. Are you sure?"

His big shoulders rose nearly to his ears and dropped again. "Ain't got nothin' else to do this mornin'."

Rori put a hand on his shoulder and squeezed. She'd known him for almost a decade and in all that time, he'd never let her down. She could trust him with anything, including her life, but she knew he abhorred violence of any kind. With his size, he easily overpowered others and it was his deepest fear that someday he'd accidentally hurt someone. She had to make sure whatever was going on in Faerie, Tug wasn't caught in the crossfire, metaphorical or physical.

She sighed and shook her head. "I can't promise it won't get dirty. As in, there might be people trying to kill me by the end of this, whatever *this* is." She eyed the bag holding the amulets. "You know what I do, and you know it's dangerous. This isn't your fight, my friend."

Tug shifted the bag to his front and wrapped his arms protectively around it. "I know."

They turned onto her street, and Rori scanned the buildings on either side. No movement and no shadows indicated they'd been followed, but the hairs on the back of her neck rose menacingly. As they rounded the corner, she chanced a glance behind them. Aside from townsfolk going about their day, nothing unusual caught her attention. Still, there was an unsettling discomfort in the shadows, a sense of being watched that she couldn't shake.

The two daggers she wore brought her some comfort. She opened the gate leading to her cottage, a cute little two-story with a thatched roof and a tidy yard that she'd bought the previous year. Tug took care of the place when she was away, always making sure it was stocked with her favorite foods and ready for when she returned. It was one of the many odd jobs he did around Cere, and she was happy for his help. Although, if she'd known how much time he'd spend there, she might've looked for a bigger place.

She unlocked the door to her cottage and again swept the street and hillside while Tug folded his body to fit through the doorway. At just five and a half feet tall, even Rori had to duck to get inside, something she'd found charming at first. Poor Tug. He was half again her height. At least the interior was high enough he could stand with comfort.

"Put those on the table." Rori pointed to the large wooden planks she used for a dining table and went to the kitchen to make tea. It was then she remembered the clover she'd picked from the forest. "Tug, what can you tell me about this?" She thrust a handful at him, smothering a grimace with a look of innocent curiosity.

Even though she'd studied botany at the Academy, Tug's innate knowledge of just about every plant that grew in Faerie far exceeded hers. His knowledge was gained from experience instead of formal education, and although she needed his expertise, she didn't want to alarm him. Despite his offer to help, it was her duty to keep him safe. He was a subject of Faerie, but more importantly, he was her friend.

Tug retrieved a bowl from her cupboard and placed the clover inside, then buried his face in the green leaves. After several grunts and long, whistling sniffs, he shook his head. "Dunno. Looks like clover, smells like clover, but it ain't clover." He pinched a leaf from the bunch and tested it with his tongue before sliding it into his mouth. For several agonizing seconds, he chewed and swished, all the while his features perplexed.

Rori put the kettle on and kept watch of her friend while he investigated the questionable plant. She'd only eaten a few leaves, and even Tug had taken a bite. It wasn't poisonous, that much she knew. If there was any chance it could've been, she wouldn't have let Tug try it. He said it wasn't clover. Then what was it?

A growl issued from her stomach loud enough to wake an ogre. Tug cast her a withering glance, and she shrugged her answer. "I haven't eaten since you saw me at the pub."

Her legs wobbled, and she swooned against the counter. The last dregs of adrenaline had worn off, and she was left with a mind-numbing exhaustion.

Tug went into maternal mode and shooed her from the kitchen. The couch looked inviting, but instead of curling up and crashing, she staggered upstairs to her room. The sounds of pots rattling and the kettle hissing were a comfort to her. These were sounds she knew, sounds of home.

While Tug cooked, she hung her jacket on a peg in the wall, making sure the sleeping fae was safe. She then stripped off her soiled clothes and stepped gingerly into the shower. *Gods bless magic and all it enabled.* The human world could have their machines and factories. Faerie had magic. Just because she herself didn't use it, that didn't mean she couldn't appreciate the gifts it gave. Hot water rained down, soaking her, cleansing her skin of debris and blood. Several cuts streaked her hands, and even more marred her face, with a particularly nasty gash on her forehead.

Rori scrubbed shampoo into her hair, luxuriating in the one item from the human realm she couldn't live without. Strict rules were put in place of what they could and could not bring back from other worlds. On the whole, soaps and cleansers weren't forbidden, just those that contained chemicals not friendly to the fauna and flora of Faerie. But Rori had found a shampoo made of natural ingredients that kept her hair silky and shiny. Fashion wasn't her thing, nor were fancy jewels or flashy cars, but her hair—that was the only part of herself she allowed any vanity.

As she turned off the water, she said a silent thanks to the elders for their wise decision centuries ago to embrace modernization. Streetlamps continued to be lit with drossfire, while kitchens and homes were powered not just by wind and water, but a collective gathering of power found all throughout Faerie. In many ways, the human realm lagged behind Faerie, except for technology. That was one discussion neither queen was willing to have. Computers, mobile phones, televisions— all banned. They had their usefulness, certainly, and there were any number of times Rori wished she'd had access to the internet, but in her heart, she knew something of Faerie would be lost if that kind of technology were introduced.

There was something more intimate, more leisurely about not having the constant blip, blip, blipping of a phone demanding attention. Someday the laws might change, but for now, she was grateful for the advances Faerie did have, and that she didn't have to heat water in the kitchen and lug it to a bathing basin like days of old. She'd heard all the stories from her mum and gran about how hard life *used* to be.

She quickly braided her hair and did her best to salve the many cuts she received from breaking through the glass. With each, she winced as she used a tincture the old healer Meg had insisted she take after her last outing to the human realm.

That time, she'd been hit by a bullet intended for someone else. Meg hadn't asked any questions as she removed the metal from Rori's body, but Meg's look of disgust told Rori exactly what the healer had been thinking. Whatever was in the tincture had worked miracles, healing the wound in a few hours instead of days. As Rori applied it to the last of her injuries, she made a mental note to pick up more—just in case.

Tug's gentle voice called her down for breakfast. She

finished plastering the nasty gash on her forehead and grabbed her battered, trusty leather jacket before heading downstairs. It might be a little worse for wear, but it was a constant in a sea of change and sometimes, familiar was exactly what she needed. She slid her arms through the sleeves and checked on the sleeping fae. Her little light illuminated the dark pocket and her wings fluttered gently with her breathing. She might not have woken up, but that little bit of movement was encouraging.

Tug stood proudly beside her table, where plates of food covered nearly the whole thing. He wore a sheet tucked around his belly like a chef's apron, his long sleeves rolled up to his elbows. A giggle tickled her insides, but she dared not laugh at her friend. Not after he'd made all this glorious food for her. Hell, he'd made enough to feed the entire Seelie Court. A cup of steaming tea beckoned her to sit and eat.

"It looks great. Thank you, Tug." She hugged him on her way to the table. His grip stopped her movement.

"Rori, yer like a sister to me. I know yer work is dangerous, but it's never followed ye home afore."

"I appreciate your concern, Tug. I really do, but you know me. I can handle it. I promise."

Tug turned her to face him. His gaze roved over the several cuts and plasters. "I'm worried for ye. That clover, or whatever it is, it's not right. And those pendants, and ye turning up out of nowhere…something's goin' on that I don't got a good feelin' about. Then there was that man—" A large hand flew to his mouth, and he shook his head.

Rori affected her best stern mother look and stared hard at her friend. "What man? Tell me now, Tug. What man?"

Again, Tug shook his head and muffled, "I can't. He'll kill ye if I do."

"He'll kill me if you tell me about him?" Rori rubbed her temples and sank into a chair. Smells, divine food scents, assaulted her, and she grabbed her mug with shaking hands. "Is that what you said? He'll kill me? There wasn't a man, Tug. Only that woman with the red dress and blonde hair. Are you sure it wasn't her who threatened me?"

She shoveled food into her mouth, barely tasting it as she chewed. Stars, but she was famished. Her withered belly protested the barrage of food, but she didn't care. It was all so good. Tug really ought to think about working as a chef. He certainly had the skill for it.

Tug took a seat opposite and shook his head slowly. "Nay, it weren't the lady. I ain't never seen her afore this morning." He blew on his tea, his eyes clouded. "It was that man. He was at the pub the night ye—well, we thought ye was ill, but then ye disappeared. He watched ye aplenty, he did." His eyes rounded to huge saucers and watered with tears. "That ain't so. I did see the lady. She was at the pub, too. He watched her a fair amount, too."

"The lady who kidnapped me was at the Shoogly Dragon?"

Tug nodded, but his lips thinned. "I don't remember. Maybe she wasn't. But the man was. And he didn't look none too friendly, not with the way he scowled over his drink and watched ye with ill intent in his beady eyes." His attention snapped to her, and he snarled like a cornered dire wolf. "Do ye think he's the one who did this to ye?" His gaze swept to the end of the table where a dozen caskets sat in neat rows. Each one held six amulets. That meant seventy-two, possibly more, victims.

"I don't know. All I do know is I woke up in a strange, silent forest." The pang of her half-full stomach begged for more sausages and eggs. She dutifully scooped more onto her plate. After several unladylike forkfuls, she slowed her pace and took a gulp of tea.

Between bites, she told Tug of her time in the forest. Of marking every third tree, and of finding the sleeping faerie, who she held out for him to see the wee thing. By the end of her tale where Tug found her in the market, and she chased after the woman, tears streamed down Tug's face, making two pale tracks over his rosy skin.

"That's like one of 'em human stories me mum used to tell me when I was a lad. She always talked about the human realm like it was a scary, mythical place I should never need venture."

"Yes, but this happened here, in Faerie." She studied him as a spoonful of pudding hovered near her lips. "The humans tell bedtime tales of Faerie, you know."

His eyes widened, disbelief crouching in the brown depths.

"But this isn't a story. This really happened to me." She pointed to the caskets. "And others. We have to find out who's behind this and why."

Tug nodded enthusiastically. "If that man at the pub is respon—" A loud knock silenced him. He looked first at the front door, and then to Rori.

She slid a dagger from its holder and gripped the hilt tight as she stepped to the door. "Who is it?"

"There's something you and I need to discuss," a male replied.

Not recognizing the voice, she turned to Tug and froze at his expression. "What is it?" she mouthed.

"The man, from the pub," he whispered.

"The man who said he'd kill me?" She stared at the door, not sure she was ready to welcome a confessed would-be murderer into her home.

"Rori," the voice—smooth, in control—came through the wood, "let me in."

Dagger in hand, Rori flipped the lock and took a step sideways. If he was going to kill her, he'd have to work for it.

11

The door handle twisted slow enough she almost shouted for him to get on with it. Instead, she rested on the balls of her feet. Her mind spun with all the options available. The back door led to a garden, then the hill beyond. A cave of sorts was half a mile away, too far to sprint, but would do if they needed to recover. Weapons of every imaginable size and shape lined the walls and ceiling of her cottage. Some obvious, some not. Swords, maces, axes, shields, and hammers hung on hooks like decorative pieces. Dishware, heavy vases, and lamps were placed around the cottage to always be within two paces.

Being a spy had its advantages, but also its pitfalls. As evidenced by the man behind the now creaking open door. His frame filled the small space, and he crouched, wary, as he entered. A glimpse beneath his hood revealed a handsome face shadowed by a day's worth of stubble. A ragged scar snaked from the corner of his lip to just below his left eye. A few strands of blond hair—a shade that reminded her of summers spent in the meadows with Cian, laughing and giggling until their sides hurt—peeked from beneath the black fabric. Her instinct told her to trust this man.

And she'd never been deceived by her instinct.

His eyes, intelligent yet wary, focused on Tug, then swept the room. Before he saw her, she slipped behind him and placed a dagger at his throat. With her free hand, she twisted his right arm up his back. "Who are you?"

The man jerked hard, but stilled when she pressed the dagger into his skin.

"Therron Mistwalker. I mean you no harm."

Tug's snort matched her own. "I heard ye at the pub. Ye said you'd kill 'er if ye ever caught up t'er."

"My giant friend," Therron's smooth voice whispered. "You are mistaken. I was looking for someone else, not her." His head angled toward Rori.

Consternation twisted Tug's features into a knot of furrows and wrinkles. "But I heard ye."

"What do you want?" Rori demanded, tired of the game of who said they'd kill whom. She maneuvered him into the room, closing the door with a kick of her boot. "Lock it, Tug. And make sure all the drapes are closed."

Tug did as told while she hooked a chair with her foot and instructed Tug to find the rope in her shed. Time dragged as she waited for him to return. Tug believed the man confessed to wanting to kill her, yet he claimed the threat was for someone else. Then why was he in her cottage? And what the devil was taking Tug so bloody long?

Therron didn't move, nor did he say anything, but she saw his eyes roving over her cottage, noted the crinkling at their edges.

"Something amuses you?"

"Aye. You."

"Me?" Rori snorted and checked her grip on his wrist. "How so?"

"Either you have a fetish for pain, or a bizarre decorating aesthetic. I'm trying to figure out which."

He made a fair point. With all of the weapons on the walls, her cottage did resemble a war room of sorts. But torture chamber? She snuffed a giggle before it reached her lips. Not likely. Although her tolerance to pain was high, higher than most fae she knew, she'd never willingly ask for it.

Tug returned with a length of sturdy rope and held Therron while Rori searched his clothing for weapons. The stash he carried on his person was impressive: four daggers, three throwing knives, six star-shaped *hira shuriken*, several wooden spikes, an iron awl, and two vials of clear liquid. And he thought her decorating odd. More likely he was mentally shopping.

Rori indicated Tug put him in the chair, and Therron sat without comment. Tug looped the rope around his torso and made several knots before giving the rope a firm yank that wobbled Therron's head. The hood slipped off to reveal slightly tipped ears. Rori stared at him with mortified fascination.

"You're an elf." It was more an accusation than a question.

"Guilty."

"What's an elf doing here?" Elves rarely involved themselves with fae business. Her already chaotic day just got more complicated.

"I seek the enchantress."

When he didn't elaborate, Rori leaned against the table, her ass half on the sturdy wood, arms crossed tightly against her chest. Several long minutes passed as she studied his features. His damn handsome features. *Focus, Rori. You're interrogating a threat.* Don't notice his full lips or the wee crinkles at the corners of those impossibly blue eyes. Or the lips that curved just so, as though he were laughing beneath that days' worth of stubble on his strong chin.

Definitely don't notice how that scar enhances instead of mars his beauty. How would someone get a scar like that? A dagger? Or perhaps a burn. The shape gave no clue—slightly curved with a sharp hook near his eye—and she found herself drawn to touch the ragged skin. She balled her hands into fists to keep from reaching out to stroke his goddamned gorgeous face. Why did elves have to be so pretty? *Oh, for fuck's sake! Focus.*

The minutes dragged to an awkward silence, and Therron met her stern gaze. "Like I said, I'm not here for you, or your friend. I'm looking for Acelyne, the enchantress who you stole those from. I'll be needing them, if you don't mind." Two fingers indicated the caskets on her table.

Tug moved to stand between Therron and the amulets.

"Why do you need them?" Rori picked up one of his daggers and idly used the tip to clean dirt from beneath her thumbnail. When he didn't answer, she glanced up with a bemused smile, a question in the raise of her brow. "You come here after possibly telling my friend you want to kill me, insist on taking something that doesn't belong to you, and for what reason?"

"I don't want to kill you. I was talking about the enchantress. As for your friends, you might want to find better ones. I believe a man named Sal was responsible for drugging your drink at the pub. As for the amulets, they don't belong to you, either."

Sal drugged her? That little gutter snipe. She'd teach him a lesson when they were done with this mess. He needed to know not to mess with her. She tilted the dagger in Therron's direction and placed it beneath his chin, forcing him to look at her. The blaze of fury in his pupils intrigued her. He hated that he had to come to her and ask for the pendants. *But why?* And just there, behind the fury, was a flash of something else—fear, perhaps. Or dread. Certainly not arousal, which was a damn shame. She kind of liked him tied up.

"You intrigue me, Therron Mistwalker. I think there is much more to this story than you'd ever admit, which leaves me precious few options."

She slid the dagger over his chin to his lips, a little jealous of the blade. If Tug weren't there, she'd definitely sex the information out of him. And quite possibly enjoy it. She bit her lip to keep from grinding her mouth against his. Her heart stuttered a beat, that damn pinch returning with a vengeance. A slow and steady pulse thrummed, low and needy, between her legs. Oh, yes, she'd enjoy interrogating him thoroughly and completely and for long, long hours.

"Why were you following the enchantress?" She cleared her throat and forced herself to look away from his lips.

"I'm not at liberty to say."

"Well then, what *can* you say? You told me there was something we need to discuss. I'm listening."

He swallowed and glanced at the dagger. Apprehension crossed his features.

A satisfied smirk curled her lips. This was better, much better than fawning like a schoolgirl over his good looks.

"I find it's easier to have a chat when everyone is, shall we say, amicable. Would you mind?" His sky-colored eyes darkened as they flashed from his blade back to her face.

Rori straightened, arms loose at her sides, ready. "Is this amicable enough for you?"

A curt laugh came from those deliciously kissable lips. "For our purposes, yes."

Focus, Rori.

"For *our* purposes? What's that supposed to mean?" Rori had the distinct impression Therron was in control and not her, despite him being tied to a chair. This wasn't going well, and she was at a loss how to take the advantage. She'd never encountered a situation quite like this. And that damned mirth was back in his eyes. As if he were laughing at her still. *Blasted bloody man.*

Therron's hands spread, hampered by the tight ropes. "I certainly wouldn't mind a plate of whatever you've got over there." He closed his eyes and inhaled deeply. "It smells wonderful."

Tug moved toward the table, but Rori stopped him. "Not until we've got our answers." The nerve of the man. To ask for food when he was the one being interrogated. A dreadful chill started down her neck, curling into a circle at the base of her spine, where it spun out in all directions and prickled her skin.

Therron watched her, not Tug, his eyes never leaving her face. "How about a cup of tea for the first answer?" He lowered his head in a silent challenge.

She could deny him—then what? He'd ask again. She knew this game.

"I don't negotiate with those who are trying to kill me." *Best to set the tone from the outset. Regain control.* From the corner of her eye, she saw Tug balancing a mug in one hand, the kettle in another. *Sweet, sweet Tug.* He was nothing but a giant softy. After a moment's hesitation, he set both mug and kettle on the counter.

The interplay between Therron and Tug intrigued Rori. It was as if Tug were completely under his spell. She studied the pair. Elves were uncommon enough in Faerie that she doubted Tug had ever seen one. He probably thought they were a myth, until now.

Therron's clothes were typical kit: sturdy boots, layers of dark fabrics from cotton shirt to sturdy tunic and trousers. Indistinguishable from any other man in Faerie. The only thing that set him apart would be the embroidered tree on his black leather coat. Something tickled her memory about the tree, but it was just beyond her recollection. Still, she would guess he blended well with his surroundings. Almost as if he were trying hard not to be noticed.

Rori stood straighter, her focus solely on Therron's face. The laughter in his eyes faded, replaced by a guarded wariness. She studied his dagger—the shape, size, and metal of the blade. This was not elven made. Nor was it forged by dwarves. Stamped just beneath the hilt was a symbol few in Faerie understood.

Not only was Therron an elf, he belonged to a thieves' guild sworn to serve the Unseelie queen. A force not entirely her own compelled her to place the soft part of her forefinger against the tip and press down. *A challenge to the elf, yes. Of course that's what it was.* Her gaze flicked to Therron, whose impassive face stared at her. She continued to press until the skin began to tear. A slip of pain ricocheted to her heart. As she'd guessed, the blade had either been dipped in poison, or had an enchantment placed on it. Her bet was the former. Now, it was a matter of whether or not Therron would let her continue or whether he'd—

"If you value your life, you won't proceed." Still reticent, curiosity had entered his eyes.

Rori released her finger and resisted the urge to suck the drop of blood that formed there. Pain radiated from the tiny hole in her skin, far too much pain for a simple prick. She figured she had about three minutes before the poison entered her bloodstream and reached her heart.

Rori gambled her life to see whether Therron could be trusted. Her instincts had said he could, but an elf thief loyal to Midna raised grave concerns. It might be extreme, but she had to know where Therron's loyalties lay.

Tug wavered by the table, his eyes darting from Rori to Therron. Rori watched them both. Her friend was definitely under some form of enchantment, but she began to suspect it wasn't from Therron.

Her prisoner struggled against the ropes without making any progress. Tug was known for his skill at knots. In fact, many a fisherman had hired the giant to fix their nets. Despite the size of his hands, and sausage-like fingers, Tug's dexterity was legend.

Again and again Therron twisted, madness settling over his features.

Something wasn't right.

Tug inched closer to the boxes, and Rori shook her head, warning him not to touch them. The whimpering was clue enough, but when her friend drooped his shoulders to pout, Rori's senses went on full alert. Even Therron started to whine. Like two stray puppies, their pitiful cries were meant to elicit sympathy from her, but they did the exact opposite.

Without warning, the pair stopped making noises.

Rori tensed, her attention torn between the two men. First the forest, and now this. What the bloody futnucker hell was going on here?

And how did she stop whatever it was, while protecting Tug, the amulets, possibly the elf, and herself?

Rori held Therron's dagger aloft and searched the corners of her cottage. Nothing foul should've been able to penetrate the defenses she'd had installed when she bought the place. The wizard who'd placed magical wards around her cottage and garden had been selected by Eirlys personally and had guaranteed many years of protection.

Her gaze went to the two men. If the threat were internal, in their minds, there was nothing the wizard's wards could do to prevent a threat entering Rori's cottage. She swore beneath her breath. The men must be under an enchantment, some kind of mental manipulation. They had to be. But who—or what— was controlling the spell? Her gaze slid to the amulets. If this was Acelyne's doing, the enchantress had to be near. She'd certainly proved she was strong enough to exploit minds and make what wasn't there seem real. Whatever enchantment she'd placed on the men, Rori needed to break it before they lost themselves to Acelyne forever.

"Tug." Rori stepped between her friend and the caskets. "I need you to do me a favor."

Dark pupils filled his eyes. This was serious magic.

Fully aware of the ticking clock and the scant amount of poison now in her system, Rori took Tug's hand and led him to her sofa. Resisting the enchantment wouldn't be easy, but he'd never failed her before, and she had to trust he'd do as she asked now. "Stay here."

Therron's blank gaze stayed rooted on the boxes. Damn her for taking a stupid risk. She let her bravado get the best of her and it might backfire. If the poison on Therron's blade wasn't one she was immune to, well, her day would end a lot quicker than she'd planned. When she pricked her finger, she hadn't planned on Acelyne enchanting Tug and Therron. She needed to know what poison she'd ingested to make an antidote—just in case it wasn't one of the one hundred thirty-seven.

"Therron, you can feel her, can't you?" She stood in front of him, hands on knees, their faces a foot apart.

The elf shook his head, apparently not wanting to look at her or answer. Rori straddled his legs, liking how his thighs felt against hers. They were strong and firm, and she ached to lower herself onto his lap. To feel his heat against hers. To— damnit! Focus. Break the enchantment. For the first time that day, she wished Acelyne were manipulating her mind, but she didn't feel the enchantress in her thoughts. The lustful desires all came from her and the stupidly hot elf nestled between her legs.

Ever so gently, she took his chin between her fingertips and tilted his head to look at her. The scar shifted slightly, and she could've sworn she saw a claw scrape across his cheek. She blinked and the scar was exactly how she first saw it curled against his cheekbone.

Rori swallowed hard and blinked a few more times, hoping and fearing she might see it move again. When it didn't, she prodded Therron to look at her.

"Is Acelyne here?"

He gave the slightest of nods.

"And she wants you to bring her the amulets?"

Another brief movement.

"Tug, don't move."

Her friend shifted on the sofa, a pained expression on his large face. His black hair stuck straight up, as if even it were trying to obey the enchantress.

Rori sifted through possibilities. She knew every exit in town, but with Tug and Therron enchanted, she couldn't take them with her. Leaving the pair wasn't an option either, as Tug would most likely untie Therron the moment she left the cottage; then she'd have both men and Acelyne to contend with. Her options were limited, and none of them good.

"Why isn't her enchantment working on me?" The words floated from her lips, a half-formed thought made solid.

"Poison." Therron choked out the word as if he fought against himself to speak. "Counteracts."

The amount of effort it took for him to say those two words worried Rori. Acelyne was powerful. Too powerful for Rori to handle on her own. With a dagger, Rori would win hands down, but with magic? What she possessed, and her skill at weaving spells, was infantile compared to what she guessed the enchantress capable of. Unless she unloosed her wild magic. No. It was too dangerous, even if it meant saving Tug. She couldn't risk it. Especially not with the captured fae so near and Therron tied up. Perhaps she could control it this time?

Or maybe she'd kill all of Faerie.

Seconds ticked by.

"What poison is on your blade, Therron?"

His eyes narrowed and lips thinned until they were a firm white line. Deep in his pupils, Rori saw the golden waves of Acelyne's hair.

"Therron, please."

The whispered words softened the tightness in his features. Between gritted teeth, he said, "Cassaneira."

Thank the gods, it was one she was immune to. To be safe, she threw several ingredients into a mug and poured steaming water over the mess. Immunity or not, with the way her day had been going, she wasn't taking any chances.

Rori returned to Therron and stared directly into the blue depths of his eyes, past his discomfort, to the connection with Acelyne.

"You'll not get the amulets, witch. I will hunt you far and wide and once caught, you'll stand trial before the Seelie queen."

Hollow laughter echoed through the room, the same she'd heard when she was alone in the forest. It came from Therron's lips, but it was not his voice that followed. "You? Barely out of the Academy and think you can take me on? You'll never equal your brother, will you? He would never have let himself get captured." More laughter, this time tinged with madness. "Bring me the amulets."

A sound, much like a gong, reverberated in Rori's mind.

The witch knew exactly what to say to make Rori's confidence shatter. And it did. Right there, in her cottage, Rori considered for the first time that day giving up. Something in the way the elf's eyes softened, the slight pinching at the edges as if he were pained to hear the words coming from his lips, steadied her resolve. Sweat dotted his forehead, and she sensed the battle he waged in his mind with the enchantress. He didn't know Rori, yet she felt…something…a connection to him that went beyond loyalty. He would die for her. Her eyes widened in surprise. And she would give her life for him.

They were strangers. Yet she knew his loyalty would never waver. Just as she trusted Tug, she could trust this man.

Oh, the enchantress was good. To make her believe an elf would protect her? That was some serious dark magic.

She stared deep into Therron's eyes and addressed Acelyne. "Like hell I will."

Rori drew back and swung her right arm with all the force she could muster. Her open hand connected with Therron's scarred cheek. Shards of pain streaked up her arm. The impact knocked the elf sideways, and he toppled to the floor with a string of obscenities.

A moment of stunned silence followed.

"A little warning might've been nice," Therron grumbled, his face smooshed against her rug, his cheek reddened from her slap. "Drink that mess you made. Do it now." Behind the gruffness, concern laced his words.

Rori didn't want to admit how much hearing his voice relieved her. Refused to let herself feel the emotion that welled up inside her heart. Therron didn't know she was immune to the poison, and despite his concern, there wasn't time to explain. In a show of haste and worry, she darted to the counter where she'd left the brew and picked up the mug with both hands.

In one long gulp, she drank the foul liquid, grimacing at the taste as it slithered down her throat to settle in her gut. Gods, but why couldn't healers come up with better-tasting cures to life's ailments? Instantly, the poisonous burn simmered to a nuisance, nothing more. As far as Therron knew, he'd helped save her life. The realization made her belly spasm. Or it was the aftereffects of the antidote. At least, that's what she told herself. No sense in letting silly emotions get even further out of control. It was bad enough his very presence made her nerves jumpy and heart stutter.

Hopefully, he could shed light on how the poison had kept Acelyne from enchanting her, but that would have to wait. First, she needed to get the pendants safely to Queen Eirlys. Immediately, her mind raced with plans, options, details, and maneuvers she might need to achieve her objective.

"I could use some help here."

Still bound to the chair, Therron lay on his side, hair askew, that handsome face full of— Was that rat bastard laughing at her? She glared harder. He was. Jerk.

But, she reminded herself, that rat bastard also—even through Acelyne's enchantment—made certain she drank the antidote.

Tug, who'd been sitting on the couch, immobile, stood suddenly and lumbered toward the caskets. Rori lunged at the table and reached them first. She gathered the leather bag and wrapped her arms around the bundle, her mind plotting how to escape. Just then, everything went black.

13

Wind rushed past, screeching across her ears. Rori clasped the bag to her chest, careful not to squish the fae in her pocket. As far as she was concerned, all the trapped fae were the single most important thing in the universe and she'd die protecting them. They were more than kin. The imprisoned fae were helpless in their glass tombs. Somehow, she'd managed to fight off the effects of the drug Sal had given her, but she suspected the others weren't as fortunate. If Rori didn't protect them, who would?

Without warning, the sound stopped and light blinded her momentarily. Rori blinked against the blaze of a torch not more than a foot in front of her face. After a moment of letting her eyes adjust, she took in her surroundings, not recognizing the stone walls, carpeted floors, or decorative tapestries.

"What the candied nut sucker fresh hell is this?"

"Do all spies swear this much?"

Years of training kept Rori from physically jumping, but her heart leapt to her throat. Standing before her was a young woman, or tall girl—Rori wasn't sure. Her features were familiar, but not intimately. Wavy black hair cascaded over her slim shoulders to her lower back. A soft rose-colored gown hung loose from her neck to mid-calf. Crystals glittered from the folds of fabric, mesmerizing Rori. Slowly, she raised her eyes to the young woman's. Blue orbs the color of the night sky watched her intently. A smile stretched across her coppery skin.

"Your Highness." Rori curtseyed low, finally putting a name to the face. "I am sorry to have intruded on your privacy." When had the princess blossomed into a young woman? The last time Rori saw her, which must've been over a year hence, she'd been no higher than Rori's waist.

Princess Arianna giggled and waved her hand as if to brush the idea aside. "You haven't intruded, you silly. You saved me. Saved us." She pointed to the caskets in Rori's arms. "We need to get these to Mother without being seen. Follow me."

Before Rori could ask what she meant, the princess darted behind a tapestry. Unease curdled the liquid in Rori's stomach. Whatever had brought her here was magic she didn't know existed. To travel from one place to another without moving and without a special door... Her mind tried to grasp how it could be possible. Portals, she knew. Magic-enhanced doorways, she understood. Both were used in Faerie to travel space and time. But this? Whatever this was, she'd never fathomed.

"We really don't have all day, Aurora."

Spurred by Arianna's quiet voice, Rori rushed past the tapestry into a dimly lit corridor. She followed the princess through a maze of hallways, some of them barely wide enough to fit a fully grown faerie.

"Where are we?" Rori whispered and cringed at the slight echo of her voice.

"We're almost there. Wait here a moment."

A flash of golden tiara was all Rori saw before Arianna vanished. She listened for footfalls but heard nothing beyond the rapid beating of her heart.

This truly had been the most bizarre day of her life.

"Are you ready?"

Arianna's sweet face looked up at Rori, excitement and expectation lighting her midnight eyes.

"For what?"

Without answering, the princess turned away and scurried a few feet to another hallway. Five paces in, she ducked into the stone.

Upon closer inspection, Rori saw it was a small door. She pushed it open and crouched low, hampered by the bulk in her arms, to scoot through. A thick tapestry folded over the door, and she pushed it aside with her shoulder. Once clear of the fabric, she stood to her full height and adjusted the burden in her arms.

"Rori, what a delightful surprise. I wasn't expecting you today, but I am glad you're here." Laughter edged Queen Eirlys's voice. The queen stood a few paces away, her black hair and chestnut skin gleaming in the candlelight. She wore a gown in the same shade as Arianna's, but it was nearly see-through and pooled at her feet. Gems sparkled at her throat and ears, though Rori couldn't recall Eirlys ever wearing such large, gaudy stones.

"Your Majesty." Rori curtseyed as well as she could with the caskets cradled in her arms.

"Let me take those from you." The queen reached out, her slender hands gripping the boxes.

A moment of hesitation made Rori clutch them to her chest.

"Rori?"

Whereas her daughter's eyes were like a night sky, Eirlys's were the color of deep purple. But that wasn't right. Rori always remembered her queen's eyes as being the shade of summer lavender.

"I'm sorry, Your Majesty. It's been a topsy-turvy day, and I'm not at all certain what I'm seeing or hearing is true."

Eirlys released the caskets and backed away. "I understand you've had quite the adventure. Come, sit with me and let's see if we can ease your mind."

Still wary, Rori looked from Arianna to Eirlys. All was as it should be, but something was off. A smell or a touch, perhaps even a hazy vision at the perimeter of her sight, but there was something that caused Rori to use extreme caution. This could be an enchantment, one meant to lure her into a state of compliance. If nothing else made sense, one thing was clear—Acelyne would do whatever it took to get the amulets. And now that she'd rid herself of the poison, she was susceptible to the witch's spells.

As she made her way to the table, Rori took in her surroundings, recognizing the room as Queen Eirlys's private sitting room. The only way Acelyne would know what was in this room was to have been there herself.

Or she used Rori's memories against her.

Acelyne had already proved herself a powerful enchantress. Making an elaborate illusion wouldn't be difficult. Disquiet clung to Rori's thoughts as she contemplated the scene. It was the same unease that had settled over her in the forest.

"Aurora, please sit." Arianna patted the chair next to her.

The table was set for four. Tea had yet to be poured, but cakes and biscuits rested on pretty plates.

"I've interrupted a meeting."

"One that can be rescheduled. This is more important." Queen Eirlys sat opposite Rori, her chin resting on steepled fingers. Dainty diamonds rested against her flawless brown skin, cascading low to her cleavage. "Tell me what happened."

"I'm not—" The words stuck in Rori's throat. This was too easy. The queen waited, her lavender eyes soft and approachable, exactly the shade she remembered. Princess Arianna sipped her tea, her legs swinging beneath her skirts. Too normal. Too…something. "I need to use the loo."

Clutching the boxes close to her chest, Rori rose. Five doors led from the sitting room to various parts of the palace, and Rori chose one she'd never been through. It led to a darkened room. Tall, rounded windows looked out onto a twilight field.

"Who are you?" A woman, with hair of silver and skin that sparkled as if stars rested just below the surface, hovered not more than a foot in front of her. The white gown she wore wafted on a breeze Rori neither felt nor heard. The woman wore no tiara or coronet. All the same, Rori sensed great power in her.

"I, erm, who are you?" Rori eyed the stranger.

Her silver hair fanned out and for a moment, Rori thought she saw dragon's wings. She had a desire to kneel, to pledge her life to the woman. Not as though she were being coerced, but out of respect and deference. The same she felt for her queen, Eirlys. Rori's battered psyche struggled against the need to gather information and the will to survive. She couldn't be sure who this woman was, where she came from, or whether she could be trusted.

A frown tugged at the woman's lips, and her eyes drooped with sadness. "I've been asked that many times of late. No answer will suffice for your needs, nor would you understand them. For now, I'm simply Taryn." She glanced at the rough stone walls and arched windows. "Where are we?"

Outside, the view changed from night to day. Faeries strolled the gardens. "We're at Queen Eirlys's palace." Rori should've been alarmed or nervous, but she was neither. This woman, whoever she was, didn't set off Rori's defenses, nor did she feel as if she were an enemy. Quite the opposite. Rori stretched her hands to fully cover her wooden charges, but the woman wasn't interested in them.

"What a curious place." Taryn drifted to the window and placed her hands upon the glass. The scene shifted to show steep cliffs and a turquoise sea. "This is the Crystal Palace in Talaith. Who is Queen Eirlys?"

Rori's head throbbed and her throat scratched with the effort of swallowing. Perhaps she'd had it all wrong and this was the ruse to lull her into complacency. Or to drive her to madness.

"Are you the enchantress?"

The woman called Taryn turned to face her, a smile of reassurance on her lips, all traces of melancholy gone. "I promise you, I am no enchantress." Her gaze flicked to the window, where the scene changed from the sea to a bed of stars.

If she wasn't an enchantress, she was awfully good at making illusions.

Rori took a step backward, her grip secure. "Look, I mean no disrespect, but I've had the worst day ever and I'm not even sure you're real."

A robust laugh filled Rori's ears.

The fool woman held her middle and wheezed, "I often wonder about that myself." Taryn shook her head with another chuckle. "As far as I know, I'm real. When cut, I bleed the same as you." A pinch of anger flashed across her pretty face. Not just pretty—ethereal. "What I'm asking myself is, how is it possible we're here? What is it you want?" Taryn glanced at the leather satchel.

Rori gripped the bag tighter, pressing the caskets painfully against her breasts. "You'll not get these."

Taryn's eyes rested on the amulets. When they met Rori's, sadness spiraled to their depths. "What is this place? Who would do that to those poor souls?"

The walls dissipated around them until they stood on

nothing and were surrounded by the night sky. A single tear tracked its way down Taryn's cheek.

"What kind of sorcery is this? Who are you really?" The throbbing in Rori's head stopped, but her heart continued beating at an alarming rate.

"I am not a sorceress, either. I am *Darennsai*." Taryn reached out, and Rori tightened her already death-like grip on the boxes. "You're hurting her. Relax, Rori."

"How do you know my name?" Her arms slackened, as if obeying Taryn's command. She opened her mouth to protest, but stopped as Taryn reached inside her jacket to retrieve the sleeping faerie. A fierce protectiveness fought through her stunned silence. "Put her back." The words were a snarled command that the woman ignored.

"I'll not hurt her." Still curled into a tight ball, the fae's gossamer wings vibrated with Taryn's touch. A small gasp came from the strange woman.

"She's…my daughter. But that's not possible. How can this be?" Taryn said, more to herself than Rori. Tears swam in her eyes, making them look like polished blue marble.

Panic raced through Rori's blood, and the roaring returned to drown out all sound. "She was trapped with me in the forest. I didn't know who she was." If the woman thought she'd had something to do with her daughter's kidnapping, this could be bad. *Breathe, MacNair. Use your training.*

Understanding dawned on Taryn's face. "But you do know her, Rori. This is Princess Arianna."

"What? You said she was your daughter. How do you know it's Arianna? I mean, no, it can't be. I just left the princess with her mother—" Her head swiveled to the door that was no longer there. Sickness churned in her belly. "Was that an illusion? Or is this the illusion? What the actual fuck?" Everything was upside down and sideways. How did the woman know Arianna, but not Eirlys? And why did she say the princess was her daughter?

Taryn nodded and placed her lips upon the still sleeping princess. "I'm not sure how or why or what's happening, but this is your present and my future. Or my past. I'm not entirely sure." She carefully returned Arianna to Rori's pocket. "Where did you say your queen's palace is?"

"In Faerie. The Seelie Court."

"You're fae?" Another gasp, followed by a wide smile. "Of course."

"Of course, what?"

"Quiet your mind, Rori MacNair of Faerie. Use your ShantiMari to know what is true and what is not."

"What's shawnty mawri?" Rori desperately wanted out of the nightmare. The woman seemed kind, and she hadn't hurt Arianna, but there was something dangerous about Taryn.

"Your wild magic, Rori."

And, there it was. Taryn saw into her, past her defenses to the place she'd buried her grief and guilt. Tears pricked her eyes, and she shook her head.

"No, I can't. It's too unpredictable. I can't trust it."

"Oh, but you can, my darling. Your ShantiMari will save them all, but you have to trust yourself, first, young one." Taryn placed her hand over Rori's heart. "What you seek is here. Believe in yourself. Trust this. It will always lead you true."

Young one? They looked to be of similar age.

A tingling, like when a limb has reawakened from a brief sleep, curled itself around her heart. "What are you doing to me?" Her wild magic yawned and stretched like a cat, its claws exposed. She desperately willed it back to the hiding place, back to the darkness where it couldn't hurt anyone. "Stop, please."

"You're stronger than you think. You have great power, but

you've locked yourself away from it. Do not fear your Shanti-Mari, Rori. Nurture it. Treat it with respect, always. Embrace that which is part of you."

Tears streaked over her cheeks to drip on the leather satchel. "But I'll hurt people. I'll be punished."

"Only if that is your intention. You were born for peace, not destruction." Taryn's eyes widened, then her brows pinched. "You need his help, Rori. Accept it freely, and you will defeat the enchantress of illusion."

The stars began to fade, and Taryn removed her hand from Rori's chest. A cold emptiness filled the place where her warmth had been.

"Wait! Whose help?"

"The elf, Therron. Trust him, Rori."

"How do you know me? Are you an elf? Where did you come from?" Even more questions rushed to her lips, but Taryn was little more than a shadow drifting to nothingness.

"Trust your power, your ShantiMari. You call it magic, but it is so much more. Protect the princess, *mi carae*. Faerie depends upon it. Not just Faerie..."

But the words were lost when the room spun with terrifying speed, turning from the night sky to bright white to inky blackness.

The air stilled, and Rori trembled uncontrollably. No training could prepare her for what had just happened. Hell, even she wasn't sure what had happened.

"Rori! Come back. Please." Therron's voice echoed in the hollowness of her mind.

14

Rough hands gripped Rori's face, followed by even rougher lips crushing against her own. Searing heat ripped down her body, turning her insides to nothing but gooey bits. It had been so long since anyone had kissed her, she'd almost forgotten how it felt. And it had never felt this good. Tenderness laced between the coarse scratch of stubble and the fierce grip of his fingers on her cheeks. Worry. She sensed worry in his kiss, but also trepidation. Fear of losing something—a connection or a curse. Or was it fear of losing a life? His? Hers?

Wait. Who was kissing her? She couldn't see anything in the darkness.

"Rori, open your eyes," Therron whispered.

She did and there, standing in her kitchen, was the elf. Close enough she could smell the scent of whetstone on the fingers that held her tight. Dark concern danced in his eyes, followed by cautious relief.

"I didn't give you permission to kiss me." As if he'd ever need it. But Rori didn't want him to get too cocky.

"Would you rather I did it your way?"

Her cheeks flamed at the memory of striking him. "If those are my options, I suppose your way is preferable to a slap to the face."

"I reckon it is."

"Hmmm, I'm thinking one more kiss will remove all traces of the enchantress."

A wicked grin lifted the corners of his lips. "Medicinal purposes only?"

A rush of adrenaline spiked her already escalated heartbeat as she nodded. Therron closed the gap between them, his lips seeking hers, cautious, unsure. She opened herself to him, delighting in the feel and taste of his tongue. This time when the room spun, it wasn't from any sort of illusion—it was from her own wicked thoughts and desires. Whatever the strange woman Taryn had done to her opened a magic far deeper than what she thought she possessed. It swirled and coalesced into a protective bubble around the pair.

If this was her wild magic, she embraced it with every part of her. It fueled her with a desire to heal, not hurt.

From far away, Rori heard the frustrated wailing of the enchantress. Like ice cracking on a warmed window, Acelyne's spell dissolved and the world became clearer, crisper.

Therron's body shuddered against hers, upsetting the boxes still in her grip. Her body ached with hunger food wouldn't fulfill. A long dormant neediness warmed her blood, and she tilted her pelvis just enough to brush his trousers. One hour, no, just one day, that's all she needed to satisfy the cravings that throbbed in all the right places.

His hands went from her face to stroke her hair, and down her back to hold her firmly in his grasp. A small moan escaped her lips, and she shushed the voice in her head that said this was dangerous. No personal attachments. Bang him and be done with it.

Letting him in was a risk she wasn't ready to take. But damn, this felt so good. She held the amulets, and Therron held her. It was as it should be.

Somehow, she knew this to be true. Never in her life had she allowed anyone to take this kind of liberty with her person, but it *felt* right. Rori ended the kiss reluctantly. A silent war waged in her mind, surprising in its intensity. She gladly would've stayed in Therron's arms all day, but she had a duty to her queen. They needed to get the amulets to Eirlys.

"Where's Tug?" Her gaze went to the sofa where Tug sat hunched, his eyes downcast.

"He's still under her control. When you stiffened, he lumbered off and has been sitting quietly ever since. What happened?"

"We have to help him, Therron." She glanced at the satchel, her breath catching. "Arianna," Rori whispered.

"The Seelie princess? What about her?"

"Just now, before the kiss, I had a vision. If it was real, and I was actually in Eirlys's palace, then she would've been frantic to have her daughter returned. Right? Because if Arianna is here, then she couldn't have been there. Which means, either Acelyne doesn't know I know about Arianna, or she didn't know she had the fae princess. Either way, we need to hurry."

"Wait a minute. You're not making sense. A vision? Arianna? Where are we going?" He still held her, his hands spanning her lower and upper back.

Even through her clothes, where he touched sent warm tingles across her skin. Just one quickie would satisfy the urges. And risk destroying the walls she'd spent years building? No thanks. No elf, hot as he might be, was worth that price. What was wrong with her? Not the time, not the priority. Maybe later, after she burned that witch's behind, then she could think about canoodling. Right now, she had to focus on getting the pendants to Eirlys.

If only he wasn't so damn cute.

Rori cleared her throat to dissolve the treacherous thoughts swarming in her brain. "When I froze, just now, I was thrust into an illusion. I believe it was Acelyne's doing, at least to start. I was at the Seelie palace with Arianna and the queen, but it felt off. Like when you walk in a room and can tell something's been moved, but you're not sure what. I tried to escape the illusion by going into a room I'd never been in and there..." She eyed him with a raised brow. "Promise not to think I'm mad?"

"Oh, I think you're well and truly mad, but go on." A tiny dimple appeared just above his quirked lips.

"That's not at all encouraging. So, this other room... there was a woman there. Gorgeous, with long silver hair and eyes as blue as the ocean. She said we—you and me— had to work together, that I should trust you, but I don't know about that." Now it was her turn to grin. "In the vision, or illusion, or whatever it was, she said we could defeat the enchantress. I'm fairly confident it wasn't one of Acelyne's illusions. The vision felt real. Unlike the forest, or when I sat with Eirlys, when I was talking to the woman, I had an overwhelming sense of hope. Then you kissed me and now I'm back in my kitchen, trying to explain the unexplainable."

How else could she describe what she herself didn't understand? The woman, Taryn, was real, of that she was certain. And not of this world or one Rori had been to, but a world connected to Faerie in some way. She'd known Rori, known Arianna, but didn't know Faerie. How that was possible was something she'd research later, after the imprisoned fae were safe. She hadn't realized it at the time, but what she told Therron was true—Taryn gave her hope. And now, she hoped she'd meet Taryn again one day. Maybe then she'd get more answers to her eleventy billion questions.

Trust the elf, she'd said. Right then, Rori also had to trust a complete stranger based on nothing more than faith and a gut feeling.

"Did she say how we would defeat Acelyne?" Therron traced his forefinger along his upper lip, his eyes narrowed.

"Not exactly." Rori couldn't tell him about her wild magic, or the other things Taryn had said about her. Not yet. Not until he proved his fidelity. "We can talk about it more later. Right now, we need the fastest route to the Seelie Court. We must get these to the queen."

As if stung by an asp, Therron snapped his head up, his stern gaze burning to her core. "We have to take them to Midna at the Unseelie Court."

"I'll take them." Tug lumbered into view, his arms outstretched.

"Nay, lad. They're my responsibility."

Rori eyed the pair, suspicion mounting. She tightened her grip. "No one is taking them anywhere until we sort this out. Who are you working for?" She leveled a gaze at Therron. "And why do they want these?"

Therron shook his head in answer. "I was hired to capture Acelyne. Why? I don't know." At Rori's glare, he continued. "Midna wanted Acelyne, and since I obviously don't have the enchantress, then the amulets might keep me alive. As you know, elves aren't exactly welcome in your lands. Your politics are your own. I'm just trying to do what I was hired to do and not create a fuss. I needed cash…there was a job…you see where this is going, right?"

"Do you know what's inside these pendants?"

"No, and I don't need to know. I only need to return them to Midna."

Rori searched his eyes and his features for signs he was

lying and found none. "They're kidnapped faeries, Therron. Kidnapped, drugged, hopefully alive. I was in one of these until I broke free in the market."

His eyes widened and filled with horror. "Trapped? In one of those?" He pointed to the caskets clutched at her chest.

"Yes. Now you know why I need to get them to Eirlys."

"I swear on my honor as a thief, I had no knowledge of pendants or kidnappings."

His sincerity mollified her suspicions, but only just. He was a thief, after all, and their word was only marginally better than a spy's. It would be just like Midna to hire an elf to do her bidding. She really had no decency at all. Why not have Cian hunt the enchantress? There had to be some other reason Midna would drag an elf into Faerie business. The Unseelie queen never did anything that didn't serve her throne first and foremost. Taryn had said to trust the elf, but Rori couldn't give loyalty to someone who was possibly working to undermine Faerie's peace. What was Midna's role in all of this?

Tug wavered, as if still under a spell. "Ye told me ye'd kill her if I said anything."

"I was talking about Acelyne, you dolt."

"Don't call him that." Low enough only Therron could hear, she added, "We can't leave him if he's still enchanted. Perhaps you should kiss him, too. To break his spell, naturally."

The look of stunned curiosity that crossed Therron's face was enough to make Rori laugh out loud.

"Would that work?" Therron's voice trailed off, uncertain.

"I really have no idea, but it worked for me. And only the gods know what other surprises you might be hiding, mysterious elf named Therron who claims to know nothing of Faerie politics."

"Sarcasm?"

Again, Rori's laughter filled the room. It had been ages

since this cottage had heard the sound of unfettered lightness. Damn, it felt good to laugh. To let the bubbles inside her belly free and not care who was watching or listening. Being a spy definitely had its drawbacks.

Rori huffed a final chuckle and waved a hand toward the kitchen. "Make him a cup of thornbarrow root and lemon whisp. It should clear the enchantment from his mind. More or less. I think. We'll see, won't we?" It was her go-to remedy for any kind of magic gone wrong. With any luck, it would help Tug.

Therron eyed the giant with a high degree of apprehension.

"Are you seriously considering kissing him?"

"If you think it would work." Therron's shoulders lifted in an exaggerated shrug.

"No way. Make yer concoction." Tug crossed his arms over his chest and clamped his lips shut.

"Suit yourself. What are you going to do?" Therron asked Rori.

"Sort out what we should do with these. Tug, sit down."

Tug situated his large body until it was hanging off the stool she'd indicated.

"Drink what Therron gives you. Don't argue—do as you're told."

Tug nodded miserably.

She could only imagine the battle raging inside his head. The enchantress was powerful, indeed, but there were some things magic couldn't erase. Love and loyalty, for a start. If Tug didn't have the deep connection with Rori, would Acelyne's spell have worked better? She touched her lips. How had Therron's kiss broken through the enchantment? She didn't know him or have any kind of bond with him. Was it an elven and fae thing? Did Tug being a giant make it easier to manipulate his mind? Giants had a childlike enthusiasm for life, but that didn't mean they were simple-minded.

Did the illusions go beyond a person's intelligence to something deeper, perhaps even deep enough to mine their insecurities and make them appear real? She'd certainly experienced that in the forest.

So why had Therron's kiss brought her out of the illusion? She shook her head at yet another mystery she couldn't solve. She was grateful it had worked and hoped his kiss would be enough to thwart any further attempts from Acelyne to manipulate her thoughts. If not, they'd all be needing more than a simple concoction of herbs.

While Therron made Tug's brew, she set the caskets carefully on a side table. She spun a dagger between her fingertips, thinking. If they took the pendants to Midna, perhaps she could find out whether Cian was still at the Unseelie Court. But then Midna would have the pendants and all the fae trapped inside.

Again, the question of why amulets and why the fae nagged at Rori's thoughts. Why would Acelyne do this? To what end? And if Acelyne wasn't acting alone, then who were the amulets for? She'd been in the market with the caskets displayed on a table. Did that mean Acelyne was planning to sell the amulets as macabre trinkets? Or was she meeting a buyer? Snickertits. This was a riddle without a beginning or end.

"We need to see Meg." Tug's scratchy voice pulled Rori from her thoughts.

"Mad Meg?" The offensive nickname sprang from her lips before she could stop it. Some folks called her Mad Meg, others Miracle Meg. To Rori, she was simply Meg. Why she'd used the disrespectful nickname, she wasn't sure. She liked Meg, genuinely as a person and not just because she was a wicked good healer.

"People shouldn't call her that. She's not mad, just...you know...odd." Tug's baritone voice held a softness she'd never heard.

Odd wasn't half off describing the witch. Even so, Tug had a good idea. Meg could help with Tug's attachment to Acelyne's enchantment and, with any luck, might be able to release the fae from their glass prisons. She lived alone in the woods, a good five or so miles from where they were. It would take what was left of the morning to walk there. By Rori's reckoning, the brew Therron made should last that long, but it would be close. When it wore off, Tug would be drawn back into Acelyne's spell. And then he might give their location away and they could be trapped. Her gut rippled with sourness. She'd never let that happen. Not ever again.

"People say yer odd, too. Does that mean yer mad, Rori?"

Was Tug actually insulting her? It was a day of revelations and possible miracles.

"What did you add to that mixture, Therron?" She scanned the ingredients scattered on her counter. A jar of jacksass sat off to the side. One of the side effects—and the only reason Rori kept it near—was it induced an overwhelming desire to speak the truth. It came in handy when extracting a confession otherwise proved difficult. Cian used sex, others used torture; Rori chose fighting, or if that wasn't possible, rare and difficult to find herbs. Along with the one hundred thirty-seven poisons, she was also immune to jacksass.

Therron shrugged and idly watched her and Tug, a devious smile teasing the corners of his lips.

"You fiendish bastard." The insult sounded like a compliment the way she said it. "Let me put these in a sturdier bag, then we can go. Wrap some of this food for the walk. Tug, stay here with Therron." Rori didn't wait for an answer. Instead, she gathered the pendants and took the stairs two at a time to the landing. In a cupboard, she found a battered leather bag that fit all of the boxes. She touched her breast pocket and whispered, "Soon," to the sleeping faerie.

The poor lass. She didn't know whether the princess had

been in the amulet before her, or whether she'd been imprisoned when Rori was unconscious. In the end, it didn't matter. No fae deserved to be captured.

A ripple of anger vibrated from her sternum. The enchantress, whether acting alone or with someone else—whoever was doing this was vile. They now became Rori's enemy. In all her missions, she'd never let emotions attach themselves to the job, but this was personal. She and the other fae needed to be avenged. She'd find Acelyne and everyone she was working with, and kill them.

She descended the stairs slower than she'd ascended them, allowing her breathing to slow, her heart rate to calm. By the time she reached the bottom, the rage pounding against her skull had dimmed to a steady thrum.

Therron and Tug waited for her by the front door. A canvas bag hung from Tug's left shoulder. By the looks of it, he'd packed all the breakfast remains, and the entire contents of her cold box. Their breakfast dishes had been washed and put away in the brief time she'd been upstairs. Sweet Tug. He didn't have the same aversion to magic that Rori had. Bless his overlarge heart.

"Right. Let's go then. Tug, you lead the way."

Try as she might, she couldn't shake the feeling they were walking into a trap. If it was Acelyne's intention to get them to leave Rori's cottage, she'd succeeded. And that made the three of them easy targets.

※ 15 ※

They strode through the narrow streets, past the town square with its ancient well and the fanciful houses that looked as though they were made of marshmallow fluff and licorice ropes. Therron kept close to Rori as the trio slipped between the two tallest buildings, the town hall and inn, without incident. He watched her scan the buildings, her eyes constantly roving, but her face passive. The giant lumbered at her side, struggling to keep up with her pace.

Therron peered into the shadows and nooks where Acelyne might be hiding. She'd somehow managed to enchant him, and that didn't settle well in his gut. Elves weren't like faeries. He should've been impervious to any of her machinations and the fact he wasn't, well, that irritated him.

An unexpected grin pulled his lips upward. At least he'd gotten a kiss for his trouble. When Rori's face went slack and eyes dazed, he knew something was wrong. She'd stood still, as if touched by frost. He hadn't meant to kiss her, but she'd looked fragile and his instinct led his lips to hers. It was the second kiss, the one Rori instigated, that made his magic coil and his heart gallop.

He couldn't hope for more, not yet. And he couldn't force it. For the curse to be broken, she had to love him unconditionally, without provocation or manipulation of any kind. That's why the kiss had surprised him as much as her. He'd meant to stay neutral, let her decide her feelings without him muddying up her emotions.

It wouldn't be easy, but that's how it had to be—completely at Rori's pace.

The scar on his cheek burned, and his heart pinched with a vicious jag. He couldn't tell her about the curse, or her role in breaking it. He glanced at the headstrong faerie and grinned. Telling her that he bore a curse set upon his family by a faerie princess thousands of years ago, and that he had three moon-turns to gain her love or he would die horribly, might not be the best way to woo the lass. He'd run away from Elvenwood in the hopes he would escape the curse by never falling in love. By the twinging of his heart, that hadn't worked out so well.

They passed through the city proper and under the gate onto the open road. Therron kept his nerves to himself, with only the occasional twitching of fingertips toward his sword.

Rori jerked her head in his direction and eyed the weapon.

"Why'd you hide your sword from me? Back at my place, you had no sword." Her tone, challenging and confrontational, didn't match the confusion in her eyes.

Therron cocked his head. "I hid nothing. You handed it to me before we left your cottage." Blood and ashes, how could she forget?

They shared a look, then both studied the long blade.

"Or did you?" Therron tapped his temple. He couldn't sense an enchantment, but that didn't mean Acelyne wasn't tampering still.

The howling agony he'd shown at Rori's was true—he'd delved into Acelyne's mind only a fraction, but he saw there filth and abominations aplenty. Enough to torment him for several lifetimes. He'd sensed in her dark magic, but hadn't risked probing further for fear she'd discover his intrusion. Acelyne suffered from the same affliction as his kin—she believed herself above everyone else. A flaw easily countered with the proper tools.

Rori's smack had startled Acelyne as much as him, and had allowed Therron to regain complete control. A few minutes longer, and he might have slipped into the abyss of Acelyne's mind forever. He rubbed his cheek where her hand had connected, knocking him sideways. Was it worry that had made her slap him? Or simply expediency? He hoped for the former, and suspected it was the latter. At least she'd cared enough to save him from Acelyne's grasping magic.

Thus far, the enchantress thought him only an elf. Like Rori, she didn't know who he was, or what he was capable of, and he meant to keep it that way. He'd played along with the enchantment to make it appear that Acelyne was in control. Now, he hoped he hadn't opened himself too much, allowing a path for her to follow whenever she desired.

"I gave ye the sword," Tug said matter-of-factly. "I also have the other weapons Rori took off ye. Since she doesn't like swords, and it belonged to ye anyway, I gave it to ye. It only seemed logical."

Rori's narrowed gaze and tight lips told Therron that Tug had just shared a secret she didn't want told.

"It's not that I don't like them. They're clunky, and daggers are much simpler." She shook her head and placed a hand on her hip, where a dagger was secured in a leather holster. "Since I don't remember seeing you give it to him, and Therron doesn't recall you handing it to him, I think we all need to assume Acelyne's enchantments aren't fully negated."

"Agreed." A slight murkiness lingered in his thoughts. He fought it, but the more he fought, the murkier his thoughts became. Trying not to fight the spell was almost as hard as fighting it. A damned snake eating its tail. For the time being, he'd allow Acelyne's connection. If it threatened them, he'd sever it.

Tug shrugged his great shaggy shoulders. "I guess maybe the two of ye should've had some of that vile liquid then instead o' just snogging. Mayhaps the enchantress is clouding more than yer judgment."

A lovely blush stained Rori's cheeks, and she leaned close to Therron. "Seriously, did you put jacksass in that mixture? I've never known Tug to speak so bluntly."

"Didn't need to. Thornbarrow is known to act oddly with different species."

"Tug not odd." His bottom lip protruded with a pout.

"You're right, friend. I was hasty in my speech." He hadn't meant it as an insult. Nor was he accustomed to the giant's ways and needed to be mindful of the words he chose.

Tug clapped him on the back, and he stumbled forward from the impact. "Tug like Therron Mistwalker."

"And Therron likes you, too."

Tug grinned and started to hum the song Rori had sung in the Shoogly Dragon—something about milking goats. Therron slid his glance to the beauty and tensed. Her eyes darted everywhere and perspiration dotted her forehead.

"Are you well?"

She cast him a dark scowl. "Of course. Don't be daft." With the back of her hand, she wiped her brow and increased her pace. "We should hurry. It'll only get hotter, and we have a lot to accomplish today."

Therron and Tug flanked Rori, each protective for their own reasons. He really did like the giant. From what he saw at the pub and at the cottage, Tug and Rori were close. She allowed the giant certain liberties she'd not allowed anyone else. That night at the pub, only Tug had put an arm around her shoulders. Therron thought back through the entire evening.

He couldn't recall anyone besides Tug even touching Rori. She'd drank with her mates, played darts, sang, but never made physical contact.

He slid a glance to his left and studied her profile. Tight lips, jaw tense, eyes focused. His gaze lowered to where she gripped the leather bag with one hand, the other on her dagger. It must be exhausting to be on alert at all times. Therron sighed and returned to scanning the trees for trouble.

If he hadn't seen it with his own eyes, he wouldn't have believed she'd been in one of the glass vials. But she'd broken free. What of the others? Were they alive? What a horrible fate for them. They had to find a way to release the fae. Acelyne would know the spell necessary to free the faeries.

A dark nagging pulled at his magic, the source of which came from the bag Rori carried. He'd sensed it in her cottage, but here, on the open road, it became more insistent. It was a darkness he shouldn't find in Faerie. Shouldn't find at all, really. Yet it was there, hidden within the pendants, he was certain of it.

His mind raced to the night at the Shoogly Dragon when Rori disappeared. Sal had drugged her drink to allow Acelyne to kidnap her. Suddenly, he didn't feel so bad about killing the man.

Rori must've gone through hell in the glass prison. His gaze lingered on the set of her jaw. There was so much to learn about her, but he'd never doubt her fierceness and strength. She was a fighter, to be sure. Something else lingered beneath the disquiet of her anger. Power, raw and pure, unlike any he'd encountered before. The elves had a term for that kind of magic—ShantiMari. It was older than even the elvenwood tree, and equally as revered. Perhaps that was what had allowed her to escape Acelyne's confinement. If the pinging of his heart were any indication, maybe her power might be the key to breaking his curse. In a way, he, too, was a captive, with her as his only means of escape.

They kept the conversation to a minimum, only speaking to indicate a turn, or to remark about a passerby. Therron used the time to work through the whys and hows of his situation. Out of curiosity, he'd followed Acelyne from town to town, but now, he needed to know how she was linked to Midna and what the amulets had to do with anything. He could feel Acelyne's desperation to regain them, and it took a strong will to deny her. His fingers itched to snatch the bag Rori held.

"Why did Midna hire you to find Acelyne?" Rori broke the silence, startling him from his musings.

They were off the main road and deeper into the forest. A perfect place for an ambush. He needed to stay alert if he wanted to stay alive.

"In truth, I don't know." Midna had hired him to find Acelyne, yes, but he'd taken the job for other reasons he couldn't share with Rori.

She didn't need to know that he'd been in too much of a hurry to escape Midna's roving hands to demand details. The Unseelie queen was desperate to conceive an heir, but Therron wasn't meant to be her stud. She had plenty of those in her palace of fornication and debauchery. The place was absolutely teeming with naked bodies, all for the asking, all there of their own volition. He'd never understood why someone would want to give themselves in service in that particular way, but Midna had no shortage of álainn obedience to fawn over her and satisfy her every desire.

"Why do you think the enchantress is kidnapping fae and keeping them barely alive in glass vials?" Rori tilted her head as she asked and a lock of blue hair fell over her face. She blew it off, but it remained.

Therron reached over and, after she jerked away with a snarl, gently tucked the strand behind her ear. Her snarl turned to a shy smile, and Therron's knees wobbled as if he were a schoolboy with his first crush. Ridiculous.

Tug whistled and ambled on, apparently ignoring their discussion.

"I've been asking myself that since I saw you burst free in the market square. I don't like where my answers are taking me." Therron kicked a rock in frustration. His answers all led back to Midna. She'd better give him a solid reason why she sent him searching for Acelyne, and what, exactly the enchantress stole from her. And—his heart beat in his throat—she'd better tell him honestly if she knew Rori was meant to be one of the captured.

"Tug, what do you think?" Rori prodded.

"Aw, no. Tug's not got a worry about them pendants. Rori's safe, that's what matters. Might rain this afternoon."

Rori shared a look with him. His gaze went to the leather satchel at her waist. Acelyne was still heavily enchanting Tug. As if reading his thoughts, Rori nodded and placed a hand over the bag. She studied the trees and scanned the sky.

"How much farther?" Therron didn't trust saying more.

"Not long. Just over this ridge."

The path narrowed until they had to walk single file. Just as Rori said, at the top of the ridge, Therron saw a small thatched roof cottage in the middle of a clearing. It reminded him of Rori's house, except this cottage was only one story and surrounded by several gardens. Smoke funneled from a chimney pot, and he breathed a sigh of relief.

The closer they drew near the cottage, the harder it became to move forward. He fought the urge to turn back and silently swore at Acelyne's magic. Tempted to release his own, he kept it in check—using elven magic in Faerie came with far too many complications. They might be gifted healers, but the other side of their power was equally as adept at killing. In the same way that fae magic nurtured the elements, they could twist the earth to poison, or warp the air to strangle. Each race had their own magic touched by good and evil. The laws of Faerie and Elvenwood were what kept everyone from abusing their power.

But people like Acelyne cared little for rules, it would seem. More than that, he sensed Acelyne's desire to steal his power. Once he fully opened a thread, she could easily snatch every ounce he possessed and destroy not just him, but Rori and Tug as well.

After what he witnessed that morning, he believed Acelyne would use every dirty trick she possibly could to get her hands on the stolen amulets. What she didn't know was that he'd read all the forbidden books in Elvenwood's library. Millennia of dark spells and corrupted sorcerers' tales filled volumes of leather-bound tomes. Not only had he read them all, but he was fully versed in the dark arts. As heir to the elven throne, it was his duty to be prepared for any situation, including encountering someone as vile as Acelyne. The nagging darkness he'd sensed around the pendants had to be from Acelyne. If she were indeed using dark magic, he'd use extreme caution. He intimately understood what dark magic was capable of, and wouldn't play into Acelyne's hands.

What concerned him most was, how had Acelyne come into contact with elven dark arts? He turned to tell Rori of his theory, but they were at the door to the cottage and Tug rapped on the thick door with his knuckle. The sound echoed beyond the cottage into the surrounding forest. The giant shifted and glanced nervously around.

"Paranoid much?" Rori stood with arms crossed, fingers tapping out her impatience.

"Meg doesn't like to be surprised."

Rori squinted at him, her head cocked.

Therron watched the pair, intrigued by the interplay.

Clearly Tug was a frequent visitor to the cottage, but not with Rori.

A square block opened, and a woman's scrunched face peered through. "Ahey, Tug. Who's this you be bringing 'round my place?"

Therron stepped forward, but Rori put a hand on his arm to stop him from speaking. At his glare, she shook her head and rolled her eyes toward Tug.

"These my friends. Rori, you know, and this be Therron. He either wants to kill Rori or kiss her some more, I can't decide."

Therron's jaw tightened so hard he nearly cracked his back teeth. A flush swept up his neck to settle upon his cheeks. Damn fool man. It wasn't right to go around spouting truths that ought not to be said aloud.

For her part, Rori remained outwardly unaffected, and that annoyed Therron even more. At least she could be insulted or excited. Something—anything—was better than the bored expression she wore.

Tug blathered on about thornbarrow and how it made his tummy feel funny, but Therron was more interested in what was happening between the two women. Rori's features shifted and she glanced at Meg as if they were having a private conversation. Tug continued speaking, and Meg nodded in the tiny opening, her eyes locked to Rori.

Rori's gaze shifted to Therron. "Fae don't mate with elves. Ever."

16

The air stilled and the birds in the trees stopped their chirping. Even Tug stopped his rambling to gape at Rori. Therron blinked, a nervous chuckle threatening to burst from his lips. He searched for something to say, but his mind caught on the use of "mate" and stopped there. Did she have feelings for him? He dared not hope, only to be disappointed.

Or was this Rori's way of letting him know that the kiss was just that and nothing more? Would never be more despite him wishing it could be so very much more. The jab in his heart turned to a wretched tearing. So be it. She'd made her declaration, and he'd respect boundaries.

"If you're suggesting I mate with the witch, I propose we don't need her help that much." He tried for humor, but couldn't lift his mirth past his disappointment.

"No, I—bollocks." Rori made an embarrassed cough and kicked the stone pavers. "We need your help, Meg. Can we come in?"

"All you needed was but to ask." Meg's face disappeared from the opening and a moment later, the door swung open.

Tug had to duck low to enter, but once inside, he stood to his full height. Unlike Rori's cottage, the space around them was cavernous. Tall ceilings, rooms that rolled one into the other for days, and in the center of it all was a huge stone pit with a raging fire. Hanging from a pole was a kettle and set around the stones were four cups, one large enough for Tug.

"Were ye expectin' us?"

"I like to be ready for company, whenever they may show up." Meg patted Tug on his huge hand before she turned to Rori. "Tis good to see you again, young Rori, although it would be nice if you weren't always bleeding when you came 'round."

Tug's expression turned from happy contentment to consternation. "She broke through glass this mornin'."

Rori shot him a look to silence his tongue, and Therron snickered. Thornbarrow worked even better than jacksass on giants. He'd have to remember that.

Oblivious of Rori's glare, Tug looked past her to Meg's kitchen, where heavenly smells drifted toward them. A smile widened from one chubby cheek to the other. His chocolate-brown eyes bulged with expectation.

"Meg's the best baker in all of Faerie. Wait till yer taste her treats."

"Oh Tug, you're too sweet. Oh, I made a pun." Meg chortled and beckoned them to sit. "I doubt you're here for my witty wordplay. What is it you came to see me about?"

"I've a feeling you already know," Therron grumbled, half to himself. Something about the witch, even just being in her space, made the hairs on his neck rise. Rori and Tug trusted her, but Therron didn't know Meg and that put him on edge.

"We've encountered an enchantress," Rori explained. "A powerful one, too. We've yet to fully counteract her spell, and I was hoping you'd have something for us."

Meg tapped a finger along her bottom lip and nodded.

Streaks of grey wove in and out of her auburn locks. A few snowdrops clung to wisps of hair as she danced away toward her kitchen. "I've just the thing for you. Stay there. I won't be a moment. Pour yourselves some tea while you're waiting."

Tug lifted the heavy kettle off the rod and poured the steaming liquid into their cups. Rori removed the leather bag and placed it between her feet as she sat down in one of the overstuffed chairs that seemed to be everywhere in Meg's cottage. The sound of humming came from the rear of the room and a moment later, Meg emerged with a platter full of biscuits.

"For the tea, love. These won't help with the enchantments," she said as Rori poked a biscuit with the tip of her dagger. Meg smiled and gave a shake of her head. "Always so mistrustful."

"Kin I have me biscuits now, Meg?"

"Certainly, Tug." She patted his thick forearm with affection before she handed him the tray of cookies.

The way Rori studied the pair—as if she'd only now realized they had feelings for each other—intrigued him. Meg looked old enough to be Tug's gran, but that meant nothing. Some fae lived several thousand years. Besides, who was he to judge another's relationship? Love came in all shapes and colors. When someone found it, they should hold it close and protect the preciousness of what they had. Dear gods, was he getting sappy now? He sniffed and eyed the cookies with fresh suspicion.

Meg caught Rori watching and a girlish smile crept across her face. She even blushed. Rori's slight nod—in a kind of permission granting way—was for Meg alone. Rori turned away from the healer and flushed when their eyes met. He kept the chuckle from escaping, but didn't stop a playful grin from touching his lips. She was a sweet lass, Rori, but too bottled up to know how much these two not only adored, but respected her.

A fierce protectiveness crossed her features, and Therron tipped his head in a sign he wouldn't interfere. What transpired between the couple was no concern of his. It was Rori who he looked to care for, if she'd let him. Now he knew she was his fated mate. Whether she chose to accept that was still undecided on her part, but his choice was already made.

"Now then, Tug is obviously fighting the effects of the enchantment, but what about the two of you?" Meg peered at Rori and then Therron, her face unreadable. A moment later, her cheek twitched, and she made a tsking sound.

The fire in her eyes wasn't from Tug alone, and Therron sat straighter, all senses on alert. Somewhere, a clock ticked a slow death beat. He ran a hand through his hair and shifted in the comfortable chair.

Tick, tick, tick.

No one spoke. Therron shrugged against the heaviness of his coat. The air warmed, and he licked his dry lips.

"This enchantress, what does she look like?"

"Light hair, red robes. Pretty face, slender frame," Therron replied quickly. The sooner they left Meg's cottage, the better.

"I see." Meg leveled her gaze at him, and it felt like a dagger to his belly.

He crossed his arms and legs, to keep himself from bolting for the door.

After a moment, her attention snapped to Rori. "What's in that bag?"

Rori placed her legs over the leather satchel. "These don't concern you. We only need to counteract the spells."

Therron eyed Rori, apprehension coiling in his gut. They'd come to Meg for help—why would she say otherwise? The surprise and consternation on Rori's features mirrored his thoughts. He glanced at the ceiling, the walls, and the furniture. Acelyne's presence was everywhere. He sent a thread of his magic to Rori as a protective measure.

"They're glass amulets," Rori forced out.

A visible battle etched across her lovely face. Consternation twisted her lips and determination shone from her sapphire-hued eyes. Therron started to reach for her, but stopped himself. If Acelyne's enchantments had snared Rori, physical contact might trap him as well. It was dangerous enough to keep his thread of magic tethered to her, but he would protect her at all costs.

Not just because of her role in the curse, but because she was goodness and kindness coiled around a woman who desperately tried to push others away. He saw it in her actions the night at the pub, and in the subtle ways she'd flip-flopped emotions with him. Or was that just wishful thinking again?

Perhaps it was because of her dichotomous behavior that he felt the need to guard her from harm. He gripped his thigh to keep from reaching out to physically touch her. His hand was but a twitch away from her fingers. Close enough to let her know he was there if she needed him.

"Enchanted amulets," Rori wheezed, "spelled to hold fae prisoners." She sagged in her chair, as if those few words had cost her bodily as well as mentally. "I fear—" Sweat dotted her brow, and she grimaced. "I believe there are dozens trapped inside." Veins protruded on her forehead and neck. "Just as I was until this morning."

Tug started to rise, but Meg put a hand on his, and he sat. The storm cloud brewing across his features gave them pause. The enchantress was near. Therron felt her presence as if it were a pillow placed over his face, suffocating him. Acelyne was not done with them yet.

17

Therron sat rigid, expectant. Itchy tendrils crept through his hair like a million beetles bent on eating his flesh. He fought the desire to brush them away. They were an illusion, a farce meant to weaken his will. Acelyne was toying with his mind once again. By the looks of his companions, she was manipulating all of them. Or rather, she was trying to.

The compulsion to draw his sword and slay Meg was powerful. Despite everything, Acelyne still fought for control of his will. She was in for a bloody war if she thought he'd capitulate fully. He'd given her enough control to fool her once; he'd not do it again. Even so, he struggled to keep his thoughts and actions his own. With a single flick of his elven magic, he could be done with the enchantress but he needed answers only she could provide, and using magic unannounced in a fae witch's home was definitely considered rude.

But oh, how the need to slay Meg overpowered everything else. Desperate, almost manic, was the enchantress's desire to kill the witch. Therron reached for his sword, and Meg laid her hand over his. She sat between the two men—one arm stretched left, the other right—for several minutes. The only sound in the cottage was of the ticking clock.

A low growl came from Therron's throat, and his fingers twitched above the hilt of his sword as he fought off Acelyne's incessant bombarding in his mind. Beside him, Rori released the clasp of her daggers, ready. His eyes bore into hers. She must believe he wouldn't hurt her. It was Acelyne he was after, but how could she know? He forced open his mouth to speak, but Meg shook her head, silencing him with one glance.

The witch swayed where she sat, and Therron felt the physical presence of Acelyne in the room, even though he couldn't see her. A sneer lifted his upper lip, baring his teeth. Tug whimpered and shuddered, his face a mix of agony and apology.

Meg's grey-green eyes clouded, and her swaying increased. Her lips moved but no words came out. Rori cast a worried glance to Therron. He ignored Meg, focusing instead on keeping Acelyne's grasping tendrils from burrowing into his mind. Her presence grew until he was certain she stood not more than a pace away. But there was no one else besides Meg and the three of them in the cottage.

Meg's grip tightened on his hand. Her fae magic tore through his veins, rage-fueled and determined. She was as powerful as Acelyne, though they were as different as the sea and desert. One a witch, whose purpose was to nurture and heal, the other an enchantress who deceived and stole. In those few moments, one became the other, their powerful threads weaving around the group with vicious intensity. Therron couldn't see their respective magics, but he felt them as sure as if they were strands of ribbons cutting at his skin.

Tug's whimpers turned to outright howls, and Rori removed her daggers from their sheaths. She plucked the bag from between her legs and slipped the strap over her head, her face set, ready for a fight. Therron kept his thread of magic around her and closed his mind. The two women battled on an unseen field, and they were caught in the crossfire. He began to think they were pawns in an unnecessary game.

Meg wailed and swayed, her lips sputtering incoherent words, her eyes milky orbs. Rori's gaze darted from Meg to Tug to Therron, a mixture of emotions swirling in her eyes. Death. Fear. Fight. Those words twisted in Therron's thoughts. He gripped Meg's hand, beckoning her to take strength from him, but he withheld his magic for fear either one of them would siphon too much and leave him weakened, vulnerable. Meg took greedily of his physical stamina, feeding off him like a starved kitten given a teat. His adrenaline whipped like a tempest through his body and into Meg's. Later, he'd need sustenance, but for now he would provide the fuel necessary for Meg to fight.

Sweat beaded Rori's brow, and she started to rise, he assumed to battle whatever entity invaded the place.

"Rori, wait." Therron indicated the chair, and she sat, eyes wide, daggers ready. Her need to protect those around her thrummed against Therron's own will to stay settled until Meg was finished. He suspected interrupting the spell Meg cast could prove fatal for everyone in the cottage. Rori's need to help, to defend—aye, even the devotion she showed to her friends—was commendable. Perhaps she might one day consider him a friend as well. He was already past such a sentiment.

The clock chimed a hideous mocking chirp to call out the hour. One, two, three; it continued, each caw rattling through the cottage. Therron's nerves corkscrewed, ready to spring at any moment.

A hiss came from Meg, and her arms bolted outward. "You have no power here. Be gone, be gone, be gone!"

Her power roared through Therron, knocking the wind out of him.

Frigid air swooshed through the room, causing candles to flicker and the cook fire to sizzle and pop, and then vanished.

Tug quieted, unfazed. He reached for another biscuit and sipped his tea as if he were at a café in the center of town.

Adrenaline pulsed through Therron's bloodstream. The last vestiges of fog in his brain dissipated. A thick, acrid taste coated his tongue.

Rori sat frozen, stark fear etched across her features.

Meg's face softened, and her hands rested in her lap. A beatific smile spread across the healer's face.

"Rori." Now Therron did place a warm palm on her forearm. Acelyne's threat was gone, and even if it wasn't, he needed to touch Rori. To assure her she was safe. His free hand reached for his sword out of habit.

"You won't be needing that, elf. Rori is well. There is no danger here." Meg's eyes bore into Therron's. Her silver-streaked hair billowed with a shake of her head. "I know of this enchantress. She's vile of the worst sort. It won't be easy to release her spell on this one." Her head tilted toward Tug. "His connection to Rori is too established, and Acelyne has used that as her anchor. Despite Tug's will to fend her off and protect his friend, he also fears he'll somehow be responsible for Rori's death. Acelyne's used that fear to prey on his insecurities, I'm afraid. I'll keep him here with me for the time being. You," Meg kept her gaze on Therron, "must fight through her lies. Your life depends on it."

"I keep myself to myself. You've got nothing to worry about with me." The comment about Tug's connection with Rori pinched Therron's belly.

Jealousy wasn't a virtuous emotion, but he wasn't a virtuous man. How could he be jealous when he had only just met Rori that morning? Yet there was something about her that sparked emotions he'd never hoped to have. Feelings that had nothing to do with his curse, but came from the strong-willed, intelligent woman sitting beside him. If only she felt the same about him.

Alas, she didn't. Her focus was on the amulets, as they should be. Since she knew nothing of the curse or her role in his future, he couldn't begrudge the giant their friendship, or her feelings for her friend. One day, when the enchantress business was settled, perhaps she might have affection for him, too.

Meg and Rori exchanged a glance. What it meant, he could only guess.

"Keeping to yourself is the elven way, isn't it, dear? But there are others you need concern yourself with, aren't there?"

Meg's penetrating stare was meant to unnerve him, and it did that and more. She couldn't mean what he thought she meant.

He blinked hard, his chest raising and lowering with labored breaths. Images of myths long forgotten played in his mind, and his scar burned. His fingers twitched to rub the damned thing, but he kept them firmly gripping his knees.

The sound of leathery wings unfolding whispered in the still air. Impossible. How could Meg know? No one knew, not even his own parents. That wasn't true. The little girl who had told him about Aurora MacNair also told him a secret that he'd refused to believe. Until now.

"Therron, help me in the kitchen. Rori, you stay here with Tug and keep an eye on him, you hear?" Meg issued her commands and pointed toward the back of the cottage.

Rori watched her with narrowed eyes and, despite himself, Therron looked to her for some sign that she would be all right in his absence. She waved him off and took a seat beside Tug. He followed Meg to the expansive kitchen, hardly able to hear from the blood rushing through his ears and the pounding of his heart.

"I know who you are, Therron Mistwalker, but what I don't

understand is what you're doing with Rori and Tug." Meg directed him to a platter on the counter. Freshly baked cookies lined the dish. "You'll take these with us when we're finished here."

Therron debated lying for a moment, but if Meg could see the secret he'd hidden from everyone, then lying was useless. "I'm on a secret mission for Midna. Rori got involved somehow and now we're here." He met her steady gaze. "How do you know who I am?"

"I'm a witch, you silly elf. I see much of what happens on this world, and some of what happens on other worlds. You feature strongly in my dreams of late."

"Does this have to do with the little girl who cursed me?"

"Little girl?" Meg closed her eyes and hummed a moment before opening them. Sorrow embedded deep in their depths. "I do not know this girl, but she tells of a prophecy that is separate from Ishnara's curse. It would appear you are twice blessed, Therron Mistwalker. You, and Rori, are destined for great things, but first, you must live through grave danger. The pair of you have been chosen." She half-shrugged. "That is all that I can see of your future."

"Can you speak to the girl? Do you know what the prophecy is?"

"I'm afraid I can't help you with that. Nor do I think you can find any mention of it in your vast library at Elvenwood. But there, you will find the truth of Ishnara's curse. You mustn't believe the lies you've been fed for generations." She silenced his questions with a severe look. "Does Rori know she's your fated mate? That she's the one who can break the curse?"

Therron glanced over his shoulder to where Rori pretended to ignore them. Even hunched over Tug, he could tell she was trying valiantly to eavesdrop on their conversation.

"No, she doesn't, and I'd appreciate if you wouldn't say

anything to her. About my identity, or the curse. If she has feelings for me, they need to come from her, not from obligation. Anything less, and it might spell disaster for her. That's a risk I can't take."

"I can see you already care for her, so I'll do as asked. She'll find out eventually, though, and it should come from you." Meg squeezed his arm with a motherly touch. "I've known Rori since she was born, and while she puts on a good front, she's not as tough as she'd like you to believe. Physically, yes, more so than anyone I've ever met, but her father wasn't kind to her emotions. He trained her to be something she's not. Be gentle with her, please?"

Therron nodded, his heart thumping so hard he swore Rori could hear it. If the little girl wasn't Ishnara, then who was she, and how was it Rori fit into both his prophecy and his curse? Until that moment, he'd thought they were one and the same, but now he wasn't certain.

As he strolled to the sitting room, carrying the platter, he looked at Rori anew. Who the blood and ashes was she, really?

$$\text{\small ❧}\quad 18\quad \text{\small ❧}$$

Rori cocked her head to better hear what Meg and Therron discussed. She could've sworn she'd heard parchment crinkling or leather being folded, but Tug's happy munching and Therron's ragged breathing fought for dominance over an old clock ticking nearby. Then Meg dragged Therron away, and she was stuck where she sat, trying to eavesdrop beyond Tug's happy chatter.

Meg and Therron returned, their faces about as opposite as could be. Meg's was full of serenity and joy, while Therron's features were set in grim defiance. What the hell had they talked about?

"Therron?" She gripped his hand where it rested on his leg. Torment covered his features. "What did you do to him, Meg?"

"*Do* to him? Nothing. He needed a reminder, that's all."

"Of what?"

Rori searched Therron's face and looked into the bottomless wells of his eyes, where she felt a dread so strong it could destroy a kingdom. What caused the suffering was hidden from her, but it was there, lurking. The annoying pinching started in her heart. Now it felt as if someone used the organ as a pin cushion. Pain, not intolerable, but certainly unwelcome, vibrated from her chest. Therron was the cause, she was sure of it. But why? How? She barely knew him…and yet she felt a connection stronger than any bond she'd had before.

She withdrew her hand from his, hoping to sever the connection, but it remained, which pissed her off. She couldn't afford to worry about the elf. She needed no one but herself. Whatever troubled him, that was for Therron to sort out. She folded her arms across her chest and tucked her hands at her sides to keep a safe distance between them. Whatever reminder Meg thought he needed, she wanted no part. She'd had enough shenanigans for one day, thankyouverymuch.

"I'm fine," Therron grumbled. "You needn't worry about me." His focus snapped in place, and Rori was shut out from whatever it was she'd experienced.

Despite wanting to rid herself of it, the loss of their connection rattled her clear to her bones. With deliberate calm, she reached for her cup. If she was lucky, Meg had put something in the tea that would make her forget this morning. Make her forget the bizarre reality/illusion she'd stumbled into. Make her forget that magic was beyond her realm of understanding and a terrifying reminder of her failure. Her tea sloshed onto the saucer, and she bit her lip. If they didn't get answers soon, she might lose her shit. Something was happening here, something she was a part of, but also not, and that didn't sit well with her.

"Can you help us with the amulets or not? We're wasting time." Therron's gruffness was directed at Meg, but Rori felt its sting as if he punished her for the loss of the connection.

Meg's sigh wasn't of despair; quite the opposite. It was of relief. "I'm afraid not. I don't know the spell used to imprison the fae, and if I try to release them, I might kill them all. The pair of you must gather both queens at a neutral spot. Neither will want to attend, but both must."

"Impossible," Therron mumbled around a biscuit, his fourth in as many minutes. "Midna never leaves her palace."

"I'm sure you'll find a way to convince Midna, won't you, Therron? And Rori, Eirlys."

Rori's face scrunched with disbelief. "The queens haven't met for ages."

"Rori, you must convince Eirlys this is in the best interest of Faerie, and Therron, tell Midna the same. Whatever nonsense they're bickering about must be put aside."

"It goes deeper than a simple dispute. Midna is desperate to conceive an heir and, well, Eirlys has Arianna. I think the reason Midna avoids Eirlys is founded more in a sense of failure than jealousy." Rori understood far too well how that felt.

"Is that all? Because of a baby? Pfffft, you'll just have to tell Midna she's being ridiculous." Meg waved her hand as if she could wave away the notion, but babies were a serious concern to the queens. If they didn't conceive by a certain age, they never would. Meg must know this, but perhaps she didn't think it as important a matter as it actually was.

Therron was right—what Meg asked was impossible. Rori was glad he had the unpleasant task of confronting the Unseelie queen. "I adore you, Meg, but you *are* mad."

"Oh yes, quite so. Now, finish your tea, Rori. You've an impossible task to accomplish."

She finished the tea, her belly full from all the biscuits she'd eaten. Gods, but she was hungry today.

Therron rose and turned toward her. "We should be going." To Meg, he inclined his head and thanked her for the refreshments. He kept his eyes locked to Meg's, as if he tried to convey meaning in his glance. Whatever they spoke of in their secret conversation, it had unnerved him.

She kept Therron in the corner of her vision as she said goodbye to her old friend.

Meg brushed her forehead and sighed. "Please try to stay out of trouble."

They both knew that wouldn't happen. "If you've got any of that tincture, I wouldn't mind a barrelful."

Before Rori finished her sentence, Meg pulled a glass pot from her pocket. "I'll make a fresh batch for when I see you next, but Rori, I'm serious. This enchantress is dangerous. You need to protect each other." She cocked her chin toward Therron.

Rori nodded, her thoughts a swirl of emotion. She'd never needed anyone before and didn't like the idea that now, in the same morning, twice she was told she needed Therron. The Taryn woman she didn't know, but Meg was an old family friend; she'd known her all her life and trusted her implicitly. If she was worried about the enchantress and Therron's safety, Rori would take notice.

Meg clasped Rori's hands and looked deep into her eyes. "Keep those fae safe, love. If Acelyne gets hold of them, Faerie is lost." Meg's eyes clouded, and her brow dipped in worry. "War brews in the cauldron of one whose mind is not their own. A shadow hovers like death upon the sick. There will be bloodshed on soil not of our own, but our kind will pay the ultimate price. Faerie shall be no more." She spoke in a somber monotone that was quite unlike her usual cheery self.

"Meg." Rori grasped the woman's shoulders and gave a gentle shake. "What war? When? Where?"

Meg shook herself and blinked, as if she'd lost her thought. "Oh, yes, as I was saying, I'd wager those amulets are at the heart of the trouble. Do what it takes to get Eirlys and Midna to meet. They'll fight you on the idea, there's no doubt about that, but make them come together." She spoke in her natural voice, as though the awful words had never happened.

Rori glanced at Therron, whose face had gone ashen.

Meg tapped her bottom lip with a wrinkled finger. "The

Vale of Dorn will do. I know the wizard who lives there. I'll let him know to expect you in two days' time."

"You mentioned war, Meg. Between the faerie queens? Or someone else?" Rori stroked Meg's arm.

"I did? How strange." She pressed her fingers to her temple. "But then, my dreams have been upsetting of late. It's imperative the queens come together. You know where I wish you to go, Rori. Be there in two days."

"There's no way we can get to the Unseelie Court that quickly. Even with the queen's fastest horses, we'll be hard-pressed to arrive by then, forget about the journey to the vale from there." Rori's mind spun with details they'd need: food, water, change of horses, bedding—too much, with no time to plan.

"You can do it." Meg tapped Rori's leather jacket just above the spot where the sleeping princess was concealed. "You know how to traverse time and space. If ever there was a reason to break the law, it's now."

An audible gasp came from Therron, and Rori took a step backward. "I can't. I'd lose my job. I'll be exiled, or worse."

Meg's stern gaze went from Rori to Therron. "Eirlys will understand. The two of you must do this together. He's your passage into the Unseelie Court. Without him, Midna won't care who you are or what you have to say. She'll throw you into her dungeon and forget you exist."

Questions, thoughts, and images raced through Rori's mind. Not all of them terrible. The queen's pleasure dungeon, from what she'd heard, was meant to be a special kind of torture. A form of discipline for álainn obedience who forgot their place. Those who wound up in the dungeons spent their days making love to other prisoners while the court kept watch. As mortifying as that might be, it would certainly be a better option than Eirlys exiling her for breaking the oaths she'd sworn to her queen.

What Meg suggested, though, was treason. She wanted Rori to use one of the magical doorways that led to places far beyond the kingdoms of Faerie. They were portals that allowed her to travel to other realms, all strictly regulated. Very few fae were allowed to use the doorways, and they were all forbidden from using them without prior consent. It kept the borders secure and their people safe. Without the regulations, chaos between the realms would ensue. Rori might be a spy, but there were some rules she couldn't break.

"I can't, Meg. I swore to Queen Eirlys that I would never enter the human realm without her permission." She hooked a finger at Therron. "And with him? I'd take the dungeons over Eirlys's rage any day."

"Without me, the *best* you can hope for is Queen Midna's dungeons. I don't like this any more than you, but we have no choice. If the fastest way to the Unseelie Court is through the human realm, we must risk it." Therron met her gaze. His usually pale skin was the color of chalk.

The dungeons were the best she could hope for? Rori shuddered at the imagined horrors of what would be worse than serving Midna's legendary álainn obedience as a prisoner. *The rack? Isolation?* Either choice meant she would be disgraced. Her family dishonored. And Cian—what would her brother think of her? Being exiled would break his heart, but if he ever found her in Midna's dungeons...that might kill him.

Bollocks and shitshark sniffers. How the hell had she ended up in this predicament? Ever since she'd woken up in that cursed forest, her life was on a downward spiral, without an end in sight. Well, fuck that. She hadn't been trained to let life toss her willy-nilly. It might get her exiled or worse, but Rori would be damned if she'd let circumstances dictate her fate.

If only Cian had been trapped in the amulet. He positively adored the human realm, and as Eirlys's current favorite, he could break all the rules he liked and get rewarded for it. The Seelie queen liked Rori, but she doubted she'd earned enough goodwill to not be punished.

Rori wrapped her arms around the leather bag and interlaced her fingers. Having the amulets close gave her hope. This was for something greater than herself. Whatever punishment she received would be worth it if she saved the other faeries' lives. At least, that was the story she told herself. She glanced at her friend, who stood behind Meg with a sappy smile on his face. Tug would be safe here with Meg. Though the healer tried to hide it, their shared affection was sweet. In a way, she was risking exile for them, too. They deserved whatever happiness their love could bring them, and all of Faerie deserved a future without war. It made her insides go all gooey, imagining Meg and Tug together. A giant and a witch. Maybe someone would write a fairytale about them. Her imagination kicked in with the possibilities, but was cut short when reality slammed back into her mind.

The only fairytale she was living was more a cautionary tale with a grim ending.

Queen Eirlys might be a fair and tolerant queen, but Rori had witnessed what happened to those who chose to ignore Faerie's laws. If Midna's sex dungeons were bad, Eirlys's dungeons were worse—convicts were left isolated, with nothing but the clothes on their backs. Countless fae had perished beneath the Seelie queen's palace without a passing thought from the courtiers who lived in the lavish rooms upstairs. Rori refused to dwell on the fact that many of those lost to the dungeons had been convicted on far less grievous crimes than the one she was about to commit.

She was stalling, and she knew it. The human realm was twelve hours ahead of Faerie. Unless she wanted to take the elf there in the middle of the night, they needed to get moving. The doorway she needed was a couple of hours' walk away.

Taking an elf to the human realm was fraught with all kinds of potential dangers, but none as horrible as what awaited her when she returned.

Whether the rack or the dungeon, she had to break her oath to save the fae.

19

Golden circles of electric light shimmered on the wet cobblestones, and Cian stopped for a moment to breathe in the scent of the human realm. The mission could wait for a few minutes. He never tired of these cities—old like Brugge, where he found himself this night, or the sleek new places with skyscrapers and buildings buzzing with technological wonders that would make his queen's black hair turn crimson with horror.

On the surface, he understood Faerie's apprehension of industry. But if only they could see what it had done for worlds like Earth. Airplanes and automobiles…he chuckled as he lifted his face to the sky and searched the clouds for corroboration. With those two wonders alone, the need for magical doorways would be moot. The queens wouldn't have to expend vast amounts of energy guarding all the doorways found in Faerie.

His gaze slid to the humans walking around the town square, their faces bent to look at the glowing screens of their mobiles. The information they carried in their pockets was mind-blowing. Entire catalogs of knowledge at their fingertips.

He envied them their complicated, fast-paced, convenient lives.

A heavy sigh lifted his shoulders. There was a time when towns like Brugge, and bigger cities like Paris, would've had entire delegations of faeries living among the humans. But the age of myth had long past, and with it, his kin. He looked toward England and farther north to Scotland, where several generations of great-grandparents once lived in harmony with the humans. Fae were revered back then. Sought out for their wisdom.

He scuffed his bespoke dress shoe on the wet cobbles. These days, fae were thought of as fantasy creatures. Wee things with wings that sprinkle fairy dust in humans' eyes while they slept. The humans who strolled past him had no idea that the fae never left Earth, they just blended in better to keep from being discovered. And now fae like him spied on those who didn't believe in his existence.

The belfry tolled, and he shoved his hands into the pockets of his long coat, also bespoke. He'd promised Midna he would be back before midnight in the faerie realm, giving him little more than twelve hours. Plenty of time for what he sought.

Soft rain gave the night a mysterious, romantic feel, just the kind of place a missing faerie princess might find enticing. Cian couldn't let the atmosphere or humans seduce him any more than they had. He was here for information. Knowledge he wouldn't find with a few taps of his mobile.

With a deep breath and shake of his head to dispel the few drops of rain that had clung to his dark locks, he strode through the streets with purpose. The club he sought was one he knew from other missions. He stretched his shoulders as he walked, loosening them for what might come next.

The doorman stood with his beefy arms folded over a chest that had seen a few too many training sessions in the gym.

Cian smiled genially at the man, hoping he'd remember him from six months past.

"Club's full," he said in French, mistaking Cian for a tourist.

"Ah, maar niet voor mij." Cian answered in Flemish. Not for me.

"Not for you." He chuckled and stepped aside to allow Cian entry.

It was well past midnight, and the club was just getting started for a night of revelry. Lasers and neon lights flashed across the euphoric faces of those on the dancefloor. Cian side-stepped a pair of women grinding each other so thoroughly, they might've been copulating. A jealous little ping snapped against his heart. Would that he could be so free to dance with such abandon. And to love whomever he chose.

The job came with risks and rewards, he more than anyone understood what those were, but the job also demanded he not form any emotional attachments. His queen had made it clear on more than one occasion that his body belonged to the crown, and he must use this tool as needed for the mission. Sure, he fucked and sucked and fornicated for his own release, but rarely was it for pleasure. That would involve a level of commitment he couldn't afford.

He raked a hand through his hair and scanned the club for his informant. They didn't have an appointment, and he hoped she would be there.

His investigation into Mairead's disappearance hadn't produced any sustainable leads in Faerie, so he and Midna had agreed it was time he looked elsewhere. The Unseelie queen had been adamant that Mairead wouldn't go to the human realm, but he'd run out of options at home. The faerie princess had simply vanished.

An all-too commonplace occurrence lately. The queens didn't want to admit it, but they were frightened. Sometimes fae went missing, but were found in the mountains to the north, on the outskirts of the elven kingdom, or to the south where all manner of races lived in harmony. Those were the ruler-less kingdoms. Cian knew for a fact that both Eirlys and Midna would love to take over the lands, but neither were willing to risk war to claim them. War led to death. As much as the queens outwardly showed their strength, inside they were both giant softies.

Midna perhaps a little more than Eirlys, but both women cared a great deal about their subjects. He couldn't see either one doing something so monumentally stupid they'd risk the peace Faerie now had.

"I thought you'd forgotten about me, Cian." Lida's silky voice whispered in his ear, and he turned to her with a large smile.

"How could I ever forget you?" He kissed her on both cheeks and took a step back to admire her beaded mini dress. The deep V neckline reached nearly to her belly button, and the short, very short, skirt skimmed the tops of her thighs. "Stunning, as always."

Grey-gold eyes flashed against her near onyx skin. He'd always assumed she was touched by fae in her bloodline, but had never asked. It would ruin the mystery if he knew.

"I know." Her red lips parted to reveal straight white teeth. Her laugh was perfectly measured.

Vanity wasn't her only flaw. An elite model, Lida traveled the world, a perk to her job that Cian exploited as often as he could. The intel she'd provided over the years had prevented several regional skirmishes, and more global catastrophes as well. All for the price of a fuck.

"Can I buy you a drink?" He indicated the bar, but she shook her head. "Don't make me dance, Lida. You know I'm rubbish."

"I was thinking something a little more horizontal." She

drew a hand over her close-cropped hair and smiled in a knowing way. "It's been so long since I've had anyone as… enthusiastic as you."

A memory of her long limbs wrapped around his body burst to the front of his mind, and his cock stirred.

"Lead the way."

She brushed past the doorman with a sultry goodbye. He winked at Cian with a knowing gleam in his dark eyes. Cian grinned just enough to appease his curiosity. He couldn't give a flying satyr what the doorman thought of his liaison with Lida, but he'd not burn a contact just out of spite. Play the game. Win prizes.

Lida chatted as they walked the short distance from the club to her flat across the river. He half-listened, his attention attuned to several footsteps that came from behind them. Cian pressed his palm against the small of her back and urged her to the left, where he knew there was better lighting and more people.

"I thought we were going to my place?" She whirled on him, face set like marble. Her eyes widened and fear flitted across them. "We are not alone."

"I know."

Lida pressed herself against him as he turned to face the approaching men.

"Evening, gentlemen." He tipped his head in greeting, hoping he was wrong about his misgivings. Yet he rarely was, and this time was no exception.

Three men spread out in the narrow street, cutting off escape from three angles. They could make a run for it, even in the five-inch heels she wore, but where was the fun in that?

"Give us your wallets, phones, and jewelry," a medium-sized man with black hair and a goatee demanded. His gaze went to Cian's shoes and then coat. "Give us them Oxfords, too."

Cian leveled a glare at the man. "No."

"What do you mean, no? There's three of us and only one of you."

"You're assuming my lovely companion is unskilled in the physical arts. That's very sexist of you."

He could've used magic to kill them instantly, but that would cause problems back home. Or, he could've bantered with them until they became frustrated and made a clumsy attack, but he didn't have time to waste on the cretins.

Instead, he kept his magic suppressed and lashed out at the one who spoke, first. His fist connected with his jaw with a crack that echoed against the stone buildings. A second crack, this one followed by the squelch of soft tissue slamming into something hard. He went down hard, holding his bleeding nose and wailing like a child. Cian kicked a second man in his sternum. Air whooshed from his lungs, and he stumbled backward. For the third, and last man, Cian withdrew a slim blade he kept up his sleeve.

Panic filled the man's eyes, and he looked from Cian to his stunned crew. Cian prayed he would make the right choice and run off, but the man was no coward. He flicked open a switchblade and spun it between his fingers. A cocky grin accompanied a manic chortle.

A ripple of anxiety twisted Cian's gut. The man sniffed the air like a dog caught on a scent. His head whipped toward Cian, the gleam in his eyes as far from panic as could be.

Fuck. A scyver. Magic-seeking sycophants that were becoming the bane of his human realm excursions.

"Cian," Lida warned, and he saw the other two men stagger forward.

Their blades flashed in the dim light. They had the same fanaticism crossing their features as their friend. Three scyvers? He cricked his neck and calculated his next moves.

He'd never encountered a group before. They were getting bolder, and more prolific.

"What are they?" Lida asked, her voice small and frightened.

She was right to ask. The men no longer looked human, but skeletal as if starved for centuries. In a way, they were starving —for his magic. How the creatures came to be, or why, no one knew for certain. Those details didn't concern Cian half as much as how did the humans, if they even were human, know he had magic? They seemed to be able to sense it, which meant what, exactly?

Lida backed away, and one of the scyvers locked his attention to her. A whimper escaped her lips, giving credence to the man's assertion that she couldn't fight. What he wouldn't give to have Rori by his side at the moment. She'd make quick work of the men with her deadly daggers. Why hadn't he brought guns with him tonight?

Because he hadn't planned on a scyver ambush.

With a hearty sigh, he signaled Lida to stay where she was, and went to work. He reached into a hidden inner pocket of his coat and withdrew a long, slim dagger given to him as a gift from Queen Eirlys when he graduated the Academy. A perpetual coating of poison only the queen knew the origins of, glinted green in the dim light. With his two blades, he savagely attacked the men, kicking one, slicing at another, dropping to the ground to swipe his leg against the third and knocking him off-balance.

He fought with skill and intuition, but not magic. These scyvers probably were more accustomed to a brawl than outright combat, as their clumsy attacks proved. The first attack he'd made was delicate in comparison to the efficiency with which he felled the trio. A throat punch here, a kick there, several jabs to each, and one by one they slid to the ground, unconscious. To finish the job, he jammed his slim dagger into each man's chest. Reluctantly, he used his smaller knife and made a clean cut across their throats. With scyvers, it paid to be paranoid.

To her credit, Lida hadn't run off shrieking, nor did she tremble and cry.

Cian withdrew his dagger from the goateed man's chest and assessed the fight, mentally noting where he could've improved. A misty drizzle had made fighting interesting, with the four of them slipping on cobblestones. He'd underestimated the scyvers' fanatic need for magic and the fight had taken more time and energy than he'd like.

He knelt for a moment to catch his breath. This wasn't how his night was supposed to end, with his lovely designer suit soaked, his informant possibly traumatized, and three dead bodies.

As he rose, a rivulet of blood caught in the gaps of scarring on the man's neck. He tilted the scyver's head to the side where three slashes had scarred over, just below his ear. Cian turned his head to the other side, where three more identical marks were embedded in the skin. He ran a finger across the ragged edges. What was left of the man's essence reacted to Cian's touch.

"The fuck?" Cian lifted his face to the sky. His night had just gotten more complicated.

A merman. Not seen in Faerie for millennia—how the hell did one show up in the human realm?

20

For well over an hour, they walked with little conversation between them. Therron kept his head down, his long legs striking out at the dirt road as if it had personally insulted him. Each scuff and thud of his boot sounded off the tree trunks along the side of the road. There was a pattern to his stride, a cadence born from walking long distances often. Rori kept her face turned away from him but he saw her surreptitious glances.

Their pace made quick work of the distance, and Therron admired Rori's stamina. If he'd been imprisoned in a glass amulet for several days, would he be as strong as she? Perhaps Meg gave them something in their tea and cookies to boost their endurance, but he didn't believe she had. Rori's prowess came from years of hard training. Her dedication and discipline was impressive. No wonder the Seelie queen had chosen Rori as one of her personal spies.

"Have you ever been to the human realm?" The tremble of her voice belied her harsh strides.

"No, and I'd be a happy man to say I never did." Elves once inhabited the magical forests of the human realm, but left for unknown reasons. He'd been raised on stories of humans who enslaved elves to do their bidding. Whether true or not, he didn't relish the thought of finding out.

"It's not so bad. Well, once you get used to the smells and sounds. They're quite noisy, humans."

His grunt came out more like a snarl. Humans weren't known for their grace, but rather for their unceasing desire to destroy things, including his kind. He slid a glance to Rori. Did humans capture fae as well? The stories he was told only involved elves, but then, everything at Elvenwood was about his people, ignoring all the other kingdoms. It didn't used to be like this, but over the centuries, elves became myopic to only themselves.

"How can you hate them if you've never met one?"

"I didn't say I've never met one. I said I've never been to their side."

Rori shifted the bag and turned her head to better see him. "You've met a human? What, here in Faerie?"

A slight shake of his head served as answer. It wouldn't do to tell her of visions and prophecies and curses. Not yet.

"If not here, where?"

His gaze took in the thick forests of Faerie. He couldn't tell her where because he didn't know himself. The little girl had appeared in his palace, but then they'd stood on a balcony near the sea—definitely not in Elvenwood. Meg believed she wasn't Ishnara, the faerie princess who had cursed his family long ago, and he was inclined to agree. The little girl did have an etherealness to her, but she didn't look fae. Her skin had sparkled as if all the night sky dwelled beneath. He'd not remembered until just now, but at the time, he'd thought she was a goddess. Who ever heard of a child goddess? Unless she'd chosen another form to speak to him. Which would make her not human?

Excellent. Now he was imagining a child goddess had

bestowed upon him a prophecy. Not just a human, but a celestial being. As if it wasn't enough he was already cursed by a fae princess. Meg had said they were chosen. By whom? Could Ishnara defy death to pick him among all of his past kin? If so, did she do so because of the prophecy? Were they somehow related? And now Rori was mixed up in the mess. Life was so much simpler when he was nothing more than a prince who would one day die alone, without a mate, without heirs.

With a grunt, he cleared his throat. "It's hard to explain."

She accepted this without argument. A blessing he had a feeling wouldn't last long.

"How did you know a kiss would pull me from the enchantment?"

He afforded her the smallest of smiles. "I didn't. My mum read me a book once about a kiss that turned a frog into a prince. Figured it was worth a shot."

The emotions that played across her face did things to his insides. Devious little tickles that he welcomed with cautious joy.

"You risked taking liberties with me from a nursery tale?"

His smile grew. "It worked, didn't it?"

A brief grin told him it had. She raised two fingers to her lips, and her face went soft for the briefest moment. Then a frown drew her brows low.

"Am I the frog or the princess in this tale?"

His grin stretched from ear to ear. She was neither princess nor frog, but if she accepted him as her mate, she would one day become a princess of Elvenwood. He liked the sound of that. Although, he doubted she'd be satisfied sitting on a throne. Rori MacNair was a woman of action, her loyalty as fierce as the glares she gave in an attempt to frighten him away. She had no idea how endearing she was. Tough, even brittle, yet a ball of fluff in the middle. He just had to crack the hard outer shell. Challenge accepted.

"Which do you think?"

"I think you're toying with me and enjoying this far too much. A nursery tale. Bah! I'll tell you what, the next time we're in a squeeze, I'm going to think of the most absurd possibility and use that to get us out of it."

"You promised Meg you'd stay out of trouble."

Rori tilted her head. "But did I?"

He squinted, thinking back to the conversation. The little minx, she hadn't made any such promise. She'd asked for a salve. Clever girl.

"We're almost to the passage. Stay close. I'd hate to lose you to the in-between."

"The what?"

"It's the void between one doorway and another." She took his hand and squeezed. "Don't worry. I won't let you get lost. I'll protect you from those nasty humans."

He kept his hand in hers, opening a thread of magic and wrapping his power around them in a protective embrace, only a little jealous it was his magic and not his arms that encircled Rori. Her hand felt good in his, warm and comforting, steadfast and enduring. Ashes, the mate bond was making his mind turn to mush with all the loved-up thoughts and emotions. He had to rein in his feelings or risk both of their lives.

"For the record, I don't hate humans." How could he explain it wasn't humans who concerned him? Just a small girl who spoke of portents and prophecy? "You assume an awful lot for being a spy."

Her head whipped around amid a swirl of blue. "Why do you think I'm a spy? I work for the queen as an—"

"I know exactly where you work." He stopped her protestations with a raised hand. He hadn't meant to alarm her or let slip he knew who she was. Bloody well better confess now. "I know where you went to school, and why it's important for you to impress your older brother. Who, by the way, is also a spy."

Rori kept her face impassive, but a slight twitch of her eye gave away her irritation. A small fluttering of pulse in her neck drew his attention. Her heart beat wildly, but her even breaths showed great control that he admired. Was this what Meg had meant about her father's training? His admiration turned to concern. What had Hagan MacNair done to his daughter that caused her to mask her emotions with such skill?

With a reluctant, knowing smile, Rori nodded. "You work for Queen Midna. Of course you'd know about the MacNairs. What else did you uncover in your research?"

Therron raised their clasped hands to his lips and kissed her fingertips. "I never said I researched you." So much for reining in his emotions. He was lost. Utterly and completely smitten.

She snatched her fingers away and rubbed her hand against her jeans. "You're insufferable!"

"I've been called worse." He really shouldn't taunt her, but it was far too enjoyable to see her cockiness falter. She kept herself bottled up tighter than a frog's ass. Plus, it annoyed him that she wasn't feeling the mate bond at all. He was a hive of buzzing nerves, like a young lad about to court his first lass. Doomed. He was doomed.

Rori dramatically rolled her eyes and blew out a deep breath, upsetting a strand of hair as she did. It floated on the breeze a moment before settling across half her face. She watched him as if to see what he'd do. His fingers twitched to brush the hair from her face, but he'd already pushed his luck with kissing her fingers. Her right brow lifted in silent challenge. Who was he to deny her a bit of sport?

Instead of tenderly removing the lock of hair, he smoothed his hand over her head and cupped her neck. If he got a dagger in the ribs, it would be worth it. To his delight and surprise, she allowed it. Perhaps there was hope for them, after all. He ached to kiss her, but didn't push his luck.

"Midna told me you and your brother are spies. She also told me I couldn't trust you and that you'd turn me in to Queen Eirlys the moment you found out I was an elf." It was all true.

"Why would I do that?"

"Dunno. Midna seemed to think your Seelie queen has a thing against elves. She isn't as accepting of my race as the Unseelie queen is, but I can't understand why. From what I've witnessed, elves hardly bother themselves with Faerie. Why are they so hated?" He released his grip and dropped his hand to his side. Her scent intoxicated him. Berries and perspiration and vanilla all mixed together to make an elixir he couldn't resist.

Rori moved on, and he followed. "I'm not sure. No one seems to remember, but it was from something that happened long, long ago. Eirlys might know, but the half dozen times I've asked, she's evaded answering me. Even my mum wouldn't tell me. Whatever it was, it was bad."

A swirl of anxiety pooled in his belly. The reason the fae hated elves couldn't possibly be due to Ishnara's curse. Meg's warning echoed in his mind: Don't believe the lies he'd been told. What really happened between the fae and elves all those centuries ago? Was this the prophecy the little girl had mentioned? Were he and Rori the chosen ones who would bring peace to the two kingdoms? He rubbed his chest, wincing at the stabbing pain.

"What you're saying is, the fae aren't willing to let go of something they can't even remember? Even if it means persecution of an entire race? That doesn't seem right."

Rori shrugged, her gaze clouded as if her mind were elsewhere. If what she told Meg was true—she risked a lot by taking him through the human realm. He eyed the leather bag.

The risk had to be taken. The fae didn't deserve to be trapped in glass prisons. His mind spun. What was Acelyne up to? And why did she need so many faeries?

"Do you know anything about the war Meg mentioned?" Rori kicked at a root and trudged onward.

Therron bit his thumbnail, his eyes narrowed. "Like I said, I try to stay out of Faerie politics, but no. I haven't heard anything." He lied. As much as he wanted to tell her the truth, he couldn't. Not yet. Not until he knew what was happening in Faerie to cause his father's wrath. Only then could he prevent any potential conflicts.

Rori slowed and stared into his eyes, as if searching through the lies he told. "Not even from Midna? If she's planning something, we could be walking into a lot worse than exile or her dungeon."

"I've been away from the Unseelie Court for a month. I doubt anything has changed in that time, but it's always good to be prepared for the unexpected."

Her anxiety seeped into his own. Nothing about this day made sense. Amulets, trapped fae, Rori's escape, Acelyne's ability to infect their minds—it all spelled trouble, and not just to Faerie. He'd have to alert his father at some point, but he planned to delay that conversation as long as possible. If the elf king knew Faerie was weakened, he might complicate matters and hasten the war he coveted.

He'd been away from Elvenwood for several months without communication, and could only hope his father had lost his desire for bloodshed. Therron had chosen to leave the palace in search of answers, only to find, at every corner, there were more questions to riddles he didn't understand.

Rori set off again, lengthening her stride to hurry them along, and Therron jogged to catch up.

"The sooner we get Midna and Eirlys together, the sooner

everything will be worked out and I can go back to my life." She didn't sound pleased about the prospect, though.

Therron walked on, resentful of the life she'd return to that didn't include himself. Within three moonturns, his own life would end. Bloody curses and prophecies. He felt once more like a pawn, but not for Acelyne's game. He was little more than a figure to be toyed with by the whims of Fate.

Rori was his salvation—the only woman capable of breaking the curse that had haunted his family for centuries—and she wanted nothing to do with him. If she didn't fall in love with him within three moonturns, and pronounce her love in front of the elven court, then would the future of not just Faerie or Elvenwood, but the entire world, be in jeopardy?

She'd allowed a few kisses and hand-holding, but would she allow herself to truly love someone more than as a friend? He had three months to find out. The clock was ticking.

21

Cian wiped the blade of his knife against the man's track suit before tucking it into his sleeve. The dagger he slipped into the secret pocket inside his coat. He tapped his calf to make certain a second dagger hadn't fallen out of its sheath. He had several more weapons tucked away in the coat, many of which were illegal not just in the human realm, but in Faerie as well.

His thoughts were fluid as he stood to catch his breath. Lida huddled in a sheltered alcove, out of the misty drizzle, shoulders hunched and eyes wide.

"Are you okay?" Cian took off his coat to wrap around her shoulders. Fool woman had only worn the beaded mini dress and a light shawl.

"They're dead?"

He rubbed her arms. "Give me a minute, then let's get you home. Can you walk?"

Her slow nod served as answer. She'd not looked away from where the scyvers lay splayed on the wet cobbles.

Cian kissed her cheek and squeezed her arms reassuringly before going to each man to check for ID, and for more evidence of the scyvers being non-human. On the first, he found nothing but a pack of chewing gum and a set of keys. On the next, several credit cards, all with different names, two IDs, a passport, and a small handgun. Cian paused for a moment to check the gun for bullets, but it was empty. He slid the weapon into his waistband and moved to the third scyver.

Neither of them had the same scarring as the goateed man. Their faces were beginning to deteriorate and Cian didn't know why. He rushed through his search of the merman and found cash and credit cards, but no ID.

"Johannes?" Lida leaned over the merman and stared at his face. "I know him."

"Even more reason to leave before someone comes down this way." Cian led her down the empty street toward the river.

As their footsteps took them farther from the scyvers, Cian released a small amount of magic that would help in the decomposition of the bodies. He hoped there wasn't any CCTV on the street, but that was a bit too optimistic.

"How do you know Johannes?"

Lida's frantic glances to either side gave away her anxiety. "I met him in Amsterdam about a year ago." She rolled her bottom lip between her teeth, and Cian sensed her reluctance.

"Whatever you tell me, it stays between us." They stopped on a bridge over the Vesten and Cian took her face between his hands. "You're in shock. It's natural to be freaked out by what you just witnessed. But I swear to you, Lida, I won't hurt you."

"I know. I trust you, Cian."

The way she said his name, Keeeee-innn, reminded him of how Rori used to annoy him when she was younger, and he hid a smile. In the present situation, it wouldn't do to appear gleeful, but thoughts of his sister always made his heart happy.

"It's just, those men's faces—they were hopped up on something, right?"

"Most likely. They certainly had the jitteriness of an

addict."

She moved off, the scent of fear and arousal trailing in her wake. Cian walked beside her, his arm draped around her waist. At nearly his height without heels, Lida towered him by a few inches. She was a goddess among mere mortals in this world.

They walked in silence, Cian letting her sort through her thoughts without disturbance. There was more she wished to say about Johannes, but something held her tongue.

At the door to her building, she paused. "I need to process what happened tonight. I hope you understand."

"Of course." Cian reached for his coat and bumped his cock against her thigh. Her moan was throaty and full of lust. "I'll say goodnight to you, lovely Lida. I do hope our paths cross again."

He slid his coat from her shoulders and backed away, delighting in the look of needy consternation on her pretty face.

"Come up with me. If even just for a cup of coffee. Please?"

In all the time he'd known her, this was the first he could recall she ever said please. He'd have to be gentle with her if he wanted to extract her secrets.

"Whatever you need. I'm here for you." He ran the backs of his fingers up her collarbone to her jaw and then scraped a thumb over her full lips. "Use me, Lida."

Just as he would use her. Some days, he hated his job.

The promised coffee didn't happen. As soon as they walked into Lida's fashionable apartment, she pushed him against the wall and devoured his mouth in hers. Cian stripped off his coat, followed by his suit jacket, and tossed them aside without losing contact. He kept her hunger satiated just enough that she needed more.

Removing her dress took less time than a flick of his

tongue through her hot mouth. She wriggled out of the delicate fabric and jerked his buttons open with savage impatience. To keep her from ripping his clothes in her rush, he unfastened his belt and slid his slacks down his legs before stepping out of the puddle of fabric. He'd magic the wrinkles out in the morning. Eirlys would give him hell for misusing his magic, and in the human realm, too, but he'd deal with his queen later.

"Tell me about Johannes," Cian urged as he retrieved a square packet from his trouser pocket. Safety first. He couldn't risk impregnating a human with his fae seed. He lifted Lida and carried her to the bedroom. On the way, he suckled her neck, earning another lusty moan.

"Amsterdam. Crack house. But…not. Oh, there, yes, there. More."

Cian lay her on the bed and rolled the condom over his hardened cock before settling between her legs.

Desire lit in her eyes and an eager grin lifted her lips.

"You're gorgeous, Cian. And that cock." She made a chef's kiss motion with her hand. "Magic."

He didn't need actual magic. Rori had her special skill with daggers—Cian had his cock.

"Not a crack house? How do you mean?" He slid his dick into her, his eyes never leaving hers. It was part of the seduction, to keep visual contact so that she would keep talking. She wouldn't realize what she said as long as he fucked her silly and kept her focus on his face.

Lida arched into him, sucking him deeper. "They had potions there. Johannes gave me one. Ahhh, harder, faster."

Cian pulled out slowly, delighting in the look of irritation that crossed her features. It told him he was doing his job well. For him, it wasn't personal; it was just business. When done properly, Lida would remember nothing about the interrogation, only that he left her satisfied. That was the power of his magic cock. It was a tool, same as his dagger or a gun.

Besides, who was he to deny the charm of his fae blood on mere mortals?

"Tell me everything about Amsterdam. How many people were there?"

He thrust hard, and she cried out.

"A dozen, maybe three! Yes! Oh God, yes." She panted against his slow glides followed by hard thrusting, her eyes locked to his. "I've never seen more than a few people there. But the last time, big group. Scary. Like the men tonight. Not right in the mind. Thought they were just druggies."

"The potion, Lida…tell me about that." His pace slowed to a steady rocking.

"I'm going to come, Cian. Don't stop."

"Not yet, Lida. The potion." He pulled out until the tip of his cock was at the entrance to her channel.

Her agony-fueled whine filled the room, but Cian ignored it. His focus was solely on getting the information. If it caused her distress, he'd make up for it after he got what he needed.

"Some dealer—not drug dealer—artifacts and stuff. Malcolm someone. Ah! Oh, God, yes."

Cian slid his cock as deep as it would go and ground against her pelvis. "Malcolm, is he a friend of yours?"

"Not a friend, no. His company, SIRE. Artifacts, but ooh, please, please."

"The full name, Lida."

"Dagniss. Yes, that's his name. Malcolm Dagniss. SIRE Unlimited. Import-export. Please, Cian, fuck me now with that magic cock."

"I have been, Lida, and it's the best fuck you've ever had."

"It is. You're too good, Cian. Too good for me."

"The potion, what was in it?"

"I don't know. I swear to you. It made me see things, like acid, maybe? Bad trip. Didn't take again. I can't hold it. Please."

"Just one last question: where can I find Malcolm Dagniss?"

Her face twisted in agony and she closed her eyes, her head thrashing from side to side. "I need release. Please."

"Dagniss?"

"Edinburgh! I heard Johannes say he got the potion from Edinburgh. That's all I know, I swear it." Her shallow breathing came in tiny gasps, and she glared at him with wild, pleading eyes.

Of all the cities in the human realm, Edinburgh was the one place he avoided. He could deal with that information later. Just then, he had a duty to perform. Cian never left his informants wanting.

Several minutes, and a whole lot of shrieking later, Lida flung her arms out, her climax retreating. Cian shuddered against his own orgasm. Sweat beaded her forehead, and she looked even more regal laying upon her white satin bedding. For the millionth time, he wondered whether she were touched by fae blood.

He tied off his condom and tossed it toward the door for later.

"I suppose now you'll leave, and I won't see you again for another few months." There was no malice in her voice. In fact, he sensed she wanted him to go.

"I'm not in a rush, unless you'd like to be alone." In truth, he desperately wanted to get back to Faerie and tell his queen what he'd discovered. Nests of scyvers, a mysterious potion, and a dead merman were just the start.

Lida stretched like a cat, a low purr coming from her chest. "You always leave me more than satisfied, but if you've got it in you for a second round, I wouldn't complain."

Good little soldier that his cock was, it stood to attention, at the ready.

Two hours later, Cian left a thoroughly fucked and

sucked Lida sleeping in her bed. She'd given him new information that he could use for this investigation, and intel to keep for later if needed. Most importantly, he now had a name to connect to SIRE. For months, he'd heard of an antiquities dealer, but could never get a name. He was beginning to think anyone who dealt with Malcolm Dagniss was spelled or enchanted to forget who he was. Even his company was an enigma. With modern technology, there should be information for the taking, but he'd had little luck finding even an address for SIRE. At least now he had a place to start.

On the way to the belfry that housed this city's doorway to Faerie, he strolled down the street where they were attacked. As he'd hoped, the bodies had disintegrated to nothing more than bits of fabric and dust. He scanned the cobblestones, hoping to find something—anything—that would give him a clue what the potion might've been made of. And why call it a potion? That was an old world word. Why not just say drug?

He brushed a hand over the drops of rain that gathered on his coat and adjusted his trousers. Magic cock. The phrase made him chuckle. If only Lida knew. If he'd actually used magic on her, she'd be half senseless right about now. Magic and emotions were a dangerous mix. He preferred to keep a cool head, even when interrogating gorgeous, naked women.

"Be careful, son. Eirlys will expect things of you that you might not be willing to do. Set your boundaries and be specific in what you will and won't do for the throne." His father's warning echoed in his mind.

Had Rori received the same warning? He hoped so, and that she heeded it. Imagining his baby sister sexing information from someone filled his heart with dread. Not because she was a woman and shouldn't do such things. Cian was far too forward-thinking to be sexist in that respect. Rori wasn't as cold or clinical as he was, and for that, he loved her all the more. She was full of kindness and compassion, no matter how hard she tried to hide it.

Cian shook his head with disgust. He very much doubted Hagan MacNair would approve of Rori's kindness, or Cian's activities this night. Their father had trained Rori altogether differently, and often more aggressively, than he'd trained Cian. It had always irked him that Rori was pushed harder, her training nearly abusive to Cian's thinking.

For what? Why had their father pushed her so hard? To kill the compassion lurking in her heart? Certainly it wasn't because she was a woman, because their mother was one of Eirlys's fiercest warriors. Or was it punishment of some kind?

Training was training, whether with their father or at the Academy. What Cian resented was the fact that Rori could've been so much more than a spy. She had promise as a healer, at the very least. But Hagan MacNair wouldn't tolerate such a lowly position in his family.

Cian had argued strenuously with his father to let Rori choose her own path, but to no avail. When their father died, that sealed her fate. She might've dreamed of working with animals or becoming a courtier, but after their father's death, she only talked of the Academy. Her near rabid devotion to proving herself worthy had been difficult to navigate, leading him and his sister to fight on many occasions, leaving them both bitter and resentful, and in some ways, unable to mourn.

He stood outside the belfry and lifted his face to the sky. They were both adults now; it was time to put the past to rest. He'd worked his ass off to become a spy to find his father's killer. After fifteen years and still not one step closer to discovering the truth behind his father's death, it was time to move on. To forgive himself and Rori. To heal and, if not too late, mourn together.

Later—much, much later—he'd deal with returning to the place of his father's murder.

22

Rori's heart raced like a colt on the last furlong, but she kept her face placid. No sense letting Therron know how much his presence affected her. Tingles lingered on her fingers where his sweet kisses had touched her skin. Goddess help her, she wanted more. More of his elven magic wrapping her in a cocoon of safety, more of his lips upon hers, more of his touch against her, warm and inviting. She hurried their pace to alleviate the throbbing between her legs. This was bad. BAD.

As soon as they returned the amulets to the queens, he'd leave and return to whatever a thief did when not on a job. There was no room in his life for her, and certainly no room in hers for him. Their differences were too vast. Hell, faeries and elves hated each other. Wasn't that the unwritten law of her people? Therron's honest question begged an answer she didn't have. Why? Why did fae hate elves so much? And vice versa? There had to be a way to bring the kingdoms together in peace.

They came to a fork in the road, and she steered them to the left. For just one moment, she wished she hadn't been born to a warrior and spy, that she wasn't of fae blood and could follow where her heart led. But that wasn't the life she chose. She'd given an oath to her queen and would honor it. Her father had trained her for one purpose—to serve the crown. She was expected to eschew any commitments that didn't fit within her purpose. She was a spy and assassin. She did not stoop to the folly of relationships. Love was a curse not meant for her.

"Once inside, stay close and don't do anything stupid. The doorway's through there." She lifted her chin to indicate a pub nestled among the trees.

"The Queen's Horn. Are all of the passages from Faerie to the human realm in pubs?"

She thought of the doorway in the Shoogly Dragon and several others—all in pubs. Yet, they didn't lead to other pubs, necessarily. This one, for instance, led to a tinker's shop in Edinburgh's Old Town.

"You know I can't tell you that, so don't bother asking anything else about the doorways or where they lead. I swor—"

"You swore an oath to your queen. I know." Therron quirked an adorable smile at her. "I'm just curious about the doorways, but wouldn't dream of tricking you into spilling any state secrets."

She narrowed her gaze, trying to decide whether he was jesting. "You're a pest, you know that, right?"

"But a cute pest, I hope."

She shook her head and rolled her eyes, a small, giddy tickle in her belly.

They made their way through the half-empty common room to a storage area. Rori nodded a greeting to the barkeep on the way. He raised a brow at Therron but said nothing. He knew better than to question her.

The cellar was a dark, dank place that smelled of centuries-old ale and piss. She wrinkled her nose and wove between broken casks to an unobtrusive door at the end of a short hallway.

"Look away."

"What?"

"Look away. I can't let you see what I'm doing."

Therron glared at her, then turned his back.

It didn't matter whether he watched or not—opening the portals was more a matter of saying the right words than anything else—but it gave her a sense of control to have him obey her request. He'd been far too bold, and she needed that sense of balance restored. A frog, indeed! Although, she really didn't think of herself as princess material either. Still, being a princess would be better than a frog. Unless you had to kiss a frog to find your prince. Foolish nursery tales.

She took a deep breath. Could she do this? Could she defy her queen and court exile? A flutter of anxiety warmed her chest. Exile might not be so bad. If she were cast out, maybe then she could pursue something with Therron. Where would they live? The human realm would be the safest option, although, she'd have to avoid Cian and Eirlys's other spies. Perhaps another world. There had to be somewhere they could live where they wouldn't have to constantly be on alert and looking over their shoulders.

Stop it, MacNair. Stop daydreaming about a life you can't have. No matter how enticing a life with the elf might be, she couldn't betray her family and queen.

What was wrong with her? She'd never in her life allowed even the hint of something with someone else, so why now? Why Therron? Why did she feel this attraction to a man she didn't know, or know if she could trust? And why the hell did she think running away with him would be worth exile?

Before she did something stupid, she extinguished the treasonous thought and took a long, steadying breath to clear her thoughts of Therron and how much she wished he'd kiss her some more.

Focus! Gods, but it was hard with him so near and the scent of him enticing her desires. Musky with a hint of pine and spice, like a winter's night spent in front of a fire. Naked.

Seriously, get a grip, MacNair.

"Is something wrong?" Therron tilted his head to see her.

"Nope. Just making sure you're not spying on me."

He turned around. "I told you I wouldn't, and I keep my word."

Her fingertips tapped along the center line of the door and the oak warmed to her touch. This was the part of traveling through the unknown she liked best—the thread of ancient power mixed with hers. In those few seconds, hope bloomed and she felt invincible.

The words she spoke came out fluid and melodic, more of a song than a spell. She kept her voice low but had no doubt Therron's elf ears heard every syllable. It didn't matter. He could try to replicate the spell, could even tap along the frame the same as she, but if the doorway didn't recognize him, it wouldn't open. Eirlys herself had taken Rori to the castle's portal and pressed Rori's hand upon the metal knob, commanding it and all the portals in Faerie to allow Rori passage.

Which meant she had the ability to travel anywhere in Faerie, even to the Unseelie Court, through these doorways. It also meant she could travel to anywhere in the human realm.

The doorway heaved with a creak, and Therron half-turned toward it. "Can I look now?"

"Of course." She placed her hand in his, ignoring the slight quickening of her pulse when their skin connected. Daydreams and wishes would get her killed. "I was serious about not losing me. The void is infinite and who knows what horrors live there. I'd never find you once separated. This is a quick jump, so we shouldn't be more than a minute in darkness."

"Let's be off, then." His words came out nonchalant, but his grip tightened on hers.

They stepped through and were surrounded by stunning silence. The thick air choked her mouth, but she kept calm and breathed through the discomfort. Absolute blackness blotted out any light that might've come from the closing door and they stood, rooted to nothing. Rori kept the tinker's shop firmly in her mind. Within the space of several heartbeats, the air thinned and a pale radiance emanated from electric lights. She stepped down as if on stairs, her boots landing upon hardwood planks. Therron's entrance wasn't as graceful, but he didn't fall, something she begrudgingly admired.

"That wasn't so awful."

"If you say so." Therron's usually gruff voice was hoarser, his breathing labored.

"Maybe it's worse for elves."

He extricated his hand from hers and shook out his coat. "Where to now?"

"The castle." Rori rubbed her hands together, as if trying to bring back the warmth his touch had provided, but she was left cold and wanting.

She checked the fae in her pocket, relieved to see the soft glow. This was new territory for her—bringing not just an elf through the doorway, but an enchanted fae as well. She had no idea what would happen to either and breathed a sigh of relief that they'd all made it without incident.

They made their way gingerly through the back room, and Rori stopped them to peek into the shop. The owner was nowhere to be seen, and she mentally did the math to sort the time. Faerie and the human realm worked on opposites. If it was mid-afternoon in Faerie, it was early morning here. The shop wouldn't be opened for several more hours. She led

Therron to the front of the store and paused. "Do elves have Glamour?"

"Of course. Why?" His look of disgust intrigued her, but there wasn't time to quiz him about his feelings on the matter.

"Use it, please. It confuses the cameras." His brows dipped, and she explained, "Pictures. The human realm loves their moving pictures. They call it CCTV, and it captures everything. Our Glamour will show us as a blur, nothing more. It wouldn't do to have documented evidence of us creeping around, now would it?"

"I've heard rumors—about beings that eat non-humans—what are they called?"

"Scyvers?" Her nervous chuckle did little to ease her anxiety about the scourge. "You believe that poppycock?" At the fierce glare he gave, she lowered her tone and adjusted her attitude. "Totally made-up, nothing to worry about. I seriously doubt there are humans who hunt magical beings and suck out their power." Lies, lies, and more lies.

Not only were scyvers real, they weren't to be messed with. If she had to lie to Therron to keep him from freaking out, so be it. Now more than ever, she needed to make certain they used the bare minimum amount of magic. She'd seen firsthand the damage a wacked-out scyver could do.

Her mind flashed to a street in Amsterdam, not more than a year past, when she'd been cornered by a female with wild eyes and actual foam at the corners of her mouth. At first Rori thought she was a drug addict, but when the woman had sniffed the air, she'd known it wasn't drugs the woman was after. They'd fought, a hard scrabble that surprised Rori in its savagery. When a passerby happened upon them, the scyver ripped out the man's throat with her teeth.

She'd stabbed the scyver at the base of the creature's neck as she sucked out his blood. The man died because Rori hadn't killed the scyver quick enough, and she vowed to never put anyone else in that kind of danger.

The trapped fae would be like catnip to someone hungry for magic. She needed Therron to focus. The last thing they wanted was a scyver on their trail.

Accustomed to taking care of herself—and only having her safety to consider—being burdened with the lives of the fae as well as Therron sat heavily upon her conscience. One wrong move and she endangered everything. She had to win, had to best her enemies, and that meant keeping the fae safe from Acelyne's clutches, as well as returning Therron safely to Faerie. Anything less would be failure.

"I believe there are creatures some consider myth that are anything but." Therron shuddered and rubbed a thumb over his scar.

His words had the unsettling effect she guessed he'd intended. Ghostly images of flying horses drifted through her mind. When she tried to focus on them, they vanished and she was left wanting more. The sooner they were out of the human realm, the better. Then she could continue her missions alone.

Instead of addressing his statement, she challenged him. "Are you afraid your Glamour might attract the wrong sort of human? Is that why you avoid them?" It was widely known in the fae realm that humans had an unhealthy lust for elves.

He didn't answer, but she saw a subtle sheen bloom beneath his skin. An opalescent translucency gave him an ethereal appearance. For the briefest of moments, his scar wavered like a winged creature, then vanished into his skin. Words deserted her as she stared, mesmerized. She swallowed hard, forcing herself not to reach out and touch his cheek. Why did elves have to be so damn alluring? She glanced at her hands, at the normal, non-shimmery skin, and sighed.

Before she did something she'd regret, like lick him from the tips of his pointed ears to what she imagined were chiseled abs, she touched the lock. It clicked open, and Rori put a finger to her lips. She opened the door just enough to slip through. Therron, being larger than her slim body, shuffled between the door and frame with a grimace. Either he didn't realize he could open it more, or he was trying to be stealthy. Either way, it was cute.

Cute? What was wrong with her? It wasn't cute. It was ridiculous. Just open the door more.

She fidgeted the bag to a more comfortable position on her hip. A quick scan of the empty street showed no threats, and yet a creeping sensation made its way up her arms. She and Therron could control their magic, but what about the imprisoned fae? Did they give off any magical vibes? If so, she and the elf were beacons for all kinds of things she didn't wish to encounter. As Therron said, there were creatures some considered myth that roamed the streets and shadows of the human realm. A scyver would be a mercy.

S trange, horseless carriages trundled up the cobblestoned
street. A few people walked along brick pathways in
similar odd clothing to what Rori wore. Here, he was
the one with strange clothing, and no one carried a sword at
their hip. One of the humans held the end of a leather lead,
with a tiny dog, or what he believed to be a dog—it could've
been a trained rat—attached to one end. The rat-dog squatted
and left a mess on the pathway. Therron watched in horror as
the woman bent to retrieve the steaming pile and tied it up in a
small bag.

"That small creature has trained its human to retrieve its
shit." Incredulity cloaked his words.

Rori chuckled and looked at the rat-dog. "They have laws
here to keep the streets tidy. The dog didn't train the woman;
she picked up the poop out of courtesy to others."

"Ah." He watched the woman toss the bag into a large
black box and walk away, her rat-dog prancing at her side.

"Come on." Rori removed her hand from where it hovered
above her dagger and took his hand in her own. "It can be
unnerving the first time. Stay close and you'll be fine."

Stores lined the narrow lane, their windows crowded with trinkets and curious knickknacks. It wasn't as noisy as Rori had said, nor were the smells too overpowering, possibly because they removed dog messes right away. Therron glanced up and down the street, taking in the rough walls of the buildings, the cleanliness of the place. This town could've been anywhere in Faerie.

Fifty paces on, and he reconsidered his opinion. Newer buildings made not of stone, but some other material, wedged themselves between timeworn walls. A black carriage on wheels sped past and Therron kept himself from leaping in front of Rori, who didn't appear bothered by the loud vehicle. He did, however, tighten his grip on her hand.

She smiled at him and went back to scanning the street, her eyes never stopping on one place. Therron appreciated her cautiousness. She was right—the first time was unnerving. He wasn't sure he'd ever get used to a place like this.

His thumb rubbed over her surprisingly soft skin. "Thank you."

"For what?"

He held their hands up and grinned. "Making sure I'm safe, and don't try to deny it."

"I won't deny it. You're my responsibility in the human realm. What would the queens say if I returned with only your corpse?"

"I'm not sure they'd be too displeased." He furtively looked inside each shop window and shook his head. What use was a glass dome filled with figurines and water? He would never understand the folly of humans. Curious creatures.

What intrigued him even more than the humans was the sense he had of his ancestors. A heaviness settled on his shoulders. A burden of souls long past. He felt his ancestors in the stones of the streets, within the cracks of the buildings. Elves had trodden these pathways. That was long ago, before they were hunted and feared. He flexed the fingers of his free hand and whispered an elven blessing to those who had lived and died in these lands.

"Do you have anyone who would miss you in Faerie?"

"Besides my family and the queen?" She cocked her head and smiled. "Are you asking if I have a betrothed or significant other?"

"Do you?"

"Do you?"

"It's rude to answer a question with a question, but no. I don't have anyone in Elvenwood waiting for me. I mean, I have family, but no one I'm committed to at present. Nor really in the past, if I'm honest. I suppose I'm not all that desirable." *Stop talking, Therron.* He cleared his throat and looked at her expectantly. "Now you."

"No. There's no one."

"That's it? No one, as in now, or ever?"

"I mean, there have been a few guys, but nothing serious. I'm not betrothal material. I was trained for…other things."

After several minutes of walking uphill, he caught a reflection in one of the shop windows and tensed. A shadow tracked them across the street. He cast a wary glance at Rori, but she didn't appear to have noticed. Again, he saw the briefest of blurs cross his vision.

He turned his head in the direction of the shadow, but saw nothing to cause alarm. They crossed a large intersection with more of the strange carriages coming at them from all directions. With great difficulty, he kept his apprehension controlled. The speed with which the vehicles traveled could fell a man in an instant.

When Rori stepped off the curb, he followed closely. At the other side of the street, the shadow once again tracked them. Now, he did see Rori glance in that direction, her eyes narrowed. His instinct was to call forth his magic. He wavered a moment, unsure whether protecting them was worth the risk of attracting a scyver. Rori might pretend they didn't exist, but he'd heard wicked tales of what they did to magical creatures and didn't wish to meet one this day.

"Magic is all but dead here." Rori's words were laced with sadness. "Humans are to blame, naturally. Their mistrust of our ways grew until now, their lives are consumed with anger and war and death. They have so much and could use what they have to do so much good, but they choose to put their energies where it least serves them."

Therron nodded in agreement. He sensed the magic that used to flow through the city. It was long dead, as Rori said.

The road split and they veered right, up a steep incline. All the while, the shadow followed. At the top of the hill, the street opened to a vast cobbled esplanade, and Therron sucked in a breath. Beyond the open area was a hulking castle. Rori released his hand, and he ached for her touch.

"Who lives here?" He stood with thumbs hooked into his coat pockets to keep from reaching out to her, and surveyed the bulky stone structure. As castles went, it wasn't pretty. Sturdy and secure, it looked to be built for defense rather than comfort.

Rori stood beside him, her gaze drifting over the castle with a longing he might've missed had he blinked. It was an almost imperceptible change to her features, a slight softening that told him this was a place she enjoyed. She was comfortable here unlike anywhere he'd seen of her in Faerie.

She smiled to him and cocked her head to indicate they carry on walking. "No queens or kings, if that's what you mean. There's a military presence still, but royalty haven't lived here for a long time."

"They do not appreciate beauty, these humans." It wasn't

meant as an insult. All of the buildings he'd seen thus far could not compare to anything in Elvenwood or even Faerie.

"But they do. You're spoiled by what you see in Faerie. This castle, this city, is more than these stones." Pride echoed in her voice, and he wondered what her connection was to the city, to this castle.

He looked at the stones anew. To the left and above the gate, a rounded wall was pierced with large black pots made of metal. Each one was slender and long enough to stick out from the wall the length of an adult elf. Foreboding oozed from the things, and Therron turned away from a vision that pummeled his mind of fire and death. Whatever they were, they were meant to kill.

Rori didn't seem to be bothered by the death pots as they strolled across the esplanade. But then, she'd been trained to kill from an early age. Perhaps this was what Meg alluded to in her cryptic warning. Therron reached for Rori's hand and stopped before their skin touched, needing to feel her hand in his, but not wanting to force close proximity. Someone accustomed to death does not always see the benefits of life. But he didn't sense it was the killing or death that she enjoyed about this place. What it was, he hoped to discover within the grounds of the castle.

As they neared the gatehouse, Rori ignored a large covered carriage parked to the right and strode confidently to the huge wooden doors. She positioned herself so that he couldn't see what she did next, and he waited for her to open the thick door. Concentration settled in her features and she drew a deep breath, closing her eyes on the exhale. Unlike the doorway at the pub, he sensed her frustration. Without thinking, he reached for the door.

The lock clicked and the door creaked open. Rori searched the darkened entry for someone else who might've unlocked the door from the inside, but the entryway was empty. Finally, her gaze settled on Therron. He didn't try to hide his surprise.

"You did that?"

"Apparently."

"How?"

He held his hands out, fingers spread wide, then flipped them palms up. "I only meant to help, and when I reached for the door, I *connected*. I've no idea how, of that I promise you."

Unease flicked across her face, and she shoved past him into the entryway.

Therron honestly didn't know how he'd unlocked the door. He hadn't used magic, nor did he sense a lingering elven presence. He simply felt compelled to help, to ease her struggling. He matched Rori's hurried strides up past the portcullis.

"Beware the guards. They have weapons that kill instantly." Irritation clung to her words.

"Did I upset you?"

She tossed her head, sending cobalt waves into the air. "I didn't need your help."

Therron chewed on that for a moment. "Perhaps not, but you lose nothing by accepting it."

"Yes, I do." She slammed her lips together and punched her fists to her sides. "You wouldn't understand."

"Rori," he turned her to face him, "I'm not your adversary." He searched her eyes and saw in their deep blue depths a flurry of confusion. "I offer my assistance freely. Not to best you, nor to make you look incompetent…to help in whatever way you might need, with absolute sincerity." He placed his hand over his heart and bent his head in respect.

She glared at him a minute, arms crossed, eyes narrowed. "Fine."

Her protective outer shell was much thicker than he'd previously thought. Breaking through would take more than a solemn promise and a few stolen kisses.

The road wound its way around a wall dotted with more of the long metal pots, and Therron flinched from the overwhelming impression of destruction they emitted. Rori spun to her left and jogged up steep stairs. He followed a pace behind, keeping vigilant to unwanted interlopers. Human or otherwise. At the top, Rori dashed across a cobblestoned courtyard, ignoring the larger buildings to their left. Therron caught a blur of white and started to turn toward it, but Rori flicked her hand, indicating a small chapel.

"Did you see that?"

"What?" Rori searched the area, her eyes focused.

"A blur, a shadow. It's been tracking us up the street."

"I feel it, but see nothing. We should hurry." She turned and jogged to the little chapel.

Therron stared in the direction of the shadow. The shape of a large wolf ghosted from the courtyard into one of the large buildings. He shook his head and joined Rori. Something was here, at this castle, but he didn't think it was a scyver or anything malicious. The strange pinching started in his heart, and he pressed a fist against his chest.

An awareness of being part of something bigger than himself and even Faerie wormed its way into his thinking. A pit formed in his gut at the momentousness of what that might entail. Meg's words echoed in his skull. Twice blessed by a prophecy and his curse. Blessed wasn't the word he would use. His gaze slid to the bag Rori clutched. This was only the beginning—but of what, he had no idea.

"This chapel is one of the oldest in Scotland, and a favorite of Queen Eirlys," Rori whispered, her features soft again, almost beatific. "I've heard rumors that on certain occasions she comes here and grants wishes to those she deems worthy."

"What a strange and wonderful thing for her to do."

"Quite." Rori shrugged. "She's a strange and wonderful

queen. Through here." She held the chapel door open for him. "Once we're inside, don't make a sound. Everything said in this chapel can be heard in Faerie."

"Even the granting of wishes from your queen?"

A cheeky grin lit up Rori's face. "Perhaps."

"And what would you wish for?" The question slipped out before he could stop himself.

She gave him an odd look, filled with lust and apprehension. Heat radiated off her, and his heart twisted. She put a finger to her lips, and Therron imagined taking it into his mouth. He knew what he'd wish for, and it involved Rori, naked, lying beside him of her own free will. Wicked thoughts raced through his mind of what he'd like to do to Rori. Images of acts he'd witnessed at Midna's court, but never participated in. If only she'd let him, he could thaw her cold heart and warm her from the inside out. But by the glare she now cast him, that wouldn't happen soon. Her emotions ran hot and cold, sometimes within the same breath. Not a bother. He was a patient man.

They stepped into the dank space, and Rori locked the door behind her. She immediately turned and walked a few feet to another door, one not open to the public. Therron watched her in silence, his eyes adjusting to the darkness.

The small door opened at her touch, and she reached out to take Therron's hand, but hesitated. Curiously, she wavered with her hand outstretched. Heat flared between them. His face warmed and the scar he'd loathed since birth no longer felt like the mark of a demon. A sweet flush crept up Rori's face, and he saw indecision dance in her eyes. Her fingertips trembled as they hovered on empty air. If only she'd share what was causing her consternation, he might help.

With a frustrated sigh, she grabbed his hand and practically jerked him off his feet and through the doorway. A spark of emotion overrode his thoughts. Not his, but Rori's. Fear swam through her blood, but also desire. Hot and thick and needy. Not just desire, but an overwhelming sense of belonging, and yes, love, flowed from her hand to his. Nay, from her heart to his. For the first time since meeting the prickly fae, Therron had hope.

$\maltese$ 24 $\maltese$

Rori knew better than to be aggressive while making jumps, especially with where they were going. Arriving in a rush could cause injury not just to them, but to anyone nearby. And with Eirlys's room full of mirrors, she risked breaking more than the glass. But Therron's presence was doing things to her mentally and physically that threw everything into chaos. All she had to do was look at him, and her blood warmed. It went beyond the weird pinching to something much deeper, more worrying. She didn't just want him—she needed him. It was a force beyond her control and that made her wary.

They tumbled onto hard marble, and Rori angled herself to protect both the amulets and the sleeping faerie still in her breast pocket. Curses flowed like whisky on Hogmanay from Therron's mouth, then he fell ominously silent.

She cocked her head, a teasing comment at the ready, but stopped the retort when she saw his face. As pale as the alabaster floor, he looked as though he'd witnessed the slaughter of an entire race.

"What is it?" Rori scrambled to her feet and held out a

hand to help him up. She caught a reflection of herself and shuddered. The room was entirely, from floor to ceiling, covered in individual, ornately framed, gleaming mirrors. Thirteen in all. At every angle, her disheveled, bruised, and bloodied body reflected into infinity. Holy sharksniffers, she was a hot mess.

"It's her," Therron whispered.

"Who her? There's no one here but us."

Except, that wasn't true.

Therron stood, ignoring her outstretched hand, and beckoned to a young girl. Standing in the middle of the room, she wasn't a reflection.

The girl's eyes, deep as an ocean and just as blue, studied her with keen interest. She wore human clothing, but something about her was off—it wasn't her appearance, or the way she kept looking at them as if she'd known them forever. It was something else. Rori couldn't put her finger on it, but she had the distinct impression she'd met the girl before.

"Caen drath elthniss, Therron."

"Nygotien tergotten amir." Therron touched his thumb to his forehead, then to his heart and bent his head low in that way royals did when acknowledging a peer.

Rori stared, dumbfounded, her lips parted in a near gape.

"Esth eamish beforgaltin Eleri?"

Therron's grunt brought Rori back to the moment, to the strange conversation. This girl, this child, spoke a foreign language she'd never heard, but the elf understood. Whoever she was, Rori's gut told her she wasn't a threat to Faerie. Rori stood taller, her shoulders back, hands loose just in case she needed to grasp a dagger in a hurry.

Before he could answer, a commotion on the other side of the room startled them. Rori turned toward the door, then back to the girl, but she was gone. Therron's face had barely regained its natural tone before once more going pale. Clearly, the girl upset him, but why?

"Who or what was that?"

"You saw her?"

"For just a moment, I did. Where'd she go?" Dozens more questions sprang to her lips, but the door opened and they were surrounded by Queen Eirlys's personal guard.

"Should've known it'd be you, MacNair. You've done it this time. Got orders to take you to the queen herself for sentencing."

Dorchmeir. Her bully from the Academy now stood in the doorway with an arrogant sneer on his ruddy lips.

"Still bitter, Dorchmeir?" She eyed his uniform, marking the rank with a smirk. "You always were second-class. Now it's official."

"Lieutenant, asshole." The words were hissed between clenched teeth.

It was still too easy to rile him up. That temper was why he couldn't cut it in spy school.

Rori and Therron were pushed along the corridor, leaving the room of mirrors behind. They didn't speak. At least, Rori and Therron didn't, but Dorchmeir had plenty to say. He spewed obscenities at her between provocations to meet in the training yard. All of his taunts ended with a promise to kick her ass. This guy had it bad for her, which couldn't be good.

She pretended to ignore him, all the while studying his gait, the way he held his body, the hand he used to grip his sword. Her mind hastily thought of a dozen combat moves she could make to free them from the guards—none of which she would use. She needed to see the queen, and Dorchmeir was her fast-track ticket into the throne room. Naturally, she'd hoped it would be under better circumstances that she greeted her queen, but desperate times and all of that.

At the closed doors to the great hall, the group stopped.

Therron casually looked up and down the hallway and then appeared to study the huge, intricately carved wooden doors. Rori had always admired the finely sculpted ivy and the tiny creatures hidden in a forest of trees. The two doors, when closed, depicted the lands of Faerie and all of her inhabitants. Tucked behind a puff of cloud was a full moon in the upper left of the arched doorway.

Her perusal of the doors was interrupted as she heard soft footsteps rushing through the hall several moments before she was engulfed in giggles and yards of silk.

Esme, a friend from school and kindness personified, stopped just short of a full-body hug, instead patting Rori on the upper arms in an awkward greeting. Her long teal gown and matching slippers reminded Rori of why she'd longed to escape the court and adventure outside of the palace. Esme detested anything having to do with dirt, preferring instead to play cards and gossip all day. Rori's lips quirked in a wry smile. That's what made Esme one of her best informants from the palace.

"Is it true? Did you? Are you? Oooh, who is this?" Esme's half-questions came at Rori too quickly for her to answer, not that Esme needed verbal confirmation anyway. She had a way of sorting a situation with just a few quick glances. Rori was certain Esme knew exactly what Queen Eirlys was going to say even before the queen said it. It wasn't magic, but it was Esme's unique gift, and Rori took full advantage whenever possible.

"Hey, Es." Rori remembered that Esme's mother was recently made a countess and she curtseyed. "I mean Lady Asthentine. Palace life treating you well?"

"You are in so much trouble. You're aware you broke the law, aren't you?"

"I did? What law? How many?" Rori teased.

The doors opened, and Rori was shoved forward by that pinched-faced demented wanker Dorchmeir.

"Nelson, there's no need for aggression. You don't want to lose that stripe so soon after receiving it, do you?"

"Nelson?" No one ever called Dorchmeir by his given name. Rori squinted at her old Academy adversary with renewed interest.

Esme's face went all soft and dewy. "We're to be betrothed, if my father approves."

Rori stifled a surprised gasp and congratulated her friend. With her pick of all the men in Faerie, why would Esme choose him? Love wasn't something Rori would ever understand, nor did she ever want to, especially if it meant loving someone as deplorable as Dorchmeir. What did she see in the pompous ass? If nothing else, she'd get some intel from Esme about the military workings of the Seelie Court. Information Rori couldn't get through regular channels.

Dorchmeir's face wasn't the least bit lovey. In fact, he wore a half sneer that concerned Rori. Esme might be marrying for love, but what was Dorchmeir getting out of the arrangement?

Halfway through the vast hall, Rori noticed there were far more courtiers than she could recall seeing in the great hall. Not even this many showed up for Eirlys's annual gifting day. Rori's confidence slipped and for a brief moment, she almost reached for Therron's hand.

What the bloody fucking hell? Get it together, MacNair. The elf would be the death of her.

25

Queen Eirlys sat in her hulking chair, watching them with sharp eyes that missed nothing. Rori noted how her long fingers tapped a rhythm on the armrests. Her legs crossed and uncrossed several times, revealing smooth brown legs that she didn't try to hide. The ruby-encrusted black velvet slippers she wore drummed against the granite dais.

The queen was nervous. Certainly not because of Rori. It must've been due to Therron's presence. She cast a quick glance his way. He walked as if used to approaching queens who may or may not wish him harm. Shoulders back, head held high, but not too high, stride just forceful enough he looked powerful, yet approachable. He reminded Rori of a king.

Eirlys motioned and the guard stopped, but Rori and Therron were beckoned forward. Esme whispered, "Good luck," and a pit formed in her throat. She'd never wanted to be on the wrong side of her queen. Had sworn to protect Eirlys and all of her offspring with her life, if need be. And now Rori stood before the monarch, little more than a scofflaw.

Eirlys studied them a moment, and each time her head tilted, the gems in her rather magnificent crown made rainbows flutter across the floor. Her coppery velvet gown draped as she bent forward, revealing lush breasts. If she was aware she exposed herself, the queen didn't seem to mind.

"I'm told you and one other left Faerie this afternoon for the human realm. Then, the two of you returned a short time later to my palace." The queen's steely gaze went from Rori to Therron. "Am I to assume this is the person you took with you?"

"He is, Your Majesty." Rori curtseyed low, almost to the floor, the caskets hindering her gracefulness. She noted that Eirlys hadn't included Arianna or the fae in the amulets in her count of how many passed through the doorway. "If I may be permitted to explain the urgency of our mission."

"Your mission? I don't recall giving you permission to leave Faerie. And if I didn't command it, then I'm to assume, perhaps, the Unseelie queen did?" Brittle steel edged the queen's words.

"Of course not, Your Majesty. We needed to reach you with haste and using the doorways was the only way."

"What could be so important you'd risk exile? And with Midna's favorite by your side?"

Midna's favorite? Rori's mind spun with the revelation. Was Therron one of the Unseelie queen's álainn obedience? She shut down the thought before it could take root and poison her mind.

Rori tucked the leather bag under her arm. If this was all a ruse of Therron's to get close enough to the Seelie queen to either rob her or cause harm, Rori's first priority would be to protect the queen, but she also had the trapped faeries to consider. It was a no-win situation. She eyed the dozen or so guards flanking the royal dais. They could see to the queen. That was, if Therron betrayed her.

He knew what was in the pendants. He had to know how important they were to Faerie. A circle of doubt cut through her logic. The elf had been following Acelyne at the pub. His story of simply being hired to find the enchantress could've been a lie. Everything he told her could've been a lie. Yet, that strange woman inside the illusion had told her to trust Therron. So had Meg.

Rori trusted Meg, but couldn't risk the queen's safety. "Your Majesty, may I speak with you privately?"

Dorchmeir stepped forward, his hand resting on the hilt of his sword. "I would advise against it, my queen."

"Advice heard and refused." Eirlys studied Rori, her lavender eyes penetrating in their search. "Follow me." Eirlys halted mid-turn. "Only Rori. Keep this one under guard." She pointed a long nail to Therron. "I trust you will behave yourself?"

"On my honor, Your Majesty." Therron put a hand over his heart and bent low, an arm extended.

Eirlys snorted and swept from the dais to a door behind the throne.

Rori followed, her gaze riveted to the queen's retreating back. She hadn't expected Eirlys to agree to a private meeting, and relief washed over her with surprising force. Waves of black hair reached to below Eirlys's ass, and Rori was mesmerized by the satiny sheen of the locks. She'd have to ask the queen what she used to get such shiny hair. Her own could use a good conditioning.

Hell, if she survived the next few minutes, she might even book herself into one of the fancy spas she saw in the human realm. Get herself a massage by a hot guy wearing nothing but a towel. Her mind immediately envisioned Therron as the masseuse, and she cursed the elf for invading her fantasies. Even so, he probably gave excellent massages with those strong hands that she longed to hold. She shoved the thoughts deep to the back of her mind before Eirlys could pluck them out for investigation.

Once inside an antechamber, Eirlys locked the door and faced Rori. "What is it with your family? First Cian, now you! Has Midna infiltrated all of my spies?"

"What? No! Wait, you didn't send Cian to Midna's court? Then what's he doing there?"

"Never you mind about that. Tell me what you didn't want the others to know."

Rori swung the leather bag in front of her belly and held open the flap. "Have you noticed any faeries going missing lately?"

At her words, the queen's face paled until the rich brown hue was a watery ashen color.

"Your Majesty, what is it?"

A spark of tears lit the queen's eyes, but she blinked them away in an instant. "It is not yet common knowledge, but there have been several instances of fae disappearing. Over the last decade, I've counted two hundred at least, which isn't alarming, but recently that number has climbed dramatically. We're close to five hundred missing fae."

Something Eirlys said in the throne room tickled Rori's memory. "Do you know who's behind the disappearances, or why?" An idea was formulating in her mind. A dangerous scheme that made her stomach roil.

"No. Nor are we any closer to catching the person responsible." The tears returned, and this time the queen let them fall over her cheeks. "My own daughter disappeared from the gardens not more than a sennight past."

"A week?" Rori had been captured three days ago. That meant Arianna had been in the amulet four days more than Rori. No wonder she wasn't waking up. "I'm going to tell you something, and I don't think you'll like what I say, but please hear me out." She removed the caskets from the bag and opened each one. The amulets rocked in their velvet beds, but they were all intact.

"What is this?" Eirlys reached out and took one of the pendants gently between two fingers. She peered into the glass and examined the miniature forest. "I don't understand, Rori."

"I was trapped in one of these for three days, according to my friend Tug. When I woke, I had no idea where I was or how to get out. It was by sheer perseverance that I escaped." She let her words sink in while the queen continued her inspection of the amulets.

"How were you captured?"

"I think I was drugged. I remember being at the Shoogly Dragon, then waking up in a strange, silent forest." Rori took the glass vial Eirlys held. "I believe each of these holds at least one faerie. Drugged, like me, but unable to wake from the potion."

"But why?" Eirlys's gaze bore into Rori. "To what end?"

Rori took a deep breath and formulated the words before she spoke them. "At first, I didn't know why, but now I've got a theory. I still don't know exactly how they're being kidnapped, but I think I know to what end. You said your guards alerted you to two people crossing into the human realm and back into Faerie, yes?"

Eirlys nodded, her brows making a deep furrow in her rich brown skin. "Yes, you and that thief Therron."

"There weren't just the two of us. Each of these holds a faerie, possibly more. Whatever sensors you have in place didn't trigger them. What if someone is smuggling fae into the human realm?"

"No!" The queen's cheeks burned crimson, and a lick of fire shone in her steely glare. "That's forbidden."

"Which is why I think that's why they're being trapped in these pendants. You said five hundred fae are missing. That's too many to not have been seen somewhere in Faerie. Even if they're being hidden in the dwarves' mines, or Elvenwood, or Midna's dungeon, someone would've seen them. Have you heard anything at all that would make you believe the missing fae are still in Faerie?"

Eirlys stroked the side of a casket, sorrow stretching her jowls low. "I haven't. I've sent spies to every corner of this world, searching for even a scrap of evidence that the fae exist."

Protocol be damned, Rori placed a hand on her queen's forearm. "An enchantress called Acelyne is the one responsible for capturing the faeries. She placed some kind of spell on my friend Tug that Meg's working to remove. Meg told me there's a war brewing, and that you and Queen Midna must meet at the Vale of Dorn in two days."

"Mad Meg? Surely you're joking. Why would you trust the word of that woman?"

The change in tone and behavior from Eirlys surprised Rori. Genuine distrust oozed from the queen. "Meg's all right. A bit kooky at times, yes, but she's not a bad egg. Besides, if there's a chance to stop the disappearances, we need to take it."

"What if it's a trap? The two queens in the same place at the same time? That would be a remarkable opportunity for someone wishing harm to Faerie."

"It could be a trap, but I don't think Meg would be so foolhardy. I've known the woman too long to figure her for a traitor. Or..." Rori rubbed her temples, her thoughts a whirling tempest in her skull. "What if it *is* a trap, but for Acelyne? Meg is powerful, but who would refuse the strength of two queens to help capture the enchantress? We have to stop her, Your Majesty."

Rori reached into her jacket pocket and scooped out the sleeping faerie. She presented the wee lass to Eirlys. The queen's face immediately softened and fresh tears tracked down her face.

"Where—" The words choked in her throat. "Where did you find her?"

"She was in the amulet Acelyne used to capture me. I've kept her near my heart the whole time."

"Why is she not grown? Why does she remain tiny?" Eirlys curled her fingers around the sleeping fae and whispered low enough Rori could barely make out the loving words. Rori shifted uncomfortably, unused to seeing her queen in such an intimate, maternal moment. Eirlys made a pocket inside her gown and slipped the tiny bundle inside.

"I fear, Your Majesty, whatever enchantment Acelyne used keeps the fae defenseless in size and mind. Somehow, when I broke free, I released the spell on me, but why it didn't work on Arianna, I don't know."

"Your family has been loyal to the Seelie crown for many generations. I have no reason to doubt what you're telling me, but I do have questions about how you escaped when none of these others could. Why you?" Eirlys peered at Rori, and she stifled the panic that swirled through her belly and up her chest to strangle her breaths.

If Eirlys found her wild magic—she held herself still and prayed to the goddess that her queen wouldn't discover her secret. She fisted her hands to keep them from trembling.

"You're different, Aurora MacNair. There's something about you that's always intrigued me, but I can't say what. Perhaps whatever it is, that's what gave you the strength to fight off the drug and escape." Eirlys tucked a strand of hair behind Rori's ear, and she leaned into the touch automatically, missing her own mum's affection in that moment. "You are a most remarkable young lady and yet you don't even know your own power. Not yet, but someday you will."

"Thank you, ma'am." All sorts of emotions whizzed through her: elation, pride, fear, worry, confusion, and even a smidge of disbelief. "I hope you know I serve you loyally and wouldn't have broken the law if it wasn't life or death." Rori glanced at the queen's chest where Arianna slept. "I knew you would be distraught without your daughter."

"More so than you'll ever know. But I am queen, and I had to put on a brave face for my subjects. I could no more demand the return of my daughter over the return of their loved ones, but how my heart ached to know she was safe." She wiped at her eyes with a satin cloth that wasn't in her hand a moment before. "Thank you for bringing her home."

"If there are others, we need to find them as well. That's why this meeting with Midna is of utmost importance."

Eirlys placed a hand over the pocket of her gown. "I agree. For now, I shall keep Arianna near my heart until such a time as we can determine the safest way to return all the fae to their normal size. We will never forget what you've done for us, Rori. When this terrible business is concluded, you will be commended."

"I don't want accolades, ma'am. I want the witch responsible caught, and then I'd like to search for the other missing fae."

Eirlys reached out and stroked Rori's cheek. "Someday you will be my deadliest weapon, but you are still young, and passion infuses your actions. As much as you try to control your emotions, they are not yet mastered. Yes, you will hunt for the other fae, but first you must go to Midna and convince her to meet with me." Eirlys tapped a nail upon her bottom lip. "If we leave by morning, we can make it to the vale before nightfall. It doesn't give me much time, but if this Acelyne is responsible, we need to know her plans, and then she must be punished."

The queen's words stung. All of her life she'd worked hard to kill her emotions, but she was still a failure. If her father could see her now, getting chastised by the queen, he'd be disgusted as well as disappointed.

"I will find this enchantress and destroy her." A storm cloud passed over the queen's features, and Rori suppressed a shudder.

Eirlys's vast powers pulled at her, and she felt her magic spark in response. She kept it under control, but only just. Eirlys's magic swirled and gathered strength in the small room, creating a funnel of the queen's rage.

The queen tapped a long nail to her lips while the funnel spun through the room looking for a place to strike, and Rori froze where she stood, too afraid to move for fear the funnel would envelop her and cast her out of the kingdom. Or, rip her to shreds.

Eirlys snapped her fingers, and the funnel vanished with a sucking *pop*. The control Eirlys had over that much magic impressed and terrified Rori. She had been *this close* to having that anger directed at her. Only by the grace of Eirlys's love for her and her family had she been spared. She made a mental note to never, ever entice the queen's ire again. She doubted she'd get a second pass.

"Was it your magic that saved you? Is that how we can free the others?"

"I don't think so, ma'am. I only used enough magic to provide me with light. I broke through the glass with determination and the daggers you gave me. I used the butt of one to break the glass. It wasn't easy. Acelyne had spelled the amulet to give suggestions of quitting, or compelling me to sleep. The drug Acelyne used to subdue the fae is powerful. I'm afraid if we break the amulets, the other fae will be no better off than the princess." Rori placed a hand over her heart and bowed her head. "I'm truly sorry your Arianna fell victim to the enchantress."

"As am I." Eirlys swept a hand over the decorative boxes. "Never have I heard of such a nefarious deed. If there is dark magic at work, we must be extra cautious. Until I know how to safely release them, I will keep these lockets safe, but take one as proof of what Acelyne has done to betray Faerie. For all we know, Midna hired the witch. If this is the case, you must warn us before the meeting."

"Of course, Your Majesty." Spy on Midna and Therron was what the queen didn't say, but meant.

Eirlys hid the caskets behind a large painting, sealing a heavy slab of stone in front of the leather bag with several wards put in place to protect them from discovery. Whether she planned to move them again once Rori was gone, she didn't ask, nor did she want to know. It was a rule of hers to never ask more than she needed because then she couldn't betray her queen under torture.

They rejoined the court in the throne room, and Rori saw a budding redness on Dorchmeir's chin. Therron stood apart, his jaw tight, brows drawn. She drew a deep breath of relief at the sight of Therron, alive. She'd suspected Dorchmeir would abuse the elf once out of the presence of the queen. Apparently, he hadn't learned to keep his violent temper under control since the Academy. Rori met Therron's gaze, a silent question in her eyes. He half nodded and flexed his fists before his features softened.

Eirlys took her seat upon the throne, and Rori joined Therron at the foot of the dais. Her arms felt empty without the bag of amulets. The one vial in her pocket was just as important as all the other caskets, though. A hush fell over the room as the gathered nobles waited for the queen's judgment.

"In light of recent revelations, all charges against Rori MacNair and Therron Mistwalker will be dismissed." An audible groan rose from the audience. "Quiet. My gracious, did you expect a beheading? You lot really need to rethink your purpose in life."

Rori wasn't fooled by Eirlys's affable appearance. She loathed the lazy courtiers who hung around the palace, sporting for gossip. Sometimes even going so far as inventing it if they were bored enough.

Eirlys scanned the crowd, her expression impassive. "If you're so set on bloodlust, perhaps we should have a hunt, with one of you as the fox." The courtiers' gasp, followed by muttered pleading, brought a wry smile to the queen's face. "Always so willing to gamble others' lives." Eirlys swept her court with a scathing glance. "Rori, you'll go to the Unseelie queen and ask her to attend the meeting in two days' time. You, sir," she directed her attention to Therron, "will remain here."

26

Rori swallowed the shout that rose up her throat, but yelling "No!" to your queen in her throne room just wasn't done. This was a disaster. Therron couldn't stay at the Seelie Court. Meg had said Rori needed him to gain entry to Midna's palace. She was about to present her concerns when Therron's firm voice sounded beside her.

"Begging your pardon, ma'am, but I should accompany Rori to Queen Midna's palace. It would be more expedient for all involved."

"Nonsense. You'll stay here. No more arguments."

Therron growled low in his throat. "Your Majesty, I've been tracking someone for Queen Midna and must caution against sending Rori without me."

Eirlys glared at the elf a full minute before she spoke. When she opened her mouth, the room let out a collective sigh. "If you've been tracking the enchantress, you'll have valuable information to share with us. Rori is capable of handling herself." The queen leaned forward. "No. More. Arguments."

Therron's face turned stormy, but he didn't utter another word.

"Esme, you and Dorchmeir will accompany Rori to the Room of Mirrors, but you are not to enter with her. Rori, you know what to do."

Rori nodded and dropped a low curtsey before she turned on her heel to leave the throne room. Her gaze connected with Therron's for a brief moment, and she was struck by the uncertainty in his eyes.

She didn't have time to consider what he might be thinking. Her mind raced with how she was going to convince Midna to *not* throw her in the dungeon and *to* travel with her to the vale. Therron's presence would've definitely made it more expedient, but Eirlys had her reasons.

None of the three spoke during the short walk to the room where Rori could travel to anywhere in Faerie, and beyond the human realm if she'd wanted. Long ago, she'd heard her father talking about worlds beyond worlds, all connected by doorways like they had in Faerie. Rori had thought him mad at the time, but the more she learned of the mysterious portals, the more she believed he'd spoken true. At the memory of her father, her heart pinched. Despite everything, she missed him as much this day as the first.

"Well, go on, then. You heard the queen. Only you can enter the room, useless twat." Dorchmeir gave her a vicious shove, and she turned on him like a viper striking its prey.

Dagger drawn, the tip rested a hair's width from his belly. At Esme's bewildered stare, Rori relented. It was entirely possible the young woman had never seen this side of her soon-to-be betrothed.

"If there is so much as a scratch on the elf when next I see him, I will consider it a personal attack, Dorchmeir. Are we clear?"

"Aw, how cute. The wee elfy needs protection from little Rori." His singsong voice nearly broke her resolve.

Instead of responding with a boot up his ass, she turned to

Esme. "Until we meet again, my friend."

Esme nodded, but said nothing.

She started to turn, but stopped. Esme deserved to know the truth about Dorchmeir, even if she didn't want to accept that her nearly betrothed was an arrogant, selfish, wanking twatwaffle.

"You know, Dorchmeir, the queen told me that when this is all over, she's going to see that I'm rewarded. She might've said something about me becoming a duchess...or was it a baroness?" Rori shrugged bashfully. "I mean, I would be honored either way, but wouldn't that put me at a higher rank than you?"

Dorchmeir took the bait and snarled at her, his sword scraping from his scabbard. "Filthy scum! I'll kill you before you ever outrank me."

"Nelson!" Esme grabbed Dorchmeir's arm and struggled to keep him from slashing at Rori. "What's gotten into you? This isn't becoming behavior for an officer of the court." She turned to Rori with concern lacing her features. "I'm sorry, Rori. Nelson isn't usually like this."

Rori gripped her old friend's shoulder. "It's not you who owes me an apology, Es. But I'll never get one from him. Unfortunately, he's exactly the same as I remember him." Then, to add fuel to his rage, she added, "Ask him about the time I saved a baby dragon and he nearly shit his pants."

Rori chuckled at the pure venom in Dorchmeir's eyes and pivoted toward the mirror room. With a deep, calming breath, she opened the door. She could only hope she'd given Esme something to think about with her soon-to-be-betrothed. Her method might've been hurtful, but if she could save a sweet soul from being destroyed by that man, she'd sleep better at night. With that bit of difficulty managed, she set her attention to the next bit of unease.

Going to the Unseelie Court would be easy. Not getting

caught in Midna's traps, on the other hand, would most definitely not be. She gently closed the door behind her and took stock of each mirror's ornate, intricately carved frame. It was those carvings that told Rori which mirror to use. Anyone not versed in Seelie ciphers wouldn't have an inkling where to begin. The clues were ancient. As old as the palace itself, yet always changing. As long as someone knew the original key, they could decipher the code.

Rori didn't need a code to know the mirror farthest from the door, placed between two other hulking plates of glass that reflected her image, was the doorway to the Unseelie palace. When she became Eirlys's personal spy, the queen had shown Rori how to warp the mirror into a portal that would whisk her to Midna's kingdom in seconds. It was a fail-safe in case anything happened to the Seelie queen and Midna's help was needed. As much as the two queens bickered, Rori suspected there was more admiration and support than either would ever claim.

She glanced at the mirror, at the wan appearance of the girl standing before her. It had been a long day. Her wild blue hair hung across her shoulders in a wavy mess. Mud smears tracked up both arms of her leather jacket, and the beginnings of a small tear just above her knee could be seen in her jeans. She would never be as genteel as Esme, or as beautiful as Eirlys.

An uncomfortable thought floated through her mind.

It wasn't that she was afraid of what Midna might do to her that she'd been reluctant to leave Therron behind. Nor did she think Eirlys would harm the elf, which, considering her animosity toward his race, she might. It was something else. Something elusive she'd never felt before. Jealousy. Raw, emotional, disastrous jealousy. She was jealous of Eirlys spending time with the elf. Jealous of the whole damn court being with Therron when she couldn't. Jealous that some gorgeous courtier might catch his eye. *She was so fucked.*

27

Eirlys sat on her throne, her fingertips thrumming a beat only she could hear.

Therron waited for her to speak, his gaze traveling from the ornate chair, so similar in size and shape to Midna's, up to the soaring arched ceiling. Light streamed in from windows high above their heads. The entire palace was bathed in light, as if it were somehow necessary. Whereas Midna used thick fabrics to block the light, Eirlys courted it.

He took in the tapestries and paintings around the room. They, too, reflected a relationship between the Seelie Court to the light. Behind him, courtiers shuffled uneasily. Far down the hallway, he heard a door close and he knew Rori had entered the Room of Mirrors.

If Therron could've stopped her from going to Midna's palace, he would have. But deep down, in the far reaches of his soul where truth dwelled, he knew, just as Eirlys did, that Rori needed to meet the Unseelie queen on her own. She needed to understand her own strength. Therron would've been a distraction she didn't need.

A pang of guilt sliced across his chest. Maybe he should be

there. It was his duty, and his curse, to remain by Rori's side. Beneath the guilt, Therron knew that had he entered Midna's court with the girl, the Unseelie queen would've played her childish games of jealousy and ownership. It might've taken precious time they did not have to convince the queen that the threat of Acelyne was far more real, and far more dangerous, than they'd previously thought.

Even so, there were things at Midna's court that Therron hoped Rori wouldn't experience. Midna and her famed álainn obedience were difficult to deny. He was being ridiculous and preemptively jealous, which didn't suit him at all. Rori had given him no indications that she would indulge in the nightly activities. With any luck, she'd be too exhausted for any sort of entertainments, even if that meant there would be little time for her to dwell on her feelings for him.

That peculiar twinge in his heart started again, but now he welcomed the pangs. They'd started the night he first saw Rori in the pub, and became more insistent the closer she was to him. Just as his scar marked him as cursed, the stabs to his heart signified his mate bonding with Rori. Blood and ashes, if only they'd cease. But they wouldn't until Rori declared her affections. Despite his fervent desire to the opposite, that wasn't going to happen anytime soon. He'd have to live with the discomfort.

"Join me in my chambers, elf."

Therron jerked his attention to Eirlys, who now stood on the dais, her steady gaze penetrating his soul. "Your Majesty?"

"I wish to speak with you privately." Without giving him a reason, she turned and stepped down from the raised platform toward a different set of doors in the back of the throne room where she'd led Rori only minutes earlier.

His options were limited—stay in the throne room to wait for that bastard Dorchmeir to return, or follow Eirlys. As much as he'd like to continue the scuffle they'd had while

Rori was conversing with her queen, he chose the latter. He chuckled at his own folly—thinking he had a choice at the Seelie Court. Eirlys was queen here, and he was nothing but a thief.

A guard held open the door for him but did not follow Therron into the wide corridor where Eirlys strode several feet in front of him. He lengthened his gait to catch up, noting the smile she wore when he fell into step beside her.

Neither spoke as they padded along the carpeted hallway. At a set of huge, white and gilded doors, Eirlys stopped.

Two guards held pikes crossed at their tips and challenged Therron. "Who approaches with our queen?"

"Oh, let us in. If you hear me scream, you may kill him. Otherwise, we're not to be disturbed."

The pikes were moved, the doors opened, and Eirlys beckoned him into her private chambers. Soft fabrics in varying pastels covered the floors, walls, and drifted from the ceiling. The sheer femininity of the room surprised Therron. Eirlys presented herself as a hardened ruler who brooked no nonsense in her court, yet this space oozed sumptuous luxury with a decidedly feminine touch.

The furnishings practically begged to be sat upon. His gaze flicked from one mirror to the next while he tried in vain to avoid the paintings interspaced between them. In one, naked fae frolicked beside a river, their wings glistening as if they'd just emerged from the water, their bodies wet from a swim. In another, four male fae bathed their queen. Also naked, their maleness was hard to miss.

And they said Midna was the sex-crazed ruler of Faerie. If only they knew what secrets the Seelie queen hid behind her frosty façade.

"Come. Join me." Eirlys floated to a sofa, her gown swirling from a deep rust velvet to a barely there sheer fabric that left nothing to the imagination. She arranged herself on the overstuffed cushions, her gown pooling like a cloud around her.

"I'll stay here, thank you."

"Oh, please. I thought you above these silly games, Therron Mistwalker. Or, should I call you Your Highness?" A wicked smile creased her lovely face. "I make it my habit to know who's traveling within my borders. Does Rori know who you are?"

Therron shook his head. "Her attention was focused on the amulets, Your Majesty. I didn't wish to confuse the situation." He placed a hand over his heart. "It's not my wish to fool anyone, especially Rori. But it's my experience that once someone knows you're royalty, there are certain," he paused to take in the scandalous outfit, "expectations. I left my crown in Elvenwood for a reason. In Faerie, I'm Therron the Thief. I find there's freedom in anonymity."

Eirlys reclined into several pillows, exposing her pink nipples in the process. "I'm afraid I don't have that luxury. But I do understand expectations." She made a circling motion with her right hand and a nearby table filled with fruits, pastries, meats, cheeses, and bread. "Hungry?" She snapped and several jugs appeared. "Or would you prefer something to drink?"

Therron helped himself to a mug of ale. "Can I get you anything?"

Her laugh came out bitter. "Dear boy, never ask that of a queen."

"Refreshments. Do you require any food or drink?" At her slight nod, he filled a small plate and took it to her. "I'll tell you the same thing I told Midna—if you wish an heir, or a spare, you'd do well to look elsewhere." He practically dropped the plate in her lap. "I'm not a stud for your stable, nor will I share your bed." Without asking permission, he sat on a chair just out of arm's reach of Eirlys.

The queen's eyes sparkled with hidden mischief. "You denied Midna as well?" As she sat up, her gown returned to the heavy velvet folds. "Tell me, was she terribly disappointed?"

"No more so than I think you are. Fae and elves are not meant to mate."

"That's where you're wrong." She sucked the pip from a cherry and spat it into a nearby fireplace.

While she chewed, Therron had the uncomfortable sense that she was measuring him, but for what, he couldn't say.

"What were you doing working for Midna?"

"She hired me to find Acelyne. I can only assume your spy wasn't cutting it, and she needed to bring in someone new."

Eirlys chuckled at this. "I doubt very much that Cian could fail at anything. More likely, she needed you for a specific reason. No matter." She reached out and stroked his cheek. The feel of her fingertips upon the scarred flesh was like maggots writhing against the sensitive skin.

Therron held himself still. His mind screamed at him to draw his dagger and stop the assault, but that would lead to certain death. Queen or not, she had no right to touch him. The peculiar pinch in his heart turned to a stab, and his nostrils flared with suppressed anguish. When finally she lifted her fingers from his face and leaned back, he forced himself to stay seated. Every nerve in his body twisted until he was certain he would spring from the chair.

"How did you get that?" Eirlys nodded to his cheek as if nothing had happened.

He hoped she hadn't felt the rush of rage and anxiety that he'd had to quell at her touch.

"If it's all the same to you, ma'am, I'd rather not say." He rose and placed his mug on the overflowing table. "I'd appreciate it if you wouldn't tell Rori who I am. I think that would be best coming from me."

"I haven't given you permission to leave."

"Nor have I asked for it. But then, you aren't my queen."

She stood, her eyes aflame with indignation. "You will obey my laws while in my kingdom. I am the ruler here, and you will respect me."

"What I will respect, Your Majesty, is someone who understands the meaning of the word. You tried to seduce me, then you accosted me inappropriately. These are affronts I do not take lightly. Until you apologize sufficiently, I will bid you farewell."

Therron strode from the room without a glance at the queen. She could have him hanged for what he said, but he doubted very much that she would. Hangings were messy and there would be his parents to contend with. He highly doubted she'd risk war over her ego. If only his father were as restrained.

His time with Midna had served him well for his encounter with Eirlys. He'd had to learn to ignore his baser instincts and not let a pretty breast or sumptuous mouth entice him into less than moral circumstances. Not that he was a prude by any means, but he'd always known he was meant for something more than pleasuring a lusty queen.

He passed the guards outside Eirlys's rooms and quickly put as much distance between himself and the Seelie queen as possible. A page scurried out of his way, only to chase after him a moment later. He didn't wish to be distracted from his ire, but the page insisted on showing him to his room.

The palace was as large as Midna's, with as many turns and corridors. Therron had always thought the fae palaces had been built to make visitors dizzy, to keep the unsuspecting unbalanced. They were tricksters, the fae. Although elves weren't perfect, they certainly didn't behave as outlandishly as Faerie's two present queens.

At the door to his room, which thankfully was far from Eirlys's chambers, the page sniveled and whined about what an honor it was to serve him. Gossip traveled quickly in a palace, and the maids in Eirlys's chambers must've said something. No one else at the Seelie Court knew his true identity. Therron nodded and thanked the page, as befitting his station. It would've been much simpler to remain anonymous. At least Midna didn't announce to her court who Therron was or use his royal status against him. Eirlys knew as well as he that by acknowledging his royalty, he was bound by protocol and customs, something a thief could've avoided. Cunning, mischievous fae.

Instead of touring the rooms as the page would have liked, Therron peeked inside, declared them adequate, and closed the door to the helpful albeit annoying man. He'd spied a desk with paper, pen, and blotter, and did not need one of Eirlys's servants hovering over his shoulder as he wrote his note.

He sat at the desk and tapped the quill to his lips, debating the exact right words. The nib scratched across the parchment as he wrote, the ink staining the fibers with every stroke. When he'd finished, he blotted the page and, before folding it, pressed his palm against the words. It was a simple thing to spell the paper, but he added a curse to anyone who was not the intended reader.

With a smile on his lips, he left his rooms and headed for the gardens. For once, he thought perhaps he could gain footing on the enchantress.

The gardens were bathed in fading twilight when he emerged from a side door, and Therron took a minute to gaze at the multicolored sky. Swathes of pinks, purples, oranges, and blues streaked across the horizon. Soon it would be full dark and Rori would be laying her pretty head down to sleep in one of Midna's guest rooms.

Therron closed his eyes and cleared from his mind the unwelcome vision Sof Rori, alone, facing Midna. She was a warrior at heart. She did not need him to protect her. She might be a damsel, but she wasn't in distress. And even if she was, she could damn well save herself.

His heart warmed at the memory of how she'd softened at the castle in the human realm. The way she'd looked at him with desire in the little chapel had given him hope. He rubbed his chest and looked toward the east to Midna's palace. Hope would have to sustain him until he saw Rori again.

The sky darkened to a glittering field of diamonds spread across a blanket of cerulean. It was time. He lifted his face and made a silent call. Within moments, a falcon swooped from the treetops to his outstretched hand. His talons wrapped around the thick leather of his glove.

"My friend, I need you to deliver this at once." Therron spoke to the creature in the elvish tongue. The falcon ruffled his feathers and clacked his beak in reply. "Thank you."

He attached the letter to the bird's leg using a strip of leather and lifted his arm for the raptor to take flight. Silently, he wished the bird a safe journey.

The cool metal of a sword's blade touched the underside of his chin, and Therron stilled.

"What was that you sent?" Dorchmeir's voice came from Therron's side, just beyond his sight.

"A message that doesn't concern you."

"I'm sure Queen Eirlys will be interested to know what it contained."

"I'm sure she would. Why don't you take me to her, and we'll discuss it."

The blade cut into his skin, sending a wave of pain down his neck. A warm trickle of blood oozed over his days' worth of stubble.

"We don't need your kind here, elf."

"I suppose you don't. Yet here I am." Therron spun away from the blade and toward Dorchmeir, his fist connecting with the man's middle.

The soldier let out an "Ooomph!" followed by several curses. Before he could recover and attack, Therron landed several more punches to his rib cage, followed by a solid hook to his jaw. Dorchmeir stumbled backward, tripped on a raised flower bed, and fell to his side. Therron stood above him, rage wafting off him like steam. He drew his boot back and kicked the lieutenant between his legs. It was ungentlemanly but effective. Dorchmeir had been an arse to Rori and deserved nothing less.

"You'll pay for that, elf." Dorchmeir spit the words at Therron, his face the color of a beetroot.

Therron wiped blood from his neck and studied his fingers. Then he retrieved Dorchmeir's sword and held the blade above the man's heart. "I've known men like you. Small minds, with even smaller pricks. You bully and bluster to make up for your shortcomings. I haven't experienced everything I have just to take your bullshit. So no, I won't pay for this. Not in any currency." He threw the sword on the ground beside the man and strode away.

As his boots crunched against the gravel path, he heard Dorchmeir whisper, "You'll pay. She'll make sure of it."

Therron shook his head. He'd made an enemy at the Seelie Court, something he'd been trying valiantly not to do. Some days, it would be easier to return to his kingdom and take up the crown as his father hoped he would. Some days.

28

Rori pressed hard against the frame, mumbling the words needed to take her to Midna's court. Forget that. She didn't get jealous. To be jealous, she'd have to have feelings for the elf, and no way…no bloody way did she think of Therron in that way. He was using his elf mind tricks on her, but she'd have none of it. Rori MacNair was a lone fae. Even if she did find him attractive, perhaps even a little sexy, he was an elf and she a faerie. It would never work out.

She didn't need any romantic entanglements in her life. Dealing with her mum and Cian was enough of a commitment. She seriously didn't need the hassle of love or mushy feelings. Just look what it did to Esme—turned her stupid and gooey and, blech. No fucking way.

The mirror swirled, the glass becoming liquid silver, and Rori stepped through. Unlike the dark, silent doorway to the human realm, sound and light assaulted her with horrifying urgency. She'd learned to tune it out, to focus on the place she was going rather than go mad in the in-between. Some never made it to the other side alive, their bodies oozing through the portal in a sticky mess. Traveling through Faerie in this manner had its drawbacks and was not for the easily intimidated.

The air thickened, pressing upon her lungs until breathing became impossible. She held her breath and waited out the discomfort. Everything about the doorways was designed to dissuade anyone from using them. Whoever first made the portals must've been a sadist. Why make something to facilitate speedy travel, only to kill a good portion of the people who use it? Rori asked herself the same question every time she entered one of the enchanted mirrors.

A light the size of her fist brightened until it nearly blinded her, growing in size as well as force. When it fully engulfed her, she forced her body to relax and took a step forward into Midna's own Room of Mirrors.

Because it was the first time Rori entered the Unseelie palace through the doorway, she let a moment's hesitation wash over her before she glanced at each of Midna's mirrors, choosing the one she believed to be the entrance to the palace proper. At least Eirlys had an actual door in her Room of Mirrors.

Rori searched the frame and found what looked like a knob and twisted it, smiling when a satisfying click sounded. The smile left her face as soon as she jerked open the door. There, standing with five of Midna's guard, was her brother Cian.

He studied her with the practiced eye of a spy trained for pretense. He showed no recognition, nor did he seem surprised to find her standing in Midna's palace.

"Take her to the queen." His sharp voice brooked no argument, and to Rori's shock, the guard obeyed.

Fortunately, she'd been trained the same as him and pretended not to know her own brother.

She strode through the palace with the confidence of a frequent visitor. Beneath a veil of indifference, she scanned her surroundings. Everywhere she looked was another intriguing bit of art or fanciful play on furniture. Mythical creatures not seen in Faerie for generations like nymphs and mermaids, as well as more common races such as faeries, elves, and ogres, were depicted in all manner of everyday life in tapestries, paintings, even floor murals made of tiny pieces of glass.

Nowhere did Rori see any evidence of the sordid sex activities associated with Queen Midna. In fact, this palace looked much the same as the Seelie queen's: stone walls, arched ceilings, bay windows with cushioned seats. In a way, the similarities disappointed Rori. She'd bought into the rumors and had mentally built the palace into legend.

"Wait here." Cian broke through her thoughts. He gave her a curt stare for only a moment before leaving them in the middle of the hallway.

Rori checked her nails and grimaced at a snagged cuticle. She reached for her dagger and was immediately met with two drawn swords.

"Easy, fellas. I just need to trim some flesh." She slowly withdrew her dagger and showed it to them before using the tip to scrape at her nail. When satisfied with her work, she slipped the dagger into its sheath and smiled at the guards. "See? No danger."

She'd not been put into irons, nor had they taken her weapons, which meant either Midna didn't see her as a threat, or she was being tested. Either way, Rori wouldn't do anything to anger the queen. Not before she had a chance to deliver her message, at least.

Cian returned and beckoned the group to follow him. They passed through a small courtyard and into another part of the palace that took on a distinctly different look and feel than the other corridors. On these murals, the nymphs frolicked with giant phalluses protruding from their bodies. The mermaids gleefully snacked on the brains of shipwrecked pirates. This was the palace Rori had feared. This was the palace Rori had secretly longed to see. If only to satisfy her curiosity. But she knew it went far deeper than idle interest. To see the álainn obedience, to understand why they'd give up free will to become essentially a sex slave to Midna—that was at the heart of her preoccupation with the Unseelie Court. Besides an education in lovemaking, what was in it for them?

She furtively scanned the corners and shadows, but didn't witness anything unusual. A pit of disappointment lodged in her gut.

At the last door, Cian didn't bother knocking, but yanked hard on the handle and ordered her inside. Rori kept her face placid even when her heart rammed against her rib cage. For whatever reason, Therron had chosen to stay at this palace with this queen. And Eirlys had said he was Midna's favorite.

Again, that pinch of jealousy unnerved Rori. What the hell was up with that bloody elf? She shouldn't care about him or this queen or anything happening around her. Yet, she was darkly fascinated with it all.

"Why have you entered my palace uninvited?" The stern voice came from the raised dais, which was very similar in shape to the Seelie queen's, but draped in rich velvets of crimson, teal, and purple. The heavy fabrics blocked out any sunlight that might've shone down from the huge windows overhead. The only light in the room came from drossfire blazing within three huge alabaster discs suspended from the high ceilings.

"I've come from the Seelie Court, Your Majesty, with a request from Queen Eirlys."

Midna leaned forward, and Rori saw her golden eyes first. They burned as if flames danced within. Her flaxen hair and snow-kissed skin were a stark contrast to the forest-green gown she wore. Upon her head rested a crown of spring blooms, their pale shades far too innocent for this queen, Rori thought. Wings—gossamer thin and translucent, with opalescent veins making a spider's web of sorts from tip to tip—unfolded behind the queen. Despite herself, Rori stared in awe. Never had she seen the Seelie queen's wings. Nor did she expect Midna's to be as delicately beautiful. She yearned to touch them, to feel the silkiness against her skin. A soft sigh escaped her lips.

"Where's Therron?"

Rori collected her thoughts, regained control of her senses. "He's with the Seelie queen. He'll not be harmed and will be by your side once I'm returned unharmed."

A shrewd look crossed Midna's features. "What does Eirlys want with me?"

From the corner of her eye, Rori saw Cian's shoulders shift the slightest bit. She knew that movement. Knew that he was preparing for battle, as he used to say. If there was to be a fight, he was ready. Dear, sweet Cian. She had no desire to fight or die this day.

"What is your interest in the enchantress Acelyne?" It was a bold question, but one that had been nagging at Rori's mind ever since meeting Therron.

"I wish to see the witch drawn and quartered." Midna's ghostly lips turned a sickening shade of blood red. "She has stolen something from me, and I want it back."

So that's why Therron was following Acelyne. Midna sent a thief to capture a thief. Clever. Considering Midna's focus was on the enchantress, Rori would leave talk of war for later. Giving the queen a chance at revenge would better suit her need to have Midna meet with Eirlys.

"The enchantress stole something from Queen Eirlys as well. That's why I'm here. The Seelie queen would like to meet with you at the Vale of Dorn day after tomorrow. I have it on good authority that Acelyne won't pass up a chance to be near the two great queens of Faerie. I'll leave it to Your Majesties to decide the enchantress's fate."

"What makes you think Acelyne will show? Why would she risk it?"

"Because I stole something of hers, and she desperately wants it back."

Midna's lips turned a soft shade of pink and curled into a smile. With that slight shift of her features, the queen's entire countenance changed. Gone was the frosty, forbidding ruler. In her place was a relaxed, welcoming woman. Midna softened into the hulking chair as if it were a lover. The movement was at once sensual and dramatic. Warmth spread from Rori's belly to the apex of her legs, where it settled with a thrumming intensity.

Whatever the queen was doing to her, Rori wanted no part of it. She was not here to become one of her álainn obedience. Even as she forced bravery into her thoughts, desire to be lost in the dungeons pounded in her heart.

"Your Majesty, please stop."

Midna scraped her nails along the armrests, a devious smirk on her lips. She turned toward Cian and indicated Rori with a tilt of her chin. "Shall I have this one killed?"

The ease with which she said the words, the complete nonchalance of the question, irritated Rori. And that she'd ask Cian, her own brother, made her want to throttle the queen.

"Only if you want war with Queen Eirlys. I've heard this one is a favorite of sorts. She said she stole something from Acelyne. It might be prudent to find out what that was."

Internally, Rori seethed. Externally, she wore a bored expression.

"Fine. What is it you have of Acelyne's?"

Rori surveyed the room. Perhaps two dozen courtiers stood in small groups, some pretending to not pay attention, others openly watching the spectacle.

"May I approach Your Majesty?"

Midna nodded to Rori while simultaneously signaling to her guard to give them space.

When Rori was within touching distance of the monarch, she withdrew the amulet, being careful to keep her palm cupped to hide it from the onlookers.

Midna peered at the pendant. Her hand hovered close to Rori's, but she didn't reach out. "What is this?"

Rori kept her voice low, measured. "A prison, ma'am. Inside is a faerie. I believe Acelyne is capturing fae and transporting them to the human realm via these amulets."

Midna snatched her hand away as if bitten. "What makes you think this?"

Rori resisted the urge to look at Cian. She hated that she wanted his support but was also relieved he stood just a few feet away. "Because until this morning, I was imprisoned." She cast a glance over her shoulder to the crowd. "I hesitate to say more, Your Majesty."

Midna's gaze flicked to her courtiers. "You were trapped? In here?" The question was little more than a whisper.

"Not in this one, ma'am. There are more, many more, hidden and safe for now. But I fear there are even more still beyond Faerie's borders."

"But how? To what end?"

"How many people did you sense come through your doorway when I entered your palace?"

"One. Just you."

"But, if I'm correct and there's a fae trapped inside this amulet, you should've sensed two. It was the same when Therron and I went to the human realm and back to Eirlys's palace."

"Therron went to the human realm?" A glint of laughter touched her golden eyes.

"He wasn't happy about it."

"I can only imagine."

Midna took the pendant from Rori and examined it for several minutes. No one in the room spoke, nor moved. Every set of eyes was trained on the queen.

"How do you get them out?" The queen broke the silence. A collective exhale of breath stirred the air.

"I don't know, but Queen Eirlys was keen to find out."

"Can't you break the amulets?" Midna eyed the glass vial with suspicion.

Rori repeated what she told Eirlys about breaking free of the silent forest, but left out any mention of Arianna. If Eirlys wanted Midna to know her daughter had been kidnapped, it was the queen's place to tell the story, not Rori's.

Midna wrapped her fingers around the amulet and held her fist to her heart. "I shall keep this for now. Is there anything you'd like from me?"

It was a strange request, and Rori wasn't sure what, exactly, the queen was asking.

"No, ma'am. I'm exhausted, starving, I could use a loo, but otherwise, I can't think of anything that I require."

Again, that enigmatic smile from the mysterious queen.

"Cian, take your sister to a room on the second floor. I'm sure she'll be comfortable there. In the meantime, I'll send a message to my sister-queen confirming we'll meet her day after next. We'll leave early in the morning. Please try to get some rest tonight, Rori."

Rori curtseyed to the Unseelie queen, noting the use of "sister" twice in her speech. Therron had said Midna knew all about Rori and Cian, but why make it clear now? And why refer to Eirlys as her "sister-queen"? As far as Rori knew, the pair weren't related. Perhaps it was a way all queens referred to each other, as a sisterhood of sorts.

She rose and turned toward Cian. He looked like hell. Hair mussed—he hated his hair to be one strand out of place—and dark half-moons under his eyes. She hadn't time to notice earlier, but now, this close to him, she saw that his stubble was from more than just one day. Something was going on with him, and she longed to know what. In fact, she had the distinct impression far more was going on in the Unseelie Court than was visible to the innocent bystander. Rori was neither innocent nor a bystander. She'd wait until her escort left her alone to explore the palace. Whatever Midna was hiding, she'd uncover.

"What did Acelyne take from Midna?" Rori kept her tone light.

Cian's chuckle warmed Rori's spirits. She'd been half afraid the cool attitude he portrayed was due to her sudden appearance.

"Leave it, Rori. This isn't your mission, nor is it your place to go snooping. Trust me. Stay in your room and wait for morning. You'll be safest there."

"You're joking, right? You expect me to sit around and what, knit? Like hell I will. Something's going on, and I'm going to find out what. With or without your help."

They jogged up a wide staircase, with Cian a step ahead of her. At the landing, he waited until her boots touched the hardwood before he dragged her into a darkened alcove and hissed close to her ear, "Don't you dare. Midna's testing you. Hell, she's testing us both. Something *is* going on, but I can't have you involved." Rori stiffened at his words, a flurry of curses on her tongue, but he stopped them with one simple admission. "Midna's sister is missing and she believes Acelyne took her for nefarious purposes. Your story in the throne room corroborated Midna's worst fears. Right now, she's trying to decide if you can be trusted—me as well, I'd assume. For all Midna knows, you and I are working with Acelyne for Eirlys's benefit."

"You know we're not." Rori rolled her bottom lip between her teeth. "Why *are* you here?"

Cian took her elbow and moved them into the hallway where a couple strolled hand in hand. She glanced away quickly, before she started mooning over Therron again.

"Officially, I'm here to offer Midna solace and assistance in finding her sister—something that has not been made public, by the way."

"And unofficially?"

"I've been tasked with finding our lost fae and returning them to their proper homes."

Rori rolled that around in her mind a bit. Eirlys said she knew about missing fae for many years. Arianna had only been taken a few days earlier.

"How long have you been here?"

"A month, maybe a bit longer. And before you ask, Mairead has been missing for three. It's not the first time she's slipped away, but there's been no word from her, nor has Midna felt her presence in Faerie. According to Midna, Mairead always lets her know that she's safe."

They rounded a corner and immediately turned to their left, where a steep staircase, not nearly as broad or as ornately decorated, met them. Cian took the steps two at a time while Rori ran behind him. Her damn fool brother was barely winded when they reached the top. It took her a moment to catch her breath.

"I've never known you to be this out of shape, little sister."

"I've had precious little to eat for close to a week. I wasn't lying when I said I was exhausted. Or about needing the bathroom."

Cian's laughter boomed down the corridor, startling several courtiers. "Then let's get you to your room." He led her to a door and opened it for her to pass through.

Inside the large room was a four-poster with curtains and

enough furniture to make it comfortable for several guests. Her stomach churned at the thought of what other guests might've done in that room, on that bed.

Cian pointed to a door on her left. "Bathroom, and there," he indicated another door to the right of the fireplace, "is your dressing room. Although, I doubt you'll have need of that. I'll get a fire started while you use the facilities."

The bathroom was half the size of the sleeping quarters, with a huge claw-footed tub sitting in the middle. She gazed longingly at the tub, but a bath would have to wait. First, Cian had some questions to answer.

By the time she returned to the bedchamber, a roaring fire glowed steady in the grate and her brother squatted before it, hands outstretched toward the flames. The clench of his jaw, and seriousness of his gaze, stopped her heart for a beat.

"What's going on, Cian? Not just with the imprisoned fae, but why are you truly here?" She stood beside him, her palm stretched across his shoulder. Beneath her touch, his tension was felt in the tightness of his muscles, the pull of skin over bones. "Do you think—" She stopped the thought before it became real.

"Think what?"

He rose and in that moment, she saw their father. They were so alike in coloring and attitude. A deep pang of longing stole her breath.

"I keep wondering, is this what happened to Dad?"

His breath sucked in and he turned away, but not before she saw fury ghost across his features. "Don't make it personal, Rori. Remember your training."

"It's too late for that. When Acelyne drugged me, she made it far more than personal. We have to find them, Cian. All of them."

"We will."

A knock at the door startled them both, and Cian stalked across the room. "That'll be supper."

He opened the door to a servant, who brought a tray of delicious-smelling food into her room. They set the tray on a table and left without a word. Rori watched the servant leave, noting the slope of his shoulders, the downturn of his eyes. His hands were clean, his nails neatly trimmed.

They ate with very little conversation. She wanted Cian's company, enjoyed having him in her presence, but something about his melancholy threatened to drown them both.

"Have you ever heard of a company called SIRE Unlimited or even just SIRE?" Cian asked after the last bite of his pudding. He took a long drink of ale, watching her above the rim of his mug.

"I don't think so. Why?"

He shrugged and finished his drink. "I've been doing some digging into fae who've chosen to live in the human realm, and this SIRE Unlimited thing keeps coming up. I couldn't find anything on who runs it, where it's headquartered, what they do—nothing. Then recently, I had a break. Malcolm Dagniss— does the name mean anything to you?"

Rori scanned through the years of knowledge she'd either collected or read and came up with one possibility. "I remember there was a Dagniss family long ago, but that line has been extinct for centuries. I don't recall there ever being a Malcolm, though."

"Very good. You paid attention to your studies." Cian patted her on the head, and she snapped as if to bite his fingers. "Easy, little dragon."

She grinned at the nickname. "What about him? Is he involved with Mairead's disappearance? Or with SIRE?"

"He owns the company, but I'm not sure about Mairead. My gut tells me he's involved with both. Why, I couldn't say, but I'm determined to find out."

Rori stifled a yawn, and Cian's face softened. "How did you get yourself captured?"

"No freaking idea. I was at the pub with Tug, then I woke in the forest three days later. I've been told my supposed friend Sal gave me a drugged drink. Honestly, though, I don't remember anything past singing with my pals." Admitting this truth to her brother hurt. She hated that she'd failed in the one aspect of her job she should've bested anyone at—protecting herself.

"If it's Acelyne, then no wonder. She's a master enchantress. Midna thinks she's here in the palace at this very moment, but I'm not so sure."

Rori's nerves twisted, and a shudder rushed down her back. She'd die before being put into a glass prison ever again. "She made me see things, Cian. I saw the princess in her palace, but then, a woman appeared who said Arianna was *her* daughter. Queen Eirlys is the princess's mum. It was all quite confusing, like an illusion within the illusion. But it felt so real. I don't know what to believe anymore."

Cian's long fingers stroked his chin. His dark brows crowded one another as he frowned. "You're exhausted. Get some sleep, and Rori, please, don't leave your room tonight. It's a new moon and Midna is restless."

She squinted in thought, deciding not to argue with him. Besides, she had a lovely tub in the next room. She'd run a hot bath and soak away her cares.

"I promise. I'll be good."

"For once."

They both laughed, and he kissed her forehead before leaving and taking the tray with him. At the click of the door latch, she turned the key, knowing if anyone really wanted into her room, there were probably half a dozen secret passageways that would allow access. Or all they really had to do was use magic on the lock.

A little thrill ripped through her belly. She'd promised Cian she'd stay in her room, and she would. But if someone happened to sneak into her room uninvited, she'd have every right to attack them, wouldn't she? Rori patted her two daggers, still somewhat surprised Midna allowed her to remain armed. She'd make sure to sleep with a dagger under each pillow. Just in case.

$\ast$ 29 $\ast$

Screams rent the night air, waking Rori from a fitful sleep. She reached for her daggers and found nothing. The bedsheet beneath her pillows was empty. Alarmed, she sat up in the huge bed, her mind racing, eyes searching. She took a deep breath, stilling the frayed nerves that careened toward panic. The curtains were drawn on the four-poster, blocking most of the light. A faint glow could be seen beyond the fabric. She felt again beneath the pillows, gritting her teeth at the empty sheets. Those daggers were a gift from Eirlys. Priceless, yes, but of great sentimental value to her. When she found the pig-faced nipple pipe who stole them, she would rip their head off.

She stared at the bed curtains and recounted her steps after her bath. She'd sat by the fire until her hair was nearly dry, then slid beneath the covers, too exhausted to care that the wardrobes were empty and she'd had to put on her dirty clothes—a precaution she took for the sole reason that she slept in Midna's palace. If anything happened, she would be prepared.

Rori scratched her head. She hadn't closed the bed

curtains, she was certain of it. She drew another long breath to slow her hammering heart.

After Cian had left, she'd locked the door, and she'd checked it again before getting into bed. Her hands went to her neck, where she'd tied the key to a ribbon and secured it like a necklace. Frilly lace met her fingertips and she paused, unsure what she was feeling. She'd gone to bed wearing her jeans and T-shirt. What the bloody cockleberry was this Victorian dressing gown bullshit she had on?

She tugged the duvet off and shoved the curtains open. White cotton covered her from her neck to the tips of her bare toes. She curled her feet against the cold floor and shivered. The fire had died sometime during the night, leaving her room frosty. She searched the wardrobe again, hoping to find a cardigan or wrap, but it was empty. So were the two chests in the room. Her own clothes were nowhere to be found.

A breeze snaked its way up her ankle to her very naked private parts. A full-body shiver racked her body and she hopped to the bed, where she grabbed the duvet to wrap herself in its downy warmth. Next, she searched the hearth for firewood, kindling, and matches, but couldn't find anything to make a fire. She was certain Cian left the matches on the mantel, but when she looked for them, the box was empty. As was the log rack beside the fireplace, where wood had been when her brother left. It was as if someone had come in during the night and taken everything out of her room. If this had been Eirlys's palace, she would've blamed Dorchmeir, but she doubted that dimwitted boot licker would have the nerve to enter Midna's kingdom.

Rori sat with a huff on one of the stiff chairs and debated her choices—stay in her room, bundled up until morning, or go in search of answers.

Another scream pulled her attention to the door. She listened hard, but the only sounds she heard were her own breathing and the blood rushing through her veins. It went against her training to intervene when someone was in trouble. *Don't get involved* was a familiar mantra at the Academy. *Stay invisible. Keep to the mission.* She knew these words as if they were written in blood on her heart.

Her father had a different variant on the mantras: protect herself at all costs, never give an inch, and never deviate from her goal. Only step in if someone had information she needed; otherwise, don't get involved. Doing so was a great way to get dead.

Since waking up in the forest, she'd done everything except not get involved. Why start going by the rulebook now?

Her fingers flinched from the icy knob. Wisps of condensation floated on her breath. She tightened the duvet and scrambled through the doorway into the darkened hall. Lights flickered at one end of the long corridor. Voices came from the same direction, and Rori turned toward them like a poppy tracking the sun's rays.

Cocooned as she was made walking difficult, but there was no way she would traipse around Midna's palace in just the thin dressing gown. It took her several minutes to make her way along the carpeted floors, counting each door she passed. She'd come to fifteen when the hallway opened to a gallery, where she found her source of lights and voices.

A balustrade kept her from falling to the marble floors, and a thick pillar concealed the bulk of her, yet gave her a prime view of what was happening thirty feet below. At first, Rori didn't understand what she saw. Bodies—some clothed, most not—writhed like hypnotized snakes. Masked courtiers stood on the fringes, watching the spectacle. Music played from somewhere beneath the gallery where she stood. Its melodic beat set the rhythm for those below. They undulated and arched like choreographed performers on stage, their cries and moans counterpoint to the music.

The more Rori studied the scene, the more she realized these must be the rumored álainn obedience of the Unseelie queen. And there, in the center of it all, was Midna.

The queen reclined on a divan, her wings fluttering to the beat, making nearby candles flicker. The interplay of light upon those near her was both ominous and sultry. They appeared as angels, then demons, depending on where any given shadow landed. Naked servants attended the masked audience, offering drinks and refreshments from glittering gold trays. Those on the outer rim of the room chatted among themselves, sometimes pointing to one group or another. Rori wished she knew what they said. For one wild moment, she wished she were down there, as one of them.

Yet, which group did she long to be part of? The masked onlookers, or with the queen? Her gaze raked over the entwined bodies back to the queen. Her wings curled in on themselves and stretched taut. One moment, her skin appeared translucent, a pearl upon the midnight fabric. A moment later, she shimmered in rainbow hues of pinks, purples, greens, and blues. With each alteration, her wings' glow ebbed and flowed, fluttered, and furled. Rori stared, transfixed.

It had never occurred to her that wings were anything more than a status symbol. She'd never seen anyone expose them thusly before. In fact, she'd never once let her wings unfold to their full size.

A thrumming between her shoulder blades caused an itch that she sadly realized would never be scratched. She wasn't royalty. Her wings would have to stay safely protected beneath her skin. She twitched her shoulders, quelling the insistent desire to let them free. Without success, she tried to recall when it had become law that only royalty could show their wings. Her back now felt inflamed, as if someone held a torch against her skin. It was unbearable. Was it law? Was it a rumor or empirical fact? She struggled to remember. Her mind was blank, as if that specific memory had been excised. If it wasn't a law, then certainly just letting the gossamer folds open for a moment wouldn't hurt.

The queen screamed, and Rori took a half step toward the barrier. Her focus snapped to Midna, to the source of what had woken her. The itch across her back faded to nothing more than an irritation. Another cry ripped through the air, as if murder were being done, except Midna looked anything but a victim. Two faeries suckled the queen's breasts, and another settled his head between the monarch's legs. The onlookers applauded politely, their attention drawn to the divan.

Midna's arms drooped to the side, her body limp after what Rori could only guess was her release. The three fae didn't stop, not even when another fae joined them. His Glamour sparkled like glitter beneath a sheen of sweat. His tall body swayed as if drunk and the queen reached for him. Roughly, she grabbed his hardened cock and pulled him to her mouth.

Rori turned away, mortified at what she witnessed, and even more so by the dampness between her own legs.

Cian had warned her not to leave her room. A quickening of her heart kept her from turning back to the orgy. Her brother might be down there. An image of the tall fae swept through her mind. Similar in height and coloring to Cian. She hadn't been focused on his face. Every nerve pinched and tightened in on itself as she debated what to do. Knowing she could never forgive herself, she cocked her head to look past the balustrade.

Rori avoided looking at Midna, tried to ignore what the queen's mouth and hands were doing to the fae, and focused on his face. Eyes closed, his chin tilted toward the ceiling, she couldn't be certain it wasn't Cian.

Bloody hell, what are you doing, MacNair? Go back to your room. You don't need to know.

Yet she did. Had to be certain it wasn't her beloved brother servicing the Unseelie queen.

One last glimpse.

She stared harder, willing the fae not to be Cian, and was rewarded with the man turning toward her, his face illuminated by a floating candle. The look of sheer bliss marking his features tore at her heart. For an instant, she wanted it to be Cian. Wanted to know her brother had experienced this kind of rapture. Since their father's death, happiness became a stranger to her family. The fae wasn't anyone she knew. Conflicting emotions of relief and regret battled in her tumultuous thoughts.

The fae's glow captivated her. Longing feathered from low in her pelvis, over her thighs, up her abdomen, across her chest. The duvet slipped from her shoulders as one hand traveled between her legs, and the other cupped her left breast. Her thumb rubbed over her hardened nipple, creating more want, more desire.

To be with the others, to feel their hands on her, their lips caressing her skin—she craved their touch. The male fae at Midna's side arched. A long moan echoed above the music. Drums beat louder and the bodies shifted with the increased tempo. Men with men, women on women: a mix of both genders entwined. They convulsed and grunted, their bodies slick with perspiration. Rori's fingers ground against the cotton fabric in a frantic need to find release.

Another scream from the queen.

So close.

Sparks edged her vision. Her breathing came in short pulls, and her body rocked to the beat of the drums.

One of the masked onlookers turned toward her, his—her? —stare like a snare. Rori gasped, aware suddenly that she stood at the edge of the banister, where all of the crowd could see. Another step, and she would've toppled over the edge.

Her body ached for her to continue, but she couldn't. Wouldn't give in to the lust twisting like a raging storm through her body. She bent to pick up the duvet and cracked her forehead on the granite pillar. Pain ricocheted across her skull. The duvet caught in her feet, and she stumbled backward, tugging on the stupid thing as she raced down the hallway. At the grand stairway that led to the room below, a lone figure ascended the stairs. Rori sped faster, clasping the duvet to her chest.

The door to her room stood wide open, and she raced through, spinning around to slam it shut. For several minutes, she waited with her forehead pressed against the wood, listening. No footsteps followed her. No one knocked on the door. Gradually, her breathing slowed and her heartrate lowered. The lust she'd felt dissipated to a familiar wanting, nothing more. Whatever happened with the queen, she didn't want to be a part of it, even as an onlooker.

She crawled into the huge four-poster and curled the duvet around her body. A profound sadness wormed its way from her frazzled thoughts to the tips of her extremities, suffocating her in its severity. Why she felt as she did perplexed Rori. She didn't want to be part of an orgy, nor did she fancy having sex with the queen. *Then what?*

The answer lay in her denial. No stranger to sex, Rori had never allowed herself to enjoy it, at least, not in the way she'd witnessed in the queen's room. She lay her head upon the pillow to sort out the puzzling emotions. The awful truth was, she couldn't recall a time she'd enjoyed sex enough to cry out, to be completely unbridled with her body. The sadness coiled and snapped within her heart. *Duty first, pleasure never.*

$\maltese$ 30 $\maltese$

No sooner did Rori snuggle into the downy softness than a hard knock at the door rattled her anew. She sat upright, swearing a stream of curses at whoever had the nerve to disturb her in the middle of the night.

But when she glared at the door, sunlight streamed through the windows. Dying embers glowed red in the fireplace, and she was once more dressed in her own clothes.

"Rori, open up. I've got breakfast," Cian shouted from behind the thick wood.

She felt along her neck and found the ribbon with the key. Her right hand slipped between her legs where an uncomfortable warmth remained. *A dream.* She'd had a bizarre dream. Had to be.

"Give me a second," she called out and slid from the bed. At the door, she put a hand to her forehead and shook the remnants of the dream from her mind. The key made a gravelly sound as she turned it, followed by a satisfying click. The door popped open and there was Cian, looking even more haggard than the previous day, but with a huge smile lighting his face.

"I thought I was going to have to break down the door. I don't recall you sleeping so hard, but you did say you were exhausted."

"Yeah, I guess." Rori took the tray and placed it on the table. "Can you stoke the fire? It's chilly in here."

"No time, I'm afraid. We have to eat and run. Queen Midna's almost ready to leave."

Still rather distracted from her unusual night, Rori nodded and sat down to tuck in to her meal. She barely tasted the porridge and fruit as she shoveled huge spoonfuls into her mouth.

"I didn't mean it literally." Cian put a hand on hers. "Slow down. Chew, swallow, breathe." He cracked a soft-boiled egg and handed it to her. "Did you sleep well?"

She took a bite of the runny goodness and swallowed before answering. "I think you might be right about Acelyne being here. I had the strangest dream."

Cian glanced at her, his greenish-brown eyes showing concern.

"It seemed so real. Bizarre, though." She scooped another spoonful of egg into her mouth.

"You stayed in your room like I asked, right?"

"I did." *But my dream self didn't.* Her cheeks burned with the memory. She rubbed her temple, noting a tender spot on her forehead. Where she'd bumped into the column. Icy pinpricks tickled across her skin. It was a dream, she insisted. A dream—nothing more. Afraid her flushed cheeks would give her away, she changed the subject. "Will the queen provide us horses to ride?"

He eyed her for several long moments, and she prayed he didn't ask any questions. After a bite of his own egg, he said, "We're traveling in her carriage."

"With her?"

"Of course, with the queen." Cian made a face and shook

his head. "Honestly, Rori. What's gotten into you? Are you losing your edge?"

"Never!" She reached for a dagger, but they were still beneath her pillow. She hoped. "I might not have as many missions clocked as you, but there's nothing you can do that I can't."

His raised eyebrow served as an answer. She didn't argue it further. Why bother? Cian was the best. Always had been; always would be. They both knew there were several things he could do better than her—fire a gun, for one. As much as she'd tried, she hated firearms. The sound, the feel—all of it repulsed her. Knowing him, he could fire a direct shot at forty paces with his eyes closed, a cup of tea in one hand, and still hit his mark. Friggin' Mr. Perfect.

"Rori."

His voice dropped, and her body tensed, as if a trap were about to spring and she'd find herself caged. Actually, it was the fatherly tone he'd adopted after their dad died. The one she'd grown to despise and resent.

"Is this what you want? Being an intelligence officer? Or are you only doing it because of the family?"

He acted as if she'd ever really had a choice. As if their father hadn't drilled it into her that she was nothing if not a spy. That her worth, and that of the family, depended on her not failing. The truth would hurt him as much as her, so she did what she always did and lied.

"You want to know if I had a choice, right here, right now, would I choose this profession? Would I choose to put myself at risk every day for our queen?"

He nodded, his eyes focused on her.

"Yes, I would. Mum gave me a choice, you know. When I was thirteen, she asked what I'd like to be when I grew up. Kids never know, do they? They'll tell you a sorcerer, or a blacksmith, because that's what caught their attention that day, but I've always known. Even before Dad died, I knew I wanted a life bigger than Faerie." At least that much was true.

"Bigger than Faerie." A snort and shake of his head were followed by a chuckle. "You've got that, all right. But Rori, we're not in competition. Stop trying to best me, and just be you. Be Rori MacNair, not Cian MacNair's little sister." He held her chin between his thumb and forefinger, his gaze steady. "You are, as the humans are wont to say, a total badass. I'm proud to call you kin."

The intensity of his stare staggered her. His words cut straight to her heart. If she were honest with herself, she knew his words were true. She'd been in a silent competition with her brother for most of her life. Everything she did was tagged with what she thought he'd think of her. To hear him say he was proud of her meant everything. Tears stung her eyes, and she blinked hard. A flippant reply sprang to her lips, but she refused to say anything to diminish the moment.

"Thank you."

"You're harder on yourself than anyone else. Queen Eirlys knows your loyalty is without question. Mum knows how devoted you are to your work."

She traced a circle on the table, her thoughts a tangled mess. "Do you think Mum misses Dad?"

"Of course. She loved him very much."

"I miss him, too. He was hard on us, but he only wanted the best for us, right?"

"Dad did what he thought was best. But don't let his dreams become yours. You're young, Rori. You can be anything you want."

She shook her head slowly. "I think the time for that has passed. I am what I am."

"You are what you think Dad wants you to be. You mistake building walls around your heart for emotional control. They aren't the same at all. You can love and be loved and still be an excellent spy. Mum and Dad are proof of that."

"That's rich, coming from you." She wasn't the only MacNair who preferred to work alone.

"We're not talking about me right now. I know you think it's what you want, but you don't have to be alone. Believe in yourself. Trust this."

He placed his hand over her heart, and an odd wooziness swept over her. Those words, and that action, were exactly what the strange woman Taryn had said and done.

Maybe Rori had been mistaking cockiness with confidence. Maybe it was time she stopped trying to prove herself to everyone and be, as Cian said, totally badass, but not in a lethal, quiet way like her brother. In her own way. Whatever that was.

Maybe it was possible to love her father and hate him a little too. And then just maybe she could love herself. Someday.

"I will."

He removed his hand from her heart and held his mug but didn't drink from it. His fingers tapped nervously on the table.

So, even cool-headed Cian could get ruffled. Rori tucked the information aside. Seeing her brother in this light was refreshing. Instead of teasing him, she asked, "How long do you think you'll be on this mission?" She didn't want to ask him why he looked so haggard, or whether he'd ever shared Midna's bed, but the thoughts were hidden behind her question.

"I'm not sure. I think I've uncovered everything here that I can, but it's possible I missed something."

"I doubt that." Her quip was drowned by a gulp of tea. Mr. Perfect never missed a clue.

"Have you heard from Mum?"

"Not since I've been back, but then, I've been busy." Rori

still hadn't forgiven her mum for moving away from the Seelie Court when she'd retired. Labhruinn MacNair had stayed on as Eirlys's captain of the guard until Rori entered the Academy, then quietly left her position and moved to a tiny village in the middle of nowhere. To Rori, it felt like abandonment. That was only half the truth. Rori choked back the other half with a bite of toast.

"I'll send her a note letting her know you're doing well." He rested his hand over hers and gave a squeeze with his fingers.

"I'd appreciate that."

Using him as her personal messenger caused a momentary flinch of guilt. She really should take a few days and visit her mum. It wasn't Labhruinn's fault their dad went missing, and it wasn't her fault that both Cian and Rori chose to follow their dad's career path. Their mum had never been anything but understanding and supportive. She deserved more than Rori gave her. So did Cian.

"Tell her I'll come see her soon."

Surprise crossed Cian's features, and he grinned. "It's about time."

It was past time. She missed her mum more than she'd realized.

"Cian, there's something I've never told anyone and maybe you should know."

Both of his hands snaked across the table to cover hers. His eyes stayed on her face, encouragement mixed with caution.

"It's about Dad."

A strange flash cut across his features, one of agony, and then it was gone.

"What about him?"

"The day he died, I was at Gran's, in the garden." The words caught in her throat. This was harder than she'd thought it would be, but her gut told her it was time he knew the truth.

"I was practicing warping and weaving magic just like Dad taught us, to pull in all the elements surrounding us to create more powerful spells. All of a sudden, I felt like my whole body was on fire. Not just on fire, but ants crawled all over me and spiders were biting me over and over again." Tears stung the backs of her eyes with the memory. "I don't know what happened. To this day, I have no idea how, but I lost control of my magic."

She withdrew her hands from his and sat on them to hide the tremors from Cian. She was still hiding, after all this time, still terrified of what happened that day, and of what lurked inside her. She breathed out, knowing she had more to confess, but unsure how he'd respond. He might hate her, or turn away in disgust, but he had a right to know. "It was awful, Cian. I had no control, as if…someone else was in charge and using it against me."

Cian wiped the tears that rolled down her cheeks. "That happens to even the best mages. Sometimes we use more than we're ready for."

"No." She shook her head, letting several cobalt locks hide her face. "It wasn't like that. I never stretched myself too much. I always knew my limits. Dad used to commend me for my control. But that day—it hurt, Cian."

"I'm so sorry. Why haven't you told me before now?"

Rori took a deep breath. This was the hard part of her story. The part she hid even from herself. "Because, what if it was wild magic and something I did caused Dad to disappear?"

Cian left his chair to kneel beside her and enfolded her body with his strong arms. "Beautiful, sweet, lethal Rori. You had nothing to do with Dad's death. Nothing." He stroked her hair and made soft, comforting sounds until she sniffed and wiped the tears from her face.

Once the words had been spoken, they didn't weigh as

heavy in her heart, but she wasn't ready to believe him yet. Doubts lingered despite his assurances.

He pulled back and searched her eyes, nothing but love and devotion on his handsome face. "And if it was indeed wild magic, we'll sort that out. You've lived with this guilt for too long. Believe me, sweet sister, you are not to blame for Dad's death."

"How can you be so sure he's dead and not just, I don't know, kidnapped or something?" She wished she could be as confident as her brother, but guilt had many years to embed itself into every nook and cranny of her psyche.

Outside her room, a page rang a bell, loudly calling out that the queen would soon be departing.

Cian pressed his hands to the sides of her face and kissed her forehead. "Don't torture yourself over something you had no part of. Dad's dead. Just...trust me." He rose and clapped his hands, as if that were done and nothing more should be said on the matter.

% 31 %

One last shovel of porridge followed by a long drink of tea, and Rori pushed away from the table, her belly satisfied for the moment. The dour conversation had dampened the mood, but she pushed her reticence aside and focused on the here and now. Cian was right, she needed to stop punishing herself for something that happened fifteen years ago. She was a child then, barely powerful enough to create a drossfire pit. There was no way she could've made their father disappear.

The mini-pep talk worked, to a point. She had a job to do and sitting around blubbering about the past wouldn't save the trapped fae or bring her father back. Her focus was, and always should be, on serving her queen. Emotions only caused trouble.

As did a certain thief. As she blotted her mouth with a napkin, she desperately tried to ignore the flutter of excitement that she would be seeing Therron again. Yet, he was still an elf, and she was still a faerie. One night away didn't change the fact that their kingdoms didn't condone such relationships.

And why was she even considering it to begin with? Lone fae, remember?

Therron's lips, remember that?

It was useless. He was the first guy to kiss her in forever and now she had a bad case of puppy love. Figures. She'd have to ask Meg whether she had a potion for curing the malady.

"We should get a wiggle on. Wouldn't want to keep the queen waiting and all that." The gorgeous freaking queen who had hired Therron to find Acelyne. What else did she pay him to do? Rori bit her cheek to keep the awful images from invading her mind.

Midna was the Unseelie queen; she was supposed to be alluringly beautiful. To distract her from the feelings she didn't like creeping into her psyche, she retrieved her daggers from beneath the pillows where she'd left them the previous night. A good bit of steel was reminder enough of her duty to Queen Eirlys. Whatever Midna, or even Therron did, wasn't her concern.

Her leather jacket hung on the back of a chair, and she swished it up to shove her arms through. An instant of regret twisted her heart. Arianna was no longer sleeping in the hidden pocket. Even though the princess had been comatose, Rori had liked having the wee lass close. Arianna gave her purpose. She'd had someone to protect other than herself and for that brief time, it felt good to have someone to care for. To save a life rather than taking one.

Cian checked his reflection while she finished dressing. He was a handsome guy, her brother. And he knew it. In fact, he used his looks as part of his arsenal of weapons. She studied him as he adjusted his jacket. Cut like a long sport coat, or manteau, it could easily pass for human or fae clothing. Same for the dark pants he wore. His shoes, however, gave him away. Handmade Italian loafers that she knew for a fact cost just under two grand. She looked at her scuffed boots and shrugged. They were a fraction of the price and equally as functional.

"Hey," she said as they exited her room, leaving the tray on the table, "remember that weird vision in a vision I told you about?" Rori looked at Cian from beneath her lashes. "Do you know what ShantiMari is? Or what a Darennsai is? The woman said these things, and she knew me, Cian. But I've never seen her before—I would swear my life on it. Have you ever heard of someone named Taryn? Silver hair, blue eyes?"

Cian cocked his head in thought. "Can't say that I have. Why?"

"I don't know. Just, I met her within that illusion, and I have a feeling she was actually outside of the illusion."

"You're not making sense."

"None of this makes sense. An enchantress, missing fae, the queens meeting—I can't shake the feeling something big is happening to Faerie, but we're the last to know. And maybe we're pawns in some greater scheme."

Cian placed his arm around her shoulders and pulled her close. "We're intelligence officers, Rori. It's our job to know before anyone else what happens. What do you think is going on?" He tapped her heart, then her belly. "In here. Like I said, trust these." His last tap was to her forehead. "And this. In our profession, they are the only things you *can* trust."

"You can always trust me, big brother. Not even torture could make me betray you."

He kissed the top of her head before letting his arm fall away. "Nor me, you."

They wove their way through the dozen or so carriages to the only white one of the bunch. All the others were drab brown, or sickly black, but the queen's shone like a star among the rabble. Rori suppressed a shake of her head and roll of her eyes.

"Nothing like shouting to the world, 'I'm here!' Doesn't she have an ounce of humility?"

"Don't be so quick to judge. Being queen isn't just about gowns and crowns." Cian glanced down at Rori. "It's a lonely position that demands a lot physically and emotionally. Queens might look like they're receiving, but it's what they're giving that takes the toll."

The dream, of the fae suckling Midna's breasts as if being fed by the queen, crashed across her thoughts. A warm tingling spiraled from her core, and she shoved the memory to the far reaches of her mind. She did not need to think of Midna like that. *Ever.*

Cian opened the carriage door for her, and she dropped a half curtsey with a sloppy grin. He swatted her on the back of the head, and she laughed as she ducked into the cool, dark interior. The laughter died in the back of her throat when she saw the Unseelie queen sprawled on the cushions. Rori did a double-take at her now lavender hair. The queen apparently changed hair color and skin tone to match her moods. The control this woman had over her magic was impressive.

Lavender waves cascaded over her shoulders to curl around a barely concealed breast. Not that Midna's garments did much to hide her nudity. Rori scrambled into the seat opposite and averted her eyes. The warmth spread from her core to her outer extremities. It was going to be a long, uncomfortable trip to the vale.

"What took you? We've been waiting ages."

"You know that's not true, ma'am. The Unseelie queen waits for no one. You only just arrived before we did," Cian chided.

The queen harrumphed and sat upright, straightening the voluminous skirts of her floaty, transparent gown.

"I see you've dressed for practicality." Her brother settled into the cushions, crossing his right ankle over his left knee.

How he could remain unaffected by the queen, Rori couldn't guess. The woman's scent alone was a distraction. *Perfume? Sex?* She swallowed a bitter lump of discomfort and gazed out the window. The rest of the carriages were loaded and ready. The horses lunged forward, knocking Rori backward. A loud *thunk* sounded when her head connected with wood.

"Futnuckers!" The word was out before she could stop it, and she stared at the queen in horror. "Your Majesty, please forgive me."

Midna's laughter was unexpected but appreciated. "Please, Rori. You have nothing to fear from me. Swearing is nothing more than words said with passion. Just words." The queen leaned forward, exposing her breasts, and Rori glanced away. "Dear girl," she tilted Rori's face to look at her own, "the things I could teach you. Your brother tells me you're talented, but by the blush staining your cheeks, I don't think you're as learned as you should be. Spying isn't a game for the easily shocked."

Rori's eyes widened and again, that wonderful sound of Midna's laughter filled the carriage.

"You must learn to give in to your desires, but in a controlled way. I can help you with that."

"With all due respect, no thank you, ma'am." Mortification didn't come close to what Rori was feeling. That Midna would dangle her breasts like ripe pieces of fruit, there for the taking, and offer to school Rori in the ways of making love—it was more than an insult. The queen had called Rori innocent, at the very least, a prude at worst. The nerve of the woman. She could hardly breathe for the anger pooling inside her gut. It *was* anger, wasn't it?

The smile on Midna's face held sadness and something else —disappointment. "I sense a schism within you, Aurora MacNair. A division between your heart and your mind that serves no purpose except to court danger." Her head cocked to the side and she nodded, as if making an internal decision. "Yes, you believe the rumors. You think my álainn obedience are sex slaves. That they are to be pitied, yes? I tell you true— every one of them is there by choice. Their reasons for coming to my court are their own, but they all come of their own voli- tion. I don't force anyone into service, nor do I make them stay. Do you know why they choose to stay?"

Rori shook her head. The scent of the woman, the confines of the carriage, the images of her álainn obedience clouded her judgment, confusing her thoughts. They chose to stay? All of them?

"They stay because it isn't about sex or carnal desires. They stay to learn control—of their heart, their mind, and yes, their body. They learn how to give pleasure as well as receive it. Life is a balance, and in my court, you discover your true self—not who you pretend to be."

The sense of being on display, of being under a microscope where Midna could see into her deepest, darkest corners and shine a light on her vulnerabilities, caused her to shrink into the cushions, but the Unseelie queen gripped her face between long fingers.

"Do not hide from who you are, Rori. Never feel shame for what you desire."

Vaguely aware of Cian's presence, Rori tried to deny she desired anything, but it rang false. "I don't know what you mean."

"Well." Midna traced a finger down Rori's cheek to her lips. Her breath came in stuttered pulls, her chest rising and lowering in spurts. The queen's nail scraped into the soft skin. Adding insult, Midna moaned as if the action were sexually fulfilling. Rori struggled to calm her runaway heart. "If you ever change your mind, you know where to find me." The queen sat back, removing her touch from Rori's face, and focused on Cian. "Now then, tell me how you're progressing with the investigation."

The change of tone and attitude startled Rori. Even Midna's clothing altered with her businesslike demeanor. Her hair paled to flaxen waves and the floaty, see-through gown became soft velvet, in a deep Bordeaux color. Midna's skin shifted from a shimmery abalone to dull cream.

Rori could barely control the whorls of emotion fighting within her heart and mind. The dichotomy of desire and disgust penetrated every cell, every fiber of her body. It was enough to drive her to madness. A memory of Midna on the divan, her cries echoing to the ceiling, slipped into Rori's tangled thoughts. Perhaps sex was the only time the Unseelie queen truly let go. If she allowed herself such pleasures, would Therron make her scream and beg for more? Gods, but she longed to find out.

With grudging respect, Rori had to admit the queen could teach her many things. Not just sexually, but about so much she didn't know. She had a feeling the Unseelie queen was the greatest spy of them all.

❧ 32 ☙

T he carriage came to a halt, and Rori snapped open her eyes, senses on full alert. Cian squeezed her hand and exited the carriage to hold the door for Midna. The queen's smile was for Rori alone. Hidden in the curves of her lips was an unspoken invitation. For a second, Rori almost blurted out that she'd stay with the queen. That whatever she could teach, Rori would happily learn. But the moment passed, and Rori sat in the carriage alone with her confusion.

She couldn't remember when she'd fallen asleep, only that Cian and Midna's conversation had bored her beyond belief. After discussing Cian's findings, which Rori paid attention to, the discussion had devolved into an accounting of household business. Midna knew everything that happened at her court, down to who was bedding whom. She could recount every penny spent from her treasury and inquired after several babies born in the past month. The dullness of it all had lulled Rori into a sleep deep enough she'd no longer felt the rib-jarring ruts in the road or heard the squeaking of wheels.

"Are you coming, or did you plan to sleep in here all night?"

"Shut it, Cian." Rori slithered from the carriage and stuck out her tongue at her brother. Her boots landed in soft grass, and she looked around at her surroundings.

The Vale of Dorn sat at the very heart of Faerie, of equal distance to the two kingdoms. Rori knew the vale well, having traversed it many times both on foot and horseback. Rowan, the fae wizard who called the vale home, was a good man. Honest, humble, and smart. He'd given Rori shelter on more than one occasion and stitched her up a fair few times as well. She saw Rowan shuffling toward the queen and smiled.

Beside Rowan was her friend Tug, and to his left, Meg. Tug saw her and waved a hello as he lumbered past the pair to meet up with Rori.

"Meg's fixed me, Ror. I ain't got no more enchantress in me mind." He folded her into a hug, and she patted his expansive back.

"That's good, Tug. Was it so terrible to be cured?"

"Nah, Meg's a good lass. Gave me some potions, didn't she? They weren't too tasty, but after a while, they did the trick. I cannae feel someone else in here anymore." He tapped his skull, a wide grin on his face. "Where's Therron? Meg thought the two of ye would come together."

"He's with Eirlys. I went to the Unseelie palace alone."

Tug nodded, as if the idea didn't surprise him. "He'll be along shortly, I imagine. Don't ye worry none about him."

It was an odd thing to say, but then, Rori had just had the oddest day of her life. The startling realization hit her that from the moment she woke up in the silent forest to when she fell asleep in the Unseelie queen's palace had all been one long day. In truth, it felt like a month, at least. No wonder she was exhausted.

A shiver clawed its way down her spine, and Rori turned in time to glimpse a flash of gold and crimson dart behind a tree. She squinted into the surrounding woods but couldn't make out any movement beyond a few rabbits. Her instinct told her to wait, that Acelyne needed to be there. It took every ounce of self-control not to race after the enchantress.

"You'll stay inside with us tonight, Rori." Meg joined them and hovered close to Tug. Her glance darted to the forest, but she didn't mention Acelyne. "Rowan insists."

"I slept in the carriage on the way here. I can patrol tonight. Where's Eirlys?"

"They were detained and won't arrive until morning. You need your rest." Meg entreated Tug, "Doesn't she?"

"Ye do, Aurora. Ye've had a busy time of it, and if Rowan says ye'll sleep in the house, then ye will."

Knowing arguing would get her nowhere, Rori agreed. "There's still a few hours of sunlight. I'll see if I can help put up tents or something. I can't just stand around waiting."

"You can help me with potions. Come, I'll show you how to make that tincture you're so fond of." Meg held out her hand, and Rori followed.

Tug meandered off in the opposite direction and soon after, she heard the *thud-chunk* of a hammer hitting wooden spikes. Other sounds came to her: of the queen giving orders, forest creatures, birds cawing in the sky—natural sounds that for all the world sounded like everything was as it should be. Yet Rori had the distinct feeling nothing would ever be the same. She savored the moment, her face upturned to the sun.

At Meg's impatient huff, she took a deep breath and focused on what the healer had to teach. A small kitchen was set up outside, next to Rowan's garden. Meg had cauldrons and spits, jars with all sorts of stuff, some of which Rori wished she'd never seen. Cat's livers, chicken feet, bull scrotum— Meg had everything necessary to brew every potion ever invented.

"Here, take these." Meg handed Rori several jars. "Put them in a pot with that elk urine."

"Eww. What exactly am I making?"

"Life Everlasting." At Rori's grin, Meg added, "It doesn't actually make you live forever, but if you're injured, it will congeal your blood and heal your wounds."

"I need a wagonload full, please."

Meg chuckled and gave Rori the rest of the instructions to make the potion. She stirred one pot before adding ingredients to another. They made enough of the tincture to supply an army, several sleeping potions, two quick-acting poisons that would put a soldier out of misery in moments, and a mysterious ochre liquid that smelled fouler than an ogre after a night at the pub.

It wasn't hard graft, but it felt good to be doing something. It also kept her mind off a certain elf and his absence. Jealously wasn't a good look on her, but snickertits and stars, she missed Therron.

When the denim blanketed the night sky and the moon was the only light by which they could see, Meg called a halt to their makeshift apothecary. "I think we've got enough, don't you?"

"Are you expecting a battle?"

Meg's serene smile didn't reach her eyes. "I like to be prepared. Best to get you inside, dear."

Sumptuous aromas wafted toward Rori, and she didn't argue. It was past time for another meal. Meg carefully lined the jars on a shelf with the labels facing out. Quick as a heartbeat, she tucked the ochre bottle into her pocket. Rori pretended not to see Meg shift her skirts to hide the potion.

Inside Rowan's cottage were at least two dozen courtiers, Tug, Cian, and the queen. Chairs were shoved into the corners in an effort to fit everyone into the cramped space. Tug waved Rori over, and she wove through the tightly packed room to her friend.

He held out a plate of food, and a flood of emotions

washed over her. Overriding them all was gratitude that he'd thought of her. Beneath that lingered worry for what would happen the following day. Deeper still, anger that it had come to this because of an enchantress with a penchant for kidnapping fae. She blinked back unwelcome tears and bent her head low over her plate. What was wrong with her? She never blubbered like a fool and yet here she was, hiding her tears. The food passed over her tongue and down her throat with barely any chewing. She doubted anyone cared about her manners in the crowded house. If they did, they could suck the nipples off a bridge troll. She was hungry.

"Did you even taste Rowan's cooking?"

"Shut it, Cian."

"You keep saying that." He wedged himself between Rori and Tug. "Hey, big guy. Anything new?"

"Just ta stuff with Aurora is all."

"So, same as usual?"

The men shared a laugh at Rori's expense. She ignored them and finished her meal. When there was nothing left but a few crumbs, Tug took the plate from her and shuffled to the kitchen. A few minutes later, he returned with three plates piled high with sweets.

"Who had time to make these?" Rori took a plate from him, her full belly protesting at the abundance of confections.

"I did." Midna glided into view, her gown now pale pink with hair to match, wings nowhere to be seen. "It relieves stress," she added with a shrug. "Enjoy."

Cian put a finger under Rori's chin to close her gaping mouth.

"She's full of surprises." Her brother gave her an "I told you so" look, and she snarled. "Finish up, then it's to bed for you."

"What am I, five? I can take care of myself, you know."

He wrapped an arm around her and tilted his head to rest

on hers. "Humor your big brother. You've been at the Academy and off on missions for so long, I hardly recognize you anymore." He fluffed a strand of her hair. "I like the color. It suits you."

"Purple was my favorite," Tug said between bites of his Victoria Sponge. "Queen bakes good."

"That she does," Cian said with a little more inflection than Rori liked.

"Are you in love with her?"

"Isn't everyone?" He indicated those in the room. "Just look at the way they watch her, as if one glance, one word from their queen would make their day."

"But she's—" Rori stopped herself from saying "bad." She tried to remember why everyone told her the Unseelie queen was untrustworthy and to watch herself, to never go there. Everyone knew the Seelie Court was about light and gaiety and the Unseelie Court was full of tricksters. These were the same "everyones" who said Midna's palace was full of sex slaves, too.

The truth was probably somewhere in the middle. Rori studied Midna as she bent to speak with a courtier here, or listened to another courtier over there. Eirlys was equally as dichotomous as the Unseelie queen.

"She's not all that bad," Rori said at last. "I guess."

Cian nudged her shoulder and grinned at her like he'd done when they were kids. "Bad, good—it's all relative. Some say we're bad for what we do. Others say we're the heroes. Without context, we're both. Come on."

He unfolded himself from the long bench and walked away from the others. She followed him without argument. Not because she wanted to, but out of respect. They trudged up the stairs to a long hallway with at least a dozen doors on either side. Rori blinked at the sight. Then blinked again.

"Rowan is a wizard, you know."

"Don't be daft. He was one of Dad's oldest friends. It's just, the amount of magic it would take to extend the cottage like this is impressive."

"I agree. Rowan is quite proud of his spellcasting skills." He opened a door for her. "Here you are." He pointed to a change of clothes on the bed and then to a connecting door next to a wardrobe. "I'm just there. Don't bother locking your door. I've been able to undo the best of locks since I was five —without magic."

Rori gave him a sugary smile and a half curtsey. "Of course, m'lord."

His chuckle followed him into his room and through the closed door. He'd always been an insufferable brat. Bless him.

Unable to sleep, she paced the small room until she was sure she'd worn a path in the floorboards. It couldn't have been more than half past nine, and she was wired from all the sugar. She tiptoed to the door separating her room from her brother's and put an ear to the wood. A few times, she heard Cian clear his throat and after a minute or so, she heard a page turn. She glanced around her room for a book and didn't see anything. Knowing him, he brought one with him.

She leaned against the door and debated her choices, which were basically sleep, or lay in bed staring at the ceiling while stressing out about the fae and what Acelyne was doing with them. It was too stuffy in the room. She paced back and forth along the length of the bed, her hands fisting and flexing with her agitation. There was nothing for it—she needed to get out of this room if for no other reason than to think. Being cooped up made her brain sloshy, and she hated it when things weren't clear.

Doing her best to not make any noise, with each step, she placed her boots gently upon the floorboard with a silent prayer they wouldn't squeak. It would be just like her brother to request a room with a built-in escape detector. At the window, she stared out into the darkness, orienting herself from inside the cottage to the vale. In the distance, a soft glow came from the forest. It could've been a random campfire, or one of the soldiers', but the insistent buzzing in Rori's gut told her it was Acelyne's. The enchantress was out there, waiting.

Rori put a hand to the sash as if to push it open and paused. The fire snuffed out. Too quickly. The buzzing intensified and nausea teased the back of her throat. *Something she ate, nothing more.* Sweat slicked her palms and her fingertips tapped along the window frame. She'd never been afraid of the dark, not even as a small child, but this night she hesitated to open a bloody window.

As she debated risk versus reward, a pair of shining lights came forward from the trees. Their size and intensity grew the closer they came.

Too late, she realized they weren't lights, but flaming daggers, and they were headed right at her. She ducked a second before they crashed into the window.

33

A booming crash came from Rori's room, and Cian stood so quickly he knocked over his book and a chair. He burst through the open doorway, his magic fully released and swirling around him like an impatient warrior ready for battle. Blue-green flames danced around his hands, with small tendrils licking up his forearms.

Rori crouched low beneath the window, her eyes wide and face pale. It wasn't fear that shone from her face, but awe. She'd never seen him use this much magic and as soon as the threat was assessed, he would reassure her he was fine. He knew how much she feared using her own magic—and now he understood why—but she needed to know magic wasn't to be feared. She'd lost control, everyone did at one time or another, but he didn't think it was wild magic. At least, he hoped it wasn't. The queens forgave a lot from his family, but that? There would be no escaping prosecution if she actually did have the cursed line of magic.

His gaze went to the unbroken window and beyond to the darkened night. "What happened?"

"I don't know. There were lights in the forest, like flaming daggers, and they flew at me."

He doused the lamps in her room with a single word and nudged her aside. She started to rise, but he cast her a look that told her to stay low, out of sight. For once, she obeyed and scooted to the left, giving him access to the frame, but stayed close enough her shoulder brushed his leg. He scanned the vale and forest, but it was too dark to see anything or anyone. He silently said all the curses he hated hearing from her lips. Such a hypocrite. But wasn't that what big brothers were for?

The window wasn't broken, nor could he see any visible marks where daggers might've hit. He pressed a tentative hand to the glass, surprised by the coolness there.

A thundering of footsteps came from the stairs, and Rori groaned. "Great. Here comes an onslaught of questions and attention that I can neither answer, nor want. I'm out." She stood and walked toward his room.

"Where are you going?"

"Tell them you're sleeping here and that was meant for you." She jerked her chin toward the window. "Those were a test, and she failed. Acelyne's out there. She's not going anywhere anytime soon, and I've had enough excitement for a while."

Without waiting for his reply, she went into his room. A moment later, he heard her crawl beneath the covers of his bed. He peeked his head inside, but she shoved a pillow over her head, effectively telling him to fuck off and let her sleep. He couldn't blame her. She'd had one hell of a day, and according to Midna, she had an exciting night, too.

Though, it wasn't Rori's fault she left her room after he'd warned her to stay inside. At least the Unseelie queen was honest enough to admit that she'd compelled Rori to observe what happened at the Unseelie Court. According to the queen, she'd made Rori think it was all a dream. He glanced at the way Rori gripped the pillow and sighed. First Acelyne, and then Midna manipulating his baby sister. It didn't sit right with him that they both messed with her mind. Hadn't their father done enough of that for several lifetimes?

He stepped back and closed the door between their rooms. Rori wouldn't try to leave the cottage, nor did he think Acelyne would try to attack them again. He returned to the window. The flaming lights might've been illusions, or they could've been flaming daggers that turned to ice upon impact.

What was Acelyne's point? Why attack them in such a feeble way?

Midna entered the small room and glared at him, then at the window. "What's going on? Where's your sister?"

"She's sleeping." He cocked his head to the window. "I think Acelyne was trying to send us a message."

A guard entered with a long piece of ice in his outstretched hands. "Your Majesty, this was found on the ground below this window." He handed it to Midna, who beckoned Cian to take it.

A chill went up his arm, and not from the frozen piece of what he'd been right to suspect was an ice dagger. It didn't ease his mind that he'd guessed Acelyne's actions correctly. What else was the enchantress willing to do? His gaze went to the closed room where Rori hopefully couldn't hear their conversation.

Midna dismissed the guard and turned to Cian. "Well?"

"Ice, spelled, but for what, I'm not sure. It wasn't strong enough to kill. Perhaps her motive was to subdue."

"Do you think she was trying to capture Rori again?"

"If so, why?" He set the melting piece of dagger on a tray and wiped his hands on his trousers, wincing at the marks the liquid made on the dark fabric.

Midna sat on the edge of the bed, her fingers tapping along the side of the mattress, her face twisted in thought. "I received a rather extraordinary note last night from my thief." At Cian's frown, Midna waved a hand to indicate he was being ridiculous. Something she did far more than he liked. "Don't let your feelings for the elf cloud your otherwise impeccable judgment. Do you honestly think I'd hire someone I didn't fully trust?" She stared at him with a challenge in her glorious eyes. "I hired you, didn't I? A MacNair working discreetly for the Unseelie queen. Who would've thought it possible?" A tinkling of laughter filled the room.

"Fine. I won't tell you you're a fool for sending him to find Mairead."

"But you just did. As you have several times in the past month. Why do you hate him so?"

Cian took a long breath and let it out slowly. "A feeling," he tapped his gut, "in here. Why is a prince hiding in your court? Why is he passing himself off as a thief?"

"Not passing—he is a thief. He belongs to a reputable guild and everything."

"That you no doubt facilitated to keep up the ruse. Why is he really here, Midna? To spy on you, naturally, but he's the heir to the elven throne. Why isn't he home, where he's needed? You and I have both heard the rumors that King Thane's illness grows. He's needed there, not here chasing after an enchantress."

"Are you jealous?" Midna scoffed and shook her now crimson hair. "I never thought I'd see the day. So, there is a beating heart beneath that utterly delectable outer façade?"

She rose and stood facing him, her lips close enough if he flicked his tongue, he would taste the wine he smelled on her breath.

"I'm not jealous, Midna. It's my job to be concerned."

Her hands crept up his abs to his chest, where she tapped above his heart. "Will you still deny me?"

"Yes." He kept his face stern, his voice steady, despite

the stirring of his cock and rushing of his blood. Damn body. He was trained to fuck, even when the situation didn't call for it.

"And it's my job to keep my subjects safe."

She returned to the bed, and he breathed out a sigh of relief. He was too tired to fight off her advances.

"What did the note say?"

She arched and tilted her head toward the ceiling. "He warned that Acelyne would try to capture Rori again and that we should keep her as safe as possible."

"Why does Acelyne want my sister?"

"She stole the amulets from her, and from what I know of the enchantress, she doesn't forgive those who cross her." Midna motioned to the window. "I placed wards around the cottage just in case Therron wasn't being paranoid. I guess he was right."

"You knew and you didn't see fit to inform me?"

"What would you have done any differently?"

In truth, nothing. He would've stayed near Rori and kept a closer watch on her, perhaps. Or maybe he would've gone to the forest to confront the enchantress.

"I think you should know, Therron cares deeply for your sister."

Cian's heart buzzed, and he clenched his jaw against the unwelcome news. "Then we'll just have to convince him that Rori isn't available."

"Darling," Midna purred in that way she did when trying to seduce him, "perhaps the elf is exactly what she needs." She curled a lock of hair between her fingers, her brows gathered in thought. "Besides, it's not for you to decide her heart. Now come, let us strategize how we can best this clever enchantress."

There had to be a way to dissuade Therron from his sister, but that was a conversation for another day. He mulled over what the elf had written to Midna. If Acelyne was desperate to reclaim Rori, she might get sloppy.

An idea began to form in Cian's mind. A terrible, wicked plan that might save his sister's life, but at what cost? He pulled a chair closer to the bed and in a whispered rush, told the Unseelie queen his dangerous idea. Their heads bent close, they strategized and schemed until the moon crossed the horizon and dawn would soon break.

They were both exhausted, but also eager for the day. Once Eirlys arrived, they could set their plan in action and capture Acelyne once and for all. He left the sleeping queen and returned to his room, where Rori tossed and turned with whatever nightmares haunted her night. He placed a comforting hand on her shoulder and told her she was safe, he was nearby. Her whimpers settled, and she quieted into a peaceful slumber. Cian knelt beside her bed for a long time, listening to her breathing and stroking her head, like he'd done after their father died.

When Rori woke, Cian was sprawled across a chair, an open book in his lap. He felt her watching him for several minutes until he looked right at her. Rori held his gaze, and he smiled in a lazy, sardonic kind of way. Finally, he blinked, and she declared herself the winner with a happy little fist bump and whoop-whoop. It was a game they used to play as children and for some reason, the fact she'd remembered gave him goofy bubbles in his belly. They'd both become far too serious over the years. It was nice to recall happier, simpler times.

"Did you sleep well?" When was the last time he'd had more than a few hours' sleep?

"Why do you keep asking me that?" She sat up and hugged a pillow, looking far too young in the morning light.

"As you said, you've had an exciting few days." He tilted his chin toward the vale. "Queen Eirlys will be here soon. You might want to freshen up."

Rori yawned and stretched, her features set in a grimace. Her gaze went to the curtains, where a slip of cloudless blue sky could be seen.

"What time is it?"

"Past breakfast." At her fallen face, he added, "Tug saved some for you."

"Guess there's no time for a shower?"

"There might be if Rowan had showers. I'm afraid it's tub only here, and water needs to be brought up from the kitchen."

"How old-fashioned."

"Quite."

At least her love of baths hadn't changed. So much else had, though. He barely recognized the woman she'd become. She pulled the duvet off and swung her feet to the side of the bed. The glint of mischief he remembered from their childhood no longer lingered in her eyes. Now, a seriousness and determination set her features. She peered closely at him, her lips a thin line that reminded him so much of their mother.

"Did you sleep well?"

"I did, thank you." He lied and swatted his book at her. "Get some food in you. Today's going to be tedious. Midna's decided since both she and Eirlys are here, they should discuss more than Acelyne and the missing fae."

"Is that why Meg made so many potions? In case there's civil war?"

"There's no threat of war between the queens, of that I'm sure."

Rori chewed on a strand of hair. "I don't know. Meg warned of a coming war, and she seemed pretty serious about it."

Talk of war never ended well, but he spoke true—both Eirlys and Midna wanted peace in their kingdoms. He'd have to ask Meg what she meant by her prediction. He'd always liked Meg, and trusted her as a healer, but as a portent to the future? He needed convincing.

Rori tugged on her boots and shook out her braid. Glorious locks of sapphire fell across her shoulders. She had no idea how pretty she was, nor did he think she ever tried to use her beauty to get information. Innocent wasn't a word he'd use for his sister, but in some areas, she was delightfully pure.

"Let me get cleaned up, and I'll head down for breakfast." She sheathed her daggers and stepped over Cian's crossed legs to the doorway that separated their rooms. "What are you doing here?"

Damn. He'd forgotten to warn her that Midna slept in the bed meant for her. Cian set his book down and stood behind Rori as reassurance, but also to make sure she didn't do anything rash. Midna reclined in the small bed; her cobalt hair closely matched Rori's and she wore a black T-shirt, same as his sister.

"She's protecting you, Rori." Cian placed his hands on her shoulder and felt the tremble of rage that coursed through her body.

"Protecting me? From what?" She took a step toward the bed and he followed, but she stopped suddenly, making him bump into her. Her eyes slid to the window where hours earlier, two flaming ice daggers tried to break through the glass. "From Acelyne? Why? I don't have the amulets anymore. She and Eirlys have them." She jabbed a finger toward Midna.

"Acelyne might not know that. And besides, it could be she doesn't want just them, darling." Midna slid gracefully from the bed, her shirt barely covering her legs. "You are what she seeks. Not only did you manage to break free of her spell, you stole something from her, and we're certain she wants revenge. We brought you here to lure her out."

"You used me as bait?" Rori spun around to confront him,

anger, confusion, and hurt clear in her blue eyes. "And you allowed this?"

Guilt stole his breath. He opened his mouth to speak, but nothing came out.

"Darling," Midna purred, "it was his idea."

34

A commotion outside the windows poached the precious minutes Rori needed to process what the Unseelie queen said. Shouts and cries from below drew their attention, and as soon as Rori saw the crest of the Seelie queen, she raced from the room. Eirlys would help. She could explain to her queen why Midna was wrong. Acelyne had no interest in Rori aside from the fact she took the amulets. Last night was nothing more than an attempt to frighten her, but it hadn't. If anything, it added to Rori's annoyance with the enchantress.

But to intentionally use her as bait? That hurt. The bloody plan had been to gather the queens and Acelyne would come for them. Not her. Cian knew she hated being imprisoned in the amulet and would rather die than ever be put in one again. That was the crux of her anger—fear. Fear of Acelyne and her wealth of power. What if the queens' plan went wrong and Rori was trapped in the forest forever? What if she were spelled into an everlasting sleep? Had Cian even considered how she might feel on the subject?

Eirlys was just descending the short steps from her carriage when Rori burst through the side door and skidded to a stop a foot from her queen. "Your Majesty." She dipped a clumsy curtsey and stepped to the queen's side. "There's been some confusion while we were waiting for you. Queen Midna is under the belief that Acelyne wants something from me. Can you please inform her that she's mistaken?"

Eirlys's lips were almost colorless as they pressed into a thin line. "I asked Midna not to say anything to you." She slapped her leather gloves against the side of the carriage and glared at the house. "Where is she?"

"Wait. You knew? But I thought Acelyne would come because Faerie's queens would be in the same place and she couldn't resist such an opportunity."

"Oh, she would've come just for us, but you, my dear, you are the true treasure."

"I don't understand." And she didn't. Not at all. But Eirlys was walking away from her, toward the Unseelie queen, and Rori was left, standing speechless, on her own.

"If it means anything to you, I was against the idea."

Icicles dripped through her veins at the sound of Therron's voice. "Did you know before or after we went to the Seelie Court?"

A look of contrition crossed his features. "We only just received word an hour ago." He indicated a guard standing to the side with a gorgeous brown falcon on his gloved hand. "But at Meg's, I began to suspect Acelyne wanted more than just the amulets. Through her enchantments, I could feel her desperation. When you broke free, she lost something far more valuable than a lone fae."

"The princess was trapped with me."

Therron shook his head. "I don't think it was Arianna. I did try to reason with Eirlys that the Seelie princess was the true prize."

"I can't believe you knew, and you allowed me to be deceived. By you, by my queen, by my own brother. You could've sent me a bird, you know." Rage burned away the frost of her words. "I'm a spy, Therron. It's my bloody job to know when deception is at hand. How the hell do you think this makes me look?"

"Do you care so much what others think?"

She did. Gods help her, she did. Spying was in her blood. It was her livelihood. If she couldn't spy, what good was she? Her father's words echoed in her mind and all she heard was, *Failure, failure, failure*. She was an absolute, complete, failure.

"I trusted you, Therron." She gave him her vilest glare and stormed off.

To her right, the sounds of two queens greeting each other could be heard above the din of chatter both queens' courtiers were making. Rori pivoted away from them, toward the forest. She wasn't Acelyne's target. No way. They had it all wrong. Her boots tore grass from its roots as she kicked at the green tufts. Damn them all. She needed air and time to think.

The soldiers' tents were all in tidy little lines, and she stepped around them gingerly, not wanting to disturb anyone inside. They'd all sworn fealty to their queen, too. Why did they do it? Why give their life to someone who would so easily betray them? She'd given everything to her queen, and now they thought to use her as bait. It stung more that they kept it secret from her. Had they asked, she would've gladly volunteered, but that they didn't trust her—that hurt the most.

From a short distance away, she heard Esme call to her, but she ignored the stupid girl. Let her have that mewling shaft shiner and be miserable. Rori was done with them. This was why she worked alone. Trusting people only brought suffering.

Shadows fell across her shoulders as she passed beneath the trees. She breathed deeply of the scent. Dirt and loam filled her senses. At times, Rori thought she might be descended from elves. Her love of the forest was as great as any of Therron's kin, she'd wager.

Calm swept over her, soothing her fractured emotions, quieting her mind. She'd return to the cottage in a minute. First, she needed the solace only the trees could provide. Forests allowed her to think clearer than any other place. A breeze wove through the branches, making the leaves dance. She trailed her fingertips along the bark of an ancient spruce. Within the trunk, she felt the tree's life-force, its own special heartbeat.

"Be well, old one." She leaned her forehead against the scratchy surface and closed her eyes.

"I never had you pegged for a tree hugger."

Rori's insides curdled at the stranger's words. Tree hugger was a human term, and only someone who'd been to the human realm would know it. Or, they knew someone who traveled there frequently enough to pick up human colloquialisms.

Rori opened her eyes and turned slowly, knowing before seeing who would be standing a few feet away. Sunlit hair, crimson dress. They hadn't been properly introduced. "Acelyne, I presume?"

The enchantress gave a sassy curtsey. "The one and same." She cocked her head and grinned. "You don't recall anything, do you?"

This close, Rori could see the faint shadow of a bruise beneath her right eye, and a long scratch across her throat. Acelyne's deep-brown eyes weren't full of anger, but curiosity. Rori flexed her fingers and kept her body loose.

"I admit, I don't."

"Then my potion-making skills are getting better. You put up quite a fight, Aurora MacNair. But you were worth it."

A fight? Rori didn't remember a fight, or anything else about the enchantress. "Why?"

"Because you're perfect. Just the right amount of self-loathing and ooh, your daddy issues are delicious. You really want to prove yourself. You're a fool. So...malleable."

The words hurt, but they were meant to. Acelyne knew all of her weaknesses and triggers.

"How do you free the faeries from their prisons?"

Acelyne moved closer, and Rori gripped the dagger on her right hip.

"You won't be needing those, dearest one." Acelyne flicked her wrist, and instantly Rori felt the need to let go of the dagger. A look of annoyance crossed Acelyne's features when the dagger didn't fly from Rori's hand.

She fought the enchantress mentally, firmly setting in her mind the insistence that she needed both daggers more than she needed breath.

"Ah. You've adapted and learned. Just as I'd hoped. Perhaps not as pathetic as I'd first thought."

The sound of twigs breaking came from Rori's flank, from where the queen's carriages were moving out of the vale. She dared not look away from the enchantress, but her senses told her whoever it was that approached, they weren't an ally.

"Nelson." Acelyne beckoned Dorchmeir to join her. "Just in time. You weren't followed?"

Dorchmeir clomped a path through the mosses and ferns to stand beside Acelyne, a look of profound pride upon his face. He shook his head. "They're too busy with the queens, as you predicted."

A trap. Excellent. Her day had just begun and already it was careening into a full blown shitstorm. She'd been prepared to face Acelyne, but not for Dorchmeir's appearance, although, she wasn't all that surprised. His hatred went deep. Naturally, he'd seek out anyone wishing harm on her, and he found the jackpot with Acelyne.

What part Therron played, Rori would soon find out. If he was involved, she'd slice his nutsack clean from his body. Instinct told her he wasn't part of Acelyne's schemes, but she'd made one error too many this morning and wasn't about to make another.

Mentally, she noted the location of each tree and the most convenient path out of the woods. On her own, she could easily take Dorchmeir, but if Acelyne used magic, it was an unfair fight.

"You have your school chum to thank for bringing you to my attention." Acelyne stroked Dorchmeir's head as if he were a puppy. "I thought your brother would be better suited to our needs, but you—" She took a step toward Rori, the grin of a fanatic stretching her lips. "You are perfect."

Dorchmeir flinched at the last word, annoyance flickering through his pride.

Rori didn't have to ask why he'd help someone like the enchantress. He was still the bully he'd been when they were younger. "Still bitter about me kicking your ass at the Academy, Dorchmeir?"

His chest puffed, and his eyes narrowed. "You cheated."

She sheathed her daggers and held her hands out wide, showing they were without weapons. "I didn't, and you know it. How about a rematch?"

Acelyne turned to say something, but he ignored her and stormed forward. Rori was hoping he was just as dimwitted as he'd been at school. He couldn't pass up a taunt then, nor could he now. She would use the distraction to separate him from Acelyne. As a pair, they were formidable with her magic and his brute strength, but separate, she might have a chance. As long as they didn't play dirty.

Snickertits.

＃ 35 ＃

Rori kept her arms loose, ready. Dorchmeir sneered in that way he did that made her want to dick punch him with both fists. He actually thought he could best her. What a narcissistic ass. When he was a pace from her, he raised his fist as if to strike. She rolled to the side and sprang up, landing a kick to his midsection. An angry grunt was quickly followed by his sword being drawn. *Fine.* He'd cheated all those years ago—and yet had bellowed to anyone who would listen that Rori was the cheat—she expected no less from him now.

He spun and sliced the air with the deadly blade, but Rori hopped to his other side, taking advantage of his height and weight to slow his movements. Her nimbleness and quick jabs elicited frustrated grunts from the overgrown spunking tramp herder. He hollered to the sky and swung his sword harder, slashing the air again and again. The third time his arms stroked down, Rori sprang forward, landing a solid fist against his jaw. She heard and felt the breaking of her bones. Dorchmeir heard it, too.

His sniveling face turned to glee. He raised both arms, with the hilt held between his fists, and angled the butt toward her. The gleaming silver was on a collision course with her cheek. A second before it smashed her face, she kicked Dorchmeir's ribs and flung herself to the side. Fire ripped up her thigh as the blade cut through her jeans and rent her skin. Heat spider-webbed outward, infecting her bloodstream. The bastard had poisoned his sword.

Rori rolled from her side and up to hop on her good leg. The sensation of a million fire ants crawling inside her veins gnawed her from the inside out. Dammit, but it must've been a poison she wasn't immune to. Dorchmeir laughed, his ugly mug contorting with the effort. She reached for the dagger at her hip and pulled it free. Her hand was half-cocked when she heard a shout from behind her.

"Rori, stop." Esme entered the small area, her eyes wide and glancing from Rori to Dorchmeir to Acelyne. "What's going on here?"

The enchantress spoke before the others had a chance, but her words were not to explain the situation. They were a spell meant to silence Esme forever. Rori knew the spell, but didn't know how she knew it. It was somewhere in the back of her mind, but this wasn't the time to ponder the hows or whys. Esme's body went rigid, and her face contorted in a freaky rictus.

Esme screamed, her hands flailing against the spell Acelyne continued to whisper. Indecision racked Rori. If she attacked Acelyne now, it might break the spell, or kill both her and Esme.

She stood and angled a dagger at the enchantress. "Release her."

Acelyne's glare bore into Rori, and she shuddered. "Or what?"

Dorchmeir stood idle while his soon-to-be betrothed was put under a deadly enchantment.

Esme clutched at her chest and uttered a strangled cry for help. "Nelson, please."

A malicious grin, as if he enjoyed seeing the girl tortured, spread across his face.

Rori let the dagger loose, directing it to land right in the soft spot of Dorchmeir's throat. With a soft thud, it made its mark. Esme shrieked again—from seeing Dorchmeir's blood spurting, or from what the enchantress was doing to her, Rori didn't know. She tugged the second dagger from her thigh and spun toward Acelyne.

"Let her go, witch."

Acelyne's hyena-like laughter brushed the treetops.

"She's innocent. Your quarrel is with me, not her." Rori indicated Esme, who had gone pale and silent, her eyes bulging. She floated several feet from the forest floor, her gown billowing as if the girl were drowning.

"Little Rori, how delusional you are. No one is ever truly innocent. Her, you, or poor Nelson here. No one is without their secrets. And we know all of yours, don't we?"

Cackling laughter, the same Rori heard when she was trapped in the amulet, scratched at her ears.

Rori leapt at the woman, hands outstretched to wrap around her neck. The gash on her thigh burned anew, stealing her momentum. Acelyne sidestepped and spun out of sight. A moment later, she appeared ten paces away, behind a tree. The enchantress had the upper hand when it came to magic and spells, but Rori had her own set of skills.

Esme dropped to the ground, coughing and sputtering, her hands at her throat. Tears streamed down her face as she gasped for air. "Kill. Her." She jabbed a finger in Acelyne's direction.

Rori drew a breath and focused. Eyes closed, she saw in her mind the forest, the layout of trees, the curve of trunks. Mentally keeping Acelyne as her target, Rori gripped the tip of the blade and blew down the sharpened edge. Then, with a silent command, she pivoted while cocking her arm back. Keeping the enchantress firmly in her thoughts, she released the dagger. A moment later, she opened her eyes.

A swath of red darted between two trees, and Rori adjusted the dagger's course mid-flight. Blue-black flames burst from behind the trees, Acelyne's magic engulfing Rori in searing heat. She screamed against the burning waves. Seconds later, they turned to icy pinpricks. Pinchers tore at her clothing, shredding the fabric and burrowing into her skin. Another wail came from deep in her core and escaped her lips.

Acelyne's magic was laced with darkness that called to Rori's wild magic. But, not to join in the torture—to defeat it. If only she knew how. She'd hid that part of herself so completely, she didn't know how to bring it out, even if it meant saving her own life.

Truth be told, she was terrified of what might happen if she did. Still afraid of failure.

Sweat streamed down her face as Rori struggled to control the dagger. At the forefront of her mind, she pictured Acelyne's heart.

The sound of branches breaking and raised voices came from behind as Rori sank to the ground. Flames rose and multiplied, their hungry tips feasting upon her. Heat followed by ice. Again, and again. Heat, then ice. Pinpricks and pinchers. Torn flesh and gushing blood. The endless torment seared through her skin to the marrow of her bones.

Acelyne's screech silenced the forest, and Rori knew her dagger had struck true.

A hush fell over the woods. The flames engulfing Rori evaporated. Death once more crept through the forest. Except this forest, with its trees and birds and sunshine, wasn't a prison. And this time, she wasn't alone.

A heartbeat later, she heard Therron call her name, and she let out the breath she held. The elf broke through the trees, looking like a king of old with his sword drawn, his cloak trailing behind him. It was a magnificent sight that terrified her in ways she couldn't explain. Her heart pinched and twitched in that odd way it did recently.

Therron reached her, and she stopped herself from stroking his face. Her outstretched hands hung limp in the air, and she stared in horror at her unbroken skin, her intact clothing. Another illusion.

"Are you real?"

"Aye." His impossibly light-blue eyes searched her face and then roved over her body. "You're injured."

"I was hoping that wasn't real."

His chuckle was like a warm balm to her bruised body.

"You're bleeding."

A thin trail of blood snaked down his neck from an inch-wide cut.

"'Tis nothing. Cut myself shaving."

They both knew that wasn't true, based on the length of his stubble, but she dropped it. There were more pressing matters to attend to.

A second man crashed into the woods, and she recognized her brother as he came out of the shadows. Others were there. Both queens, Tug, Meg, and Rowan.

"Where's Acelyne?" Cian asked, and Rori pointed to the trees, where a slip of red showed through the green.

Therron put out a hand to help her up, and she gratefully accepted. Midna and Eirlys held hands, both looking more like worried mothers than the monarchs they were. Meg went to Esme's side and helped her stand. Eirlys glanced briefly at Dorchmeir's body, then turned to Rori.

"We had a plan. What were you thinking, coming here alone?"

"No one told me about a plan," Rori mumbled. "Just that I was the bait."

Eirlys cupped Rori's cheek with her palm. Her wan smile and soft eyes were the only apology Rori would get. Both queens stepped past her to where Cian crouched over the body of the enchantress. Rori limped behind, ignoring the pain in her leg out of a desperate need to see the woman who'd captured, then tried to kill her.

To her surprise—hell, to everyone's surprise—Acelyne wasn't dead. Rori's dagger protruded from the woman's chest, and blood trickled from her slack mouth, but labored breaths still came from her lungs. Acelyne used the last of her magic to keep herself from crossing the veils. Evil clung to her glare.

"You were perfect," Acelyne slurred, and everyone turned to look at Rori. "He would've been so pleased with you."

"Who would've?" Rori demanded, but the enchantress

gurgled a laugh and shook her head. Fresh blood bubbled over her lips.

"Where's my sister? What have you done with Mairead?" Midna asked, and again Acelyne cackled.

"Someplace you'd never dare look."

"I have something here to loosen her tongue." Meg held out the vial of yellow liquid she'd slipped into her pocket the night before.

"And I have something here to heal it." Acelyne knocked the cork out of a small bottle. It was one of the vials of Everlasting Life Rori had made the previous night. Before Cian could stop her, Acelyne emptied the contents into her mouth. Pinkish foam spilled from her lips to her lush golden hair.

Her eyes protruded, and she glared at Meg. "You. Tricked. Me." The words came out harsh and slurred, with a lifetime of hatred behind them.

Meg wiggled the bottle in her hand. "It was easy, sister. I knew if I left the potions where you could reach them, you'd take what you thought could help. You really should've learned to make your own potions. You'll never steal from me again."

Sister? Rori looked from Meg to Acelyne, but there was no resemblance between the two. The encounter at Meg's cottage suddenly made sense, and she made a mental note to ask Meg about it the next time they were alone. Why wouldn't her friend have confided in her? As the enchantress said, they all had their secrets.

"This might not be pretty," Meg warned.

Despite wanting to look away, Rori couldn't. Neither could any of the others, apparently. They all bore witness as the poison took effect. Acelyne's youthful features warbled and wrinkled to flaps of skin and age spots. Locks of sunlit hair fell away, leaving her pate mostly bald, with only a few silver strands covering her head. The crimson gown deteriorated to wisps of faded fabric, and Rori's dagger clattered to the ground as the enchantress's body sunk in on itself, nothing more than a rotted cadaver.

Cian retrieved her weapon and wiped it against a tuft of grass.

"Help me, Midna?" Eirlys asked the Unseelie queen.

They stood to either side of the enchantress, their hands making an arch above the lifeless body. The women began chanting and a crystal coffin ensconced the corpse. Within the clear box, Acelyne's features returned to that of an old woman, but did not regain the youth or beauty she'd had a few minutes before.

Cian stood next to Rori and handed her the dagger. After a moment's hesitation, she returned it to its sheath against her leg. She'd retrieve her other dagger from Dorchmeir's body later.

"I don't understand." None of this made sense, and now the enchantress was dead and encased in her own glass prison. It was poetic justice, but at what cost?

"Nor do I," Midna admitted, "but we've done our best to preserve her mind. I'll send her to my necromancer to see if there's anything yet to learn."

Several of Midna's men, dressed as courtiers yet behaving more like soldiers, lifted the crystal coffin from the ground and carried it out of the forest. Rori watched them leave, her heart heavy and her mind conflicted. If this had something to do with the human realm, to what end? And why did Acelyne want her bad enough she risked her life to capture Rori? Her gaze traveled up past the men to the treetops, then back down to the small group.

Meg stood beside Tug, her auburn hair hanging past her hips. Gone were the wrinkles and wiry silver hair. She looked like a maiden fresh from the milking shed. And Rori wasn't the only one to notice. Tug gaped at the healer.

"Acelyne's been stealing my youth for years. I've tried everything to overpower her, but she was too good at illusions. In the end, that's what killed her. Well, that and your dagger." Meg grinned and held the vial between her fingertips. "I knew she'd be watching you, Rori. That's why I had you help me with the potions. Acelyne never was good with them, but I made sure I told you what every bottle contained. I knew Acelyne would rob my stores, so I made my sister believe she was stealing a potion that would heal her completely."

"Remind me never to get on your bad side, Meg," Rori teased.

"Or yours," Therron quipped. "You weren't even looking at the enchantress when you threw your dagger, yet it flew true and hit its mark."

"We all have our own kind of magic, I guess." Rori shrugged and winced against a jag of pain.

"Speaking of which." Meg motioned to Rori's leg, where blood stained her jeans and dripped into the mossy ground. "Come inside. Rowan and I can get you stitched up." Meg squinted, her lips pursed. "And take care of that poison, too. You don't do things by half, Rori MacNair." She pulled a vial from another pocket and motioned for Rori to bend her knee. "This will get the healing process started until we can finish healing you properly. It might sting a little."

Rori gritted her teeth and waited for the torment to begin. Meg's elixirs didn't just sting a little—they hurt like bloody fucking hell. As expected, her leg flared when the liquid hit her skin. Fire ants were a mercy compared to the agony she suffered. She groaned and twisted her head against the pain, counting the seconds until it eased.

"That'll do, love. You just might yet live."

"Thanks so much."

Meg's beguiling smile was so full of love and compassion

that Rori couldn't be angry with the healer. Literally, without her, she would probably be dead.

"Shall I carry you?" Therron bent as if to do just that.

"Not if you like your balls attached to your body." Harsh, but she was still angry at him for going along with the ludicrous plan to make her the bait. The same plan she completely ruined because she'd let her emotions run away with her. Was she angry at him? Or herself?

Therron backed away and held up his hands as if surrendering. "Then I shan't."

He did, however, hold her around the shoulders where she could lean on him as she tried valiantly not to limp out of the woods. Cian retrieved her dagger from Dorchmeir's throat and tucked it into a pocket. One of the soldier/courtesans carefully wrapped the lieutenant's sword in a blanket and carried it away.

"What will happen to him?" Esme asked no one in particular.

Rori's heart went out to her friend. He'd deceived them all, but perhaps Esme most of all.

"There, there, child. Come inside and have a cuppa. We'll sort you right as rain." Meg took Esme's hand in her own, and indicated she follow.

"I think I'd like that." Esme tucked Meg's hand against her side, as if the woman were the only thing tethering her to reality.

Rori understood far too well how her friend was feeling. In time, she would recover, but she was in shock and needed whatever healing Meg could provide. She limped to her friend and enfolded her in a hug. Esme stiffened, then went soft and returned the embrace.

"I'm sorry, Es. He left me no choice."

"It's not your fault. I should've known he was using me, but I'd convinced myself what we had was real."

"The love you felt was real. Don't let him steal that from you. In time, you'll find someone who deserves you." Rori gave Esme a gentle hug. "You are the kindest person I know. Be kind to yourself right now, will you?"

Esme nodded against her shoulder. "Thank you, Rori. I just wish I had your strength."

"You are so much stronger than you think, Es. You survived Acelyne's spell. There aren't a lot of people who can say the same." She thought of the trapped fae and grimaced at the slice of despair that cut her heart. Acelyne hadn't told her how to free them and now their futures were uncertain.

"Was there really a dragon?" The innocence shining from Esme's eyes softened Rori's despair.

"There was, but that's a story for another day."

Rori released her friend and returned to Therron's side. His arm slid around her shoulders with ease, his grip protective and secure. She could get used to having him near. Having someone to watch her back.

Maybe Cian was right that she could love and be loved... that maybe, just maybe, she didn't need to be alone.

$\mathcal{H}$ 37 $\mathcal{H}$

Therron stood to the side while Rori comforted her friend. How the lady hadn't succumbed to Acelyne's spell was a miracle. He'd entered the forest just in time to see the girl drop to the ground and then witnessed Rori throw her dagger at the enchantress. The next few moments, when she struggled against an invisible foe, had been horrifying.

His mind had told him it was another illusion, but his heart feared it would be Rori's doom. Yet she'd persevered and somehow managed to direct her dagger to Acelyne's heart.

She returned to his side, and he wrapped his arm around her shoulders in a protective embrace. If only she would allow him more, but for now, this would suffice. She was right to be angry with him. He'd sent his note to Midna asking that Rori be protected, and when that idea became corrupted to using Rori as bait, he'd argued against it, to no avail. Still, he could've fought harder to protect her rather than giving in to the two queens. Yet there hadn't been time. They'd received Midna's note just a scant hour before arriving to the vale, and by the time he'd exited the carriage, Rori was already there, upset with her queen and him.

At the moment, he hated himself a little, too. How could he expect her to forgive him for what she saw as a betrayal?

"I'm sorry I didn't stop them from using you to lure Acelyne from hiding. I should have fought harder to protect you."

She paused in her limping and looked up at him as if she weighed his words against an unknown metric. "I can protect myself, in case you haven't noticed."

"Oh, I noticed, as did the rest of the court." He brushed a lock of hair from her forehead and gazed at her lips, wanting to kiss her more than ever. "You are special, Aurora MacNair. You told Esme to be kind to herself and that's advice you should also take."

"I said that because Esme's a nice person. I'm not."

"Why? Because you're a spy? Because you've killed people?"

"Sure, let's start there." Anger blazed in her eyes.

A warning he chose to ignore.

"You are kindness personified, but you don't allow yourself to see it. There's a lot you don't allow yourself to see or feel, for that matter."

"Feelings make you sloppy. Like today. I almost failed."

"But you didn't. And who's to say your emotions weren't what saved you?"

"Me. I say my skill with a dagger saved me."

He blew out a breath and looked over her head to the others. They were all invested in themselves and ignored him and Rori. How could he get through to her that life was about living? Loyalty was honorable, but she was too young to give everything to her queen, including her happiness.

"What do you want from me, Therron? Do you want some

kind of promise that I'll be happy and loving and all that sappy stuff? Because I can't do that."

"Can't or won't?" Anger flushed through his veins, and he fought to control the ire he felt at whomever had convinced her she wasn't capable of love.

"Does it matter?"

He held her face in his hands and rubbed his thumb over her lips. She didn't snarl or snap, but her eyes filled with tears, making her look much younger, and far more innocent than she was.

"I want you to experience life on your terms, Rori. All of it. The good, the painful, the hopeful, and the dreadful. Everything this turn of the sun has to offer, I want to you feel it with every fiber of your body. Only then will you truly know who you are and what you desire."

"What do you desire?" Husky flirtatiousness edged her words.

An invitation he couldn't resist.

"You."

His lips brushed against hers, tentative, shy even. He was taking liberties yet again, but this time, she was fully aware of his actions, if not his motivations. That would come soon, but right now, he wanted her to love him as just Therron.

She sighed into the kiss and opened her mouth to accept him fully into her. He reveled in her taste, to her touch, wishing for nothing more than this moment to last. His hand slid around her waist and pulled her against him. His thoughts unraveled with the deepening of their kiss, and he was lost to her. All of his secrets began to unfurl, as if he might spill everything into her at once, but he held back, afraid.

Once she knew the truth, would she still want him?

Her hands grasped at him, and she writhed slowly against his leg, a low whimper coming from their locked mouths. A split-second vision crashed into his mind of flying beasts, and he pulled away, instantly regretting losing contact with her.

"I'm sorry. I shouldn't have done that."

"I didn't mind." Her grin was endearing and inviting.

The group was nearly to the edge of the forest. "We should go."

"In a minute. Tell me about that cut on your neck. It looks infected."

"Acelyne's friend might've taken a dislike to me."

She glanced at her leg. "Then you've been poisoned, too. Doesn't it hurt?"

He grinned and cocked his head. "I'm immune to most poisons you use in Faerie. Call it professional paranoia."

She traced a finger over the cut, and his skin warmed to her touch. A slight itching irritated the skin, but then it stopped. He rubbed where he'd been cut, but the skin was unblemished.

"You healed me, but how?"

"Another hidden skill. Very hidden. In fact, I'd appreciate if you didn't tell anyone."

His lips brushed hers, and he whispered his vow to keep her secret. He felt her smile against his and would've stayed there for the rest of their lives if not for the court leaving them behind, and the fact she still had poison in her leg.

"Let's get you healed."

She nodded and took a step in the direction of the others.

"Rori, there's something you should know."

She turned back to him, a peacefulness he'd not seen on her face before now present.

The truth about his identity could wait. Instead, he told her another truth. "I don't know where our paths will lead us now, but know that should you wish it, I will follow you wherever you lead. You have my sword should you need it, and my person should you desire it."

"Your person?" Her lips crooked up in a grin. "Tempting."

In his heart, where dread had made a comfortable home, hope blossomed. His scar warmed, but did not burn, and for the first time, quite possibly in his entire life, he looked forward to the future.

Curse or no, he would follow her to the depths of hell if she asked.

$\approx$ 38 $\approx$

Dizzy from the kiss, and her lips still tingling from his touch, Rori steadied herself against Therron's strong body. Damn, that boy could kiss. She felt it all the way to her toes, and most assuredly at the apex of her legs. Her nethers pulsed and warmed with incessant need. He'd promised to follow her wherever her path led, but where would that be? And would it mean more kisses, because yes, please.

She looked around to see whether anyone had caught them snogging, but no one paid them any mind. Which hopefully meant no one saw her heal his cut. She hadn't meant to, but when her finger touched his skin, she knew the words that drew the poison from his blood and knit his skin together. He'd promised to keep her secret, yet another in a long line of secrets she couldn't risk becoming public knowledge.

Her heart rammed in her throat at the memory of Acelyne taunting her. She knew all of Rori's deepest regrets and her innermost shame. If Midna's necromancer dragged them out of the enchantress, what would happen to her? If it came to that, she'd deal with it then. She was tired of worrying over something she couldn't control. She suppressed a shudder and limped quickly to catch up with the others, despite the tremendous pain in her leg. Why couldn't she heal herself? Now that would be a clever trick.

Midna and Eirlys led the group through the trees, their heads bent close in conversation. When they reached the vale, Eirlys turned to the group and sighed.

"This day has been one I had hoped would never come to Faerie, yet here we are. There is malevolence growing all around us, and we need to stop it before it destroys every last one of us. Rori, since you have intimate knowledge of the amulets, I should like you to go to the human realm and uncover what you can about them. Meg, get her healed and fit. Cian, continue doing the good work you've started here. Midna and I will do what we can to uncover who is behind all of this."

Back to the human realm? She glanced at Therron, but his face was unreadable. Only a slight clenching of his jaw told her he didn't like the queen's command. She tightened her grip on his waist as a way to let him know she wasn't in favor of the order, either. Yet it was her queen, and her job to do as commanded.

Eirlys turned and signaled for the Unseelie queen to join her inside Rowan's cottage. Rori met Cian's gaze and saw the disappointment lingering there. This should be his assignment. Yes, she'd been captured by Acelyne, but he had all the intel on SIRE, and Rori knew in her gut that the company was somehow involved. She didn't believe in coincidence. Whoever Malcolm Dagniss was, he played a role somehow.

Her belly churned with indecision. Going to the human realm meant leaving Therron and his sweet kisses. He said he'd follow her anywhere. Did that include through the doorways and back to the human realm? He'd proved valuable thus far; surely Eirlys and Midna would let him continue working with her. The queens disappeared into the little house amid a flurry of gesticulating hands and raised voices.

On one side of the cottage, several forest creatures crouched low until their bellies dragged on the ground. They inched their way closer to the door. She spied two brownies among the raccoons, badgers, and wood sprites.

"What do you think they're up to?" Rori said more to herself than anyone in particular.

"I think they want ta give the queens thanks," Tug replied. "Acelyne's been poisoning their homes for too long."

Acelyne's death would stop some of the evil Eirlys sensed creeping throughout Faerie, but whoever was paying the enchantress was still out there.

Rori glanced once more at Cian and weighed her options. The best way she could help Faerie was to learn all she could. Not just about SIRE and Malcolm Dagniss, but about every-thing—including herself. She'd lived a life within blinders until now—adhering to Academy rules, living to some unseen metric set by her parents. Existing with only what was in front of her, focusing too hard on her missions. Faerie and the human realm were wider than she'd ever imagined. The enchantress might never be able to trap her again, but she'd make damn sure nobody else would either. Physically, or emotionally.

Therron supported her as she maneuvered around the forest creatures, careful not to step on any tails or paws. His arm felt good around her shoulders, and his body heat was welcome warmth. This man was dangerous. Not just because he'd conspired with the queens and Cian without telling her, but for the thoughts whipping through her brain—all culminating with images of Midna's palace. But this time it was Rori on the divan and Therron who stood beside her. She told herself it was his magic or the poison that made her heart flutter and legs wobble. Yet she knew it wasn't either of those things. On this, her gut stayed silent and let her heart speak.

Rori cleared her throat and shook her head to dispel the treasonous thoughts. She had no time for messy emotions and mushy stuff. She recalled what Midna had said in the carriage —how her álainn obedience chose to be there. Maybe she didn't have time for relationships, but she could spare a few weeks or months getting to know who she really was, what she really wanted. Wasn't that what Therron had been trying to tell her? If she was going to love someone else, she had to love herself, first.

Rori stiffened, adrenaline pushing her heartrate and flooding her brain. She'd run from love her entire life. It was a weakness, she'd told herself. Something to be avoided and even pitied in others. Therron adjusted his grip, and she fought the urge to duck beneath his arm, to run as far and as fast from the cottage as she could.

Then it hit her. In that instant, she understood. Love meant loss. The day her father died, she watched the light fade from her mum's eyes. She saw Cian step into a role he didn't deserve. She'd shielded herself from ever feeling the keening despair that comes from giving one's heart to another. Yet when she looked around the room, she saw all the emotions she'd hid from playing out on the faces of those gathered. They loved, they mourned, they grieved, they rejoiced, and through it all, they were not less than.

In fact, what if—Rori breathed deeply and allowed the thought to fully settle in her soul—what if because of their emotions, they were more?

Cian strode into the cottage, and Rori made her decision. She needed to speak to the queens before they were too far into their planning. With Therron's help, she shuffled through the courtiers to where Faerie's queens sat upon twin chairs, looking magnificent and regal despite the humble surroundings.

When she approached, both looked up, but not in surprise as Rori had thought they might. After all, she'd played her part. Eirlys had given her a command—what more could Rori have to say?

"I'd like Cian to go to the human realm to seek out the miscreant who is kidnapping fae." She dropped a low curtsey just for good measure. Pain surged from her thigh, and she grimaced. "If you approve, Your Majesties, I would like to convalesce with Queen Midna for an undetermined amount of time. Once healed, I'd like to learn everything she can teach me."

Both women raised their eyebrows at her declaration. Hell, even Rori was shocked at her words. She'd decided it was best if Cian pursued the mission, but she hadn't realized how badly she wanted to return to Midna's court until the words spilled from her lips. Not for sex, although if it involved Therron, she wouldn't mind some schooling. Her heart hiccupped at the possibilities. She didn't desire becoming an álainn obedience, but she sure as hell could learn about emotions and love and how to not let either interfere with her job.

Eirlys turned to Midna, a secret smile upon her lips. "Well, sister of my heart, do you consent to taking my Rori on as a foster?"

Her Rori? Seriously? Secretly, she liked that Eirlys showed protectiveness; she was just surprised she would do so publicly.

"Only with your approval."

"Then you shall have it." Eirlys glanced above the heads of those gathered. "Cian, what say you to your sister's request?"

Cian's eyes were huge in his handsome face. His usually tense jaw gaped and for once he was at a loss for what to say.

"I'll take that as a yes." The queen giggled when she

turned toward Rori. "You'll have your education, dearest. Learn well, but learn quickly. I have a feeling your brother will be needing your assistance soon enough."

Rori frowned at the implied meaning—that she'd be leaving Faerie soon even though she'd just tried to finagle a way to stay longer. She'd been through hell and needed to heal, surely the queen understood that. And, in the depths of her heart, she knew she wasn't ready yet to leave Therron.

There would be time later to sort out her mission and execute plans. At the moment, her leg throbbed and her stomach complained about its empty state. On top of everything, her heart beat so hard she could barely breathe.

She couldn't force Therron to go to the Unseelie Court with her, but she hoped he would. For too long she'd denied herself from caring for another. If nothing else, the past few days had taught her that compassion wasn't a dirty word. She'd loved her father with all her heart and whether he had died or not, it felt like he'd deserted her—that didn't mean Therron would.

As she turned toward the kitchen, she glanced at the elf. Something dark and mysterious lingered in his gorgeous eyes. Something she hoped wasn't an illusion. Something she desperately wanted him to unleash upon her. Her fingers traced her lips where his touch lingered, and she wanted more. It was time she learned to depend on someone besides herself. And just maybe, it was time she embraced loving unconditionally. Love didn't mean failure.

She could open her heart and take a risk, even if it meant getting messy in the process. Sometimes, the risk was worth the reward.

ABOUT THE AUTHOR

Tameri Etherton is a *USA Today* Bestselling and award-winning author of dangerous fantasy and magical ever afters. She grew up inventing fictional worlds where the impossible was possible.

It's been said she leaves a trail of glitter in her wake as she creates new adventures for her kickass heroines, and the rogues who steal their hearts.

She lives an enchanted life traveling the world with her very own prince charming and their mischievous dragon, Lady Dazzleton.

Read More from Tameri Etherton and explore the Aetherverse at

www.TameriEtherton.com

AUTHOR NOTES

I hope you enjoyed this updated and expanded version of Fatal Illusion. This is the story I always wanted book one to be, but time and circumstances prevented it until now. Not only am I excited you got to meet Cian in this version, I am forever grateful for Steph Rawlins at Rawls Reads for her insightful and thoughtful developmental edit. In addition, again my thanks go to Lynn Trahan for her beta read and also to Mariëlle Sophia Smith for challenging me to keep the intimacy of the first version in this expanded edition. Thank you ladies! All my love to you.

I'd also like to thank my readers because without them, the stories would languish in a forgotten drawer.

My first beta readers: Carly, Sarah, Koda, Nadia, Shandris, Abel, and Lynn. Thank you, my beauties! I hope I've done justice to the story and given you the Therron you requested. You rock my world!

No book is ever finished, but Faith Williams at the Atwater Group does her best to make sure mine are as polished as possible. I owe her a debt of gratitude for her editing skills

Thank you to Lori Grundy who made gorgeous covers to reflect what I saw in my mind.

And finally, my husband David. This writing gig can be fraught with all kinds of demons—loneliness, doubt, angst, sugar-driven mad sprints, and giddy excitement. David has been there through it all, by my side supporting me in every wicked adventure and half-formed idea. He's my co-shenanigator in writing and in life.

Never fall in love with your mark.

Cian MacNair is Faerie's best assassin. He knows the rules, hell, he made half of them. Rule number one: Never fall in love with your mark.

Sent to the human realm to discover who's been kidnapping fae, he's tangled in a web of deceit that threatens not only

Faerie, but the humans as well. It'll take working with the enemy to uncover who the real villain is.

There's just one problem. She's been sent to take him out before he discovers too much.

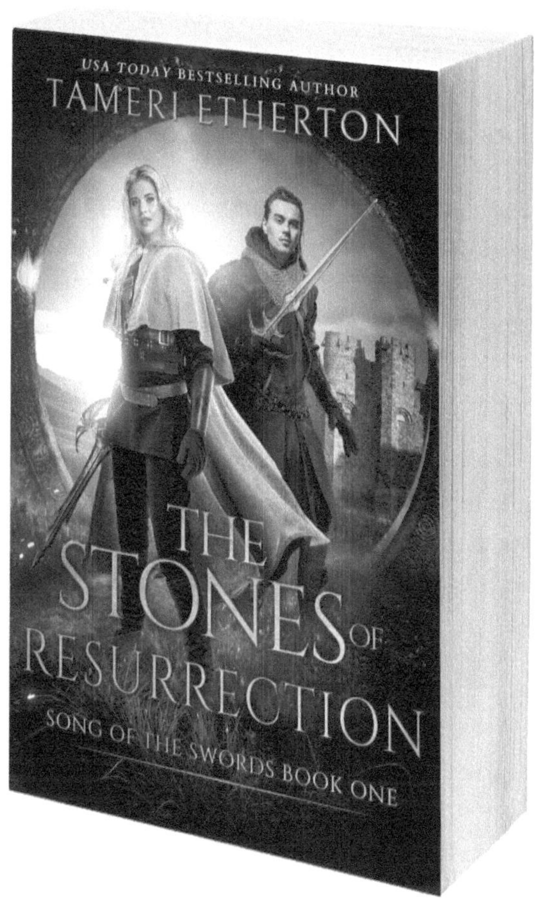

Otherworldly portals. Mysterious powers. Evil hungrily awaits her return.

Taryn's simple life is all she's ever known. Living above a busy London pub with her grandfather, they're ripped from their reality and plunged into a strange world to jumpstart an ancient prophecy. And when he's killed defending her from a vicious intruder's magic, Taryn's left nearly alone... and forced to trust a rugged savior.

Rhoane has one job. Sworn to protect the young woman who has returned to fulfill her destiny, the assassin dare not let his feelings get in the way of her training. But he knows the time will come when she accepts her power and recognizes he's her fated mate.

As Taryn learns her life on Earth was a lie, she must unlock her hidden talents to save an entire world from destruction. And though Rhoane will show no mercy to anyone who stands in her way, he fears her biggest threat comes from the family she has never known.

Will the destined pair rise to stop the annihilation of a vast kingdom?

The Stones of Resurrection is the enthralling first book in the Song of the Swords fantasy series. If you like ensemble casts, intense action, and dark family sagas, then you'll love Tameri Etherton's epic tale.

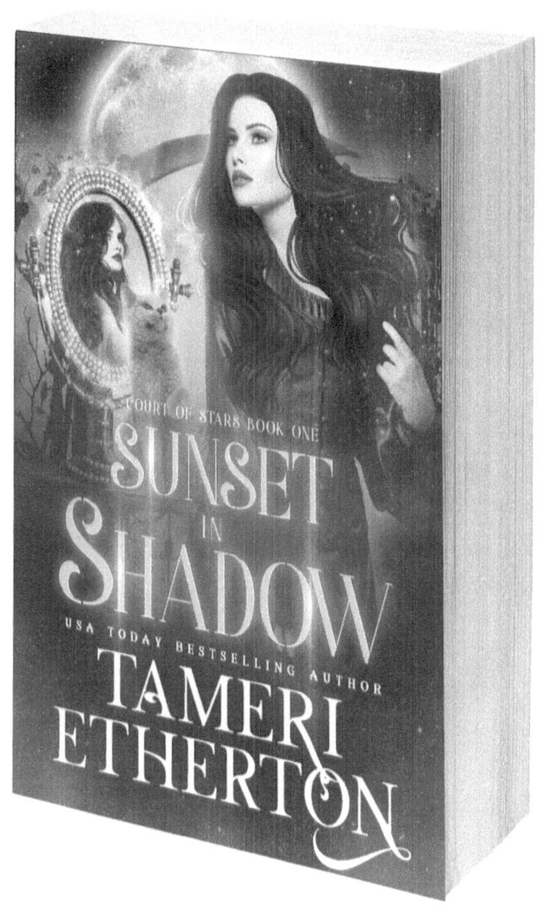

epic skills with a blade save a handsome royal from ravenous wolves, revealing her shameful form could get her killed.

Prince Theo Mistwalker would rather be in his grand library than combing the forests for his wayward brother. But after he's attacked, he's smitten by the swashbuckling rescuer who plants an alluring kiss on his lips before vanishing into the trees. Though his loyalty weakens while he heals in a local duchess's home and develops feelings for her beautiful elven daughter.

After Rainne confesses her burden to the noble man she's fallen for, she has no choice but to deal with her self-hatred or risk losing her one shot at happily-ever-after. And to be with the woman of his dreams, Theo must embark on a dangerous quest to break the spell.

Can they find a way to end Rainne's torment and surrender to their destined passions?

To unleash her dragon, she must confront her past.

In the seven years since Amaleigh failed to assassinate her best friend, she's been on the run jumping from world to world. All she truly wants is to stop running and find a place to call home. And maybe be kissed by someone who doesn't leave her feeling indifferent. Love doesn't come easily for her, yet unlocking her cold, dead heart might be a start to unleashing her inner dragon. That would mean trusting another and there's only one person she's ever trusted—the same man she couldn't kill.

Prince Gwilym knows he shouldn't risk Amaleigh's life by asking for help, especially since he's the reason she had to escape Eidyn. Now his life is in peril and she's the only person he trusts. He wouldn't blame her for not daring to return to the city that celebrated the slaughter of her kind and cast her aside.

Can she survive the very place her parents were murdered, or will palace intrigues claim another victim? If she fails Gwilym, she might lose her chance to come to terms with her past, and open her heart.

Forced to make a desperate choice, she must put aside her hatred for the man who murdered her family and sentenced her to a life of crime and loneliness.

To save those she loves, she must become the Dragon Mage the king fears most.

9 781941 955178